FATE'S SURRENDER

ETERNAL SORROWS, BOOK 3

SARRA CANNON

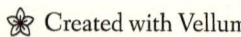

To My Hearties Community

Thank you for supporting me through the NaNoWriMo Diaries in 2020. This book was not an easy one to write, but your continued support meant the world to me.

And to those of you still dreaming of finishing that first book.

I believe in you. It's your turn.

PART ONE
THE STONE

ONE

PARRISH

Parrish Sorrows dreaded the darkness.

Her stomach knotted at the first hint of sunset. A conditioned response.

A reaction to weeks of hearing rotters out on the streets at night, searching for someone to eat.

Tonight, though, hidden away in a neighborhood near the hospital, it was completely quiet.

Almost peaceful, if such a thing still existed.

The streets were dark, but the moon was full, illuminating the rows of houses in this part of the suburbs. Each one of these homes had been someone's dream at one point. They had worked hard to decorate it and make it their own. They had made friends here and had children and created memories that they'd printed out and framed on the walls.

Now, everything was dark and still, and despite how much she hated the sounds of rotters, the silence was unsettling. Had all the rotters for miles around been in that hospital yesterday?

How many had they killed in order to survive?

Parrish still hadn't processed everything that happened at that hospital, but there was one thing she couldn't get out of her head. It ran through her mind on a constant loop.

Zoe is still alive.

Could it be real?

Lily had said a lot of things when Parrish had confronted her yesterday. She'd told them some elaborate story about an ancient evil necromancer many called The Dark One who'd tried to rule their original home world. About how the five of them—The Guardians—had somehow managed to trap the Dark One here in this foreign world, sealing away all magic forever.

Or what they'd hoped would be forever.

And yet, somehow, she'd managed to awaken her powers.

Lily hadn't told her exactly how that one had happened, but Parrish was pretty sure she'd pieced that part of the story together herself.

They'd all been dreaming of Tobias for months. He'd been the one sent here from their home world to bring the fatalis stone to them. To check on them and make sure the Dark One was still imprisoned.

Parrish knew somewhere deep down that Tobias had come here to this world many times. More than any of them remembered. And each time, the world had been peaceful. The seal held.

Until now.

This time, when he'd come through, Lily had slipped through with him, and everything had changed.

Without his training and their memories, they were lost. They needed to get to this island they'd all been dreaming of, and their full memories and powers would be returned to them.

Except there were two things standing in their way.

First, they hadn't actually found the fifth.

Parrish had seen him in her dreams, though. He'd been there on the island with them. Not Lily.

And wherever he was, he was likely alone and searching for them, too.

Parrish wasn't sure whether the magic of the island would work without the fifth or not. She had a feeling they all needed to be together, but how were they going to find him? He could be anywhere in the world.

Second, Parrish couldn't get her sister out of her mind.

It had broken her heart to lose contact with Zoe, and even though everyone had told her to forget her sister and to let go, there had always been a part of Parrish that wanted to believe Zoe was still alive. That still felt connected to her in some way.

Lily's words had given her hope, but she'd also said the Dark One knew where to find Zoe.

Had she been telling the truth? Or was this just another one of her elaborate lies? The next part of whatever trap she and the Dark One had set for them?

Parrish shook her head and held back tears. She hadn't wanted to be right about her, but Lily had been lying to them this whole time. She'd been playing them, and for what? To draw them into a trap? To kill them all?

How many times had the rotters they'd faced been because of her?

And why hadn't she just slit their throats in the middle of the night, instead? Why make them face all of those zombies?

Parrish still didn't have the answer to those questions, but

"A little warning would be nice, guys. It's not nice to just sneak up on people in the middle of a zombie apocalypse."

Crash smiled and shrugged. "Sorry."

Noah looked up, confused. "Wait, what do you mean Lily wasn't the one in the closet? There was someone else there?"

He ran a hand through his messy black hair and shook his head. "I've been going through it in my head, over and over, trying to make sense of what happened that night we met her."

He sat down across from the two of them, and Parrish pulled her knees under her body to make room for him. When he sat down, she noticed that the lightning bolt on the fatalis stone began to glow brighter.

"I've been giving this a lot of thought," Crash said. "I think Lily could see inside my dreams. She must have seen the fifth in the closet, and she knew from watching my dreams that for whatever reason, I couldn't see the fifth's face. Unlike the rest of you, I didn't have any solid information about who or where they were. She took advantage of that and set herself up to seem like the fifth. I think she basically recreated the situation from my dream and made me believe it. Then she used me to get to the rest of you."

Parrish sat in silence, taking in this new information and trying to piece together the puzzle for herself.

"So she set all of this up and then acted like a scared victim so we'd welcome her in and take care of her," Noah said.

"This whole time we looked at her like she was the weakest one in our group," Parrish said, frustration building up inside her. She wanted to scream. "She acted like she'd been through some kind of major trauma and needed us to take care of her, when what she was really doing was plotting how to kill us. I mean, how much of what we've been through over the she felt the loss of Lily's friendship more deeply than she thought she would.

They'd trusted her. Brought her into the group like she was family, and she'd betrayed them every step of the way.

Parrish ran her thumb across the smooth surface of the dark purple stone Lily had given her before the giant rotter had hauled her away.

What was the importance of this stone? Why give it to her if she was working with the Dark One?

And why did Parrish feel like she'd held it in her hand dozens of times before this?

She stepped away from the front window and paced the floor of the living room. These questions were driving her insane, looping in her mind nonstop ever since the rest of their crew had gone to sleep.

There was no way Parrish was sleeping tonight.

Instead, she'd taken first watch in the small house where they'd decided to wait things out until morning.

Whoever had lived in this house had completely emptied this front room of furniture and replaced it with a bunch of sleeping bags. From the looks of it, at least ten people had bunked out here.

Where they were now, Parrish could only guess.

For all she knew, they were among the survivors at Tank's compound on the other side of town.

But when her eyes drifted to the splintered back door that had been patched a couple of different times and was now stained with blood, she got the feeling whoever had been hiding out here had never made it to the compound.

Parrish sighed and sat down, leaning her back against the wall.

For what must have been the hundredth time that hour, she ran her finger across the infinity sign etched into the dark stone.

An image flashed through her mind. A handsome man kneeling on the ground, a mound of fresh dirt like a makeshift grave behind him, fear blossoming in his eyes.

She could almost feel his fear flow into her like a pulse of electricity.

It scared her so much, she dropped the stone onto the floor with a thud and sat up.

Something moved in the hallway, and she immediately brought her hand to the hilt of her katana, the blade already emitting a dim blue glow.

Noah's face appeared in a small stream of moonlight, and he raised his hands.

"It's just me," he said softly. "Everything okay? I thought maybe you'd want to try to get some rest."

She let her hand fall from the katana, but her heart still raced. "I can't even think about sleep right now," she said, taking several deep breaths to try to clear the image of that man from her mind.

Who was he? Another vision from her own past? Someone else tied to the stone?

"Are you sure you don't even want to try?" Noah asked. "Morning's going to come faster than you think."

Parrish shook her head and settled back against the wall.

"I should be exhausted after everything that happened yesterday at the hospital, but I can't get the whole thing out of my mind. How could we have been so stupid? The enemy was right there with us the whole time, and we didn't even know it."

"Well, we kind of did," Noah said. He leaned down and picked up the fatalis stone before sitting on the floor across from her. "As much as we didn't want to believe it, we all knew we might be walking into some kind of trap."

"Yeah, but I never dreamed it was going to be that bad," she said, shuddering as she remembered the horrible things they'd faced inside that hospital. She'd almost lost Noah back there. How would she have kept going without him? "How are you feeling, by the way? How's your head?"

"It hurts," he said, gently touching his head. "To put it mildly. That's why I can't sleep. I can't seem to shake this headache."

"Did you try healing yourself?" she asked.

"I don't think it works on me," he said. "Which kind of sucks, to be honest."

He said it with a soft laugh, and their eyes met in the semi-darkness.

"What about the supplies we grabbed from the med room?" she asked. "I'm sure we have some good pain killers in there if you need them."

"Everything in there is too strong. I don't want to dull my reactions in case we have to move quickly," he said. "I'll take something when we get back to the safety of the compound if it's not better by then."

She nodded toward the hallway. "Karmen and Crash?"

"Sleeping," he said. "Lucky jerks."

She laughed. "I would love to be sleeping right now."

He patted the floor next to him and lay back, head on the floor and knees raised. She joined him, his hand instantly reaching for hers as they lay there side by side.

They lay together in silence for a while, and Parrish was

suddenly reminded of that night when they lay just like this in the grass, listening to Zoe play her violin.

She'd been so nervous to be that close to him. She'd wanted him to kiss her or hold her hand, and the thought of it had nearly taken her breath away.

Life had been so simple back then.

"Noah, do you think Zoe really is still alive in New York like Lily said?" She turned her head to look at him. She wanted to see his reaction. "Could that really be true? Or do you think she was just playing with me?"

Noah frowned, avoiding her eyes.

She shouldn't have asked him. She already knew what everyone in their group was going to say. No one wanted to risk New York. Not after yesterday.

"I want to believe it just as much as you do," he said finally. "But even if it is true, what can we really do about it before Lily or the Dark One have a chance to get to her?"

Parrish did her best to listen to him with an open mind, but she didn't want to hear any protests. She just wanted reassurance.

"We talked openly about where Zoe is, which means Lily knows exactly where to go. She has a head start, and she's on the Dark One's side, which means she can just waltz into the city and go straight to the hotel. There's literally nothing standing in her way. If we try to rescue Zoe, we'll have to fight our way through God knows what, Parrish. We don't stand a chance at getting to your sister first."

"So then why tell me?" Parrish asked, glad for the darkness so he couldn't see the tears in her eyes. "Just to torture me? To set some kind of trap for us in New York? Why?"

"I don't know," Noah said. "But there's no doubt in my

mind Lily or one of the Dark One's other allies will be at Zoe's room before the night is over. The real question is whether they'll let her live once they have her."

Parrish blinked back tears. "You're saying you think it's too late, then? So, what? You don't want to go with me to New York, anymore?"

She reached over and took the fatalis stone from him. Somehow, it comforted her to have it.

"I didn't say that. I'm with you all the way, but if we're still planning on going after her, we need a better plan than just fighting our way through hell and hoping for the best."

She sighed and released the tension she'd been holding in her shoulders. She hadn't realized just how scared she'd been that he would refuse to go with her after what happened.

"So, we figure out a plan," she said, squeezing his hand. "Together we can do anything. I'm so glad I didn't lose you in that hospital. I was so scared, Noah."

"Me too," he said in a whisper. "If I'd had any idea just how much planning Lily must have done to set that trap for us, I never would have agreed to it. I still don't understand how she set all of that up ahead of time, but she must have had some way to communicate with the rotters, even when she was there inside the compound with us."

"What I don't understand is why Crash had been dreaming about Lily in the first place," she said. "He was right about the rest of us, and he seemed sure the fifth was hiding in that closet. He dreamed about her. It doesn't make sense."

"Lily wasn't the one I was dreaming about in that closet." Crash stood in the doorway leading back to the small bedrooms.

Parrish sat up with a start, her katana glowing again.

past few weeks is because of her? The rats? The horde on the drive here? The super zombies on the roof that night in DC were definitely because of her, right?"

"Definitely," Crash said, nodding. "She created them, somehow, from regular rotters. And then she did it again before we got to the hospital. I don't know when or how, but it was definitely her this whole time, no doubt with some help from the Dark One herself. That's what Lily called her, right? The Dark One?"

Parrish and Noah both nodded. They'd gone over everything Lily said back at the hospital several times, but it all still seemed so unreal.

"So, what do we do now?" Parrish asked, knowing there was no easy answer to that question. "Why has all of this been put on our shoulders?"

She ran her thumb across the infinity symbol again, watching the light inside flicker as if there was a fire inside it.

"I mean, why do we have these strange abilities if we don't even know how to use them?" she asked. "What are we supposed to do with them? We obviously aren't normal humans. If these visions we've had are to be believed, we never were human, which don't even get me started on that. But if we're here for a reason or if our sole job is supposed to be to stop the Dark One, we're doing a pretty crap job of it so far. Is there even much of a world to save, anymore?"

She thought of Zoe all alone in that hotel room. What if Lily had already gotten to her by now? What then?

"There are survivors everywhere right now," Crash said, patting her knee.

When he touched her, the light inside the stone flashed brighter for a moment.

"We might not be able to see them or talk to them right now, but I believe there are compounds and groups like the one we found here that have found a way to survive," he said. "If we can help save them, it will be worth it."

"There's more to it than that," Karmen said.

Parrish looked up as Karmen walked over and sat down next to her, looping her arm with Parrish's arm, as if they were the best of friends.

Which, in a world where nearly everyone else was dead, she supposed they were.

"What do you mean?" Noah asked.

"We didn't come from this world, did we?" Karmen said. "I don't understand everything we've seen in these weird visions, but I know for certain the red sand beach I've seen over and over isn't here in this world. And the Dark One didn't come from here, either. Neither did Lily."

"And neither did we," Crash said. "She's right."

"So, what does that mean?" Parrish asked.

"It means this goes further than just being put here to save this world," Karmen said. "It means there's at least one other entire world full of people that are counting on us to keep them safe, too. Our real home world."

Parrish took a deep breath, the sudden weight of this impossible responsibility falling on her shoulders. She wasn't sure why, but she knew that she was supposed to be the one leading this group. She obviously wasn't equipped for it. She'd never been a leader.

She was an outcast, at best.

And seriously, this was the last hope of two worlds and billions of people? A room full of confused teenagers?

They were screwed.

"Did we wake you up?" Crash asked, his eyes on Karmen.

She shook her head. "I couldn't really sleep with everything that's going on," she said, squeezing Parrish's arm. "What are we going to do next? And please tell me it doesn't still involve going to New York City? Because we already had that conversation, and I want to make it clear that I have absolutely no intention of walking into the most obvious trap in the history of the world. Especially not now."

"I have to go," Parrish said, her voice catching in her throat. She knew as well as anyone else how stupid it seemed. Having hope in a situation like this.

And how was she supposed to explain why she was willing to risk everything to get to her sister? Everyone in this room had lost their families and their closest friends. What was one more sister?

But to Parrish, it felt like the most important thing of her entire life. Or maybe all her lifetimes.

Zoe was too good for this. She didn't deserve to die alone. If there was even a small chance Parrish could save her, she had to try. Even if she had to do it alone.

Even if she died in the process.

What that meant for the fate of the world, she didn't know, but right now, saving Zoe was the only thing that made any sense to her.

They all sat in silence for a moment, Parrish's words hanging between them.

But then, something strange happened.

Crash began to hum.

But it wasn't just any song you'd hear on the radio. It was one of Zoe's songs. The one she'd played that night Parrish and Noah lay on the grass outside the window. The night the infected man had passed out in Parrish's front yard.

"How do you know that song?" she asked.

Crash raised an eyebrow, as if he hadn't even been aware he was humming. "Oh, uh... hmm." He seemed to think it over for a minute before he finally said, "I think I must have been dreaming about it. I actually don't think I've heard this song before tonight, but some part of it has gotten stuck in my head."

Parrish's arms erupted in goosebumps. With Crash, a dream was never just a dream. It had to mean something.

"What else can you remember?"

He closed his eyes and hummed more of the tune.

Handel. She'd heard Zoe play it so many times, she had it memorized. It was one of the violin solos Zoe played at auditions.

"Someone in a dark room," Crash said softly, turning his head as if to see it again in his mind's eye. "A child, I think. Playing as lightly and softly as possible."

"Zoe," Parrish gasped, suddenly noticing that the stone in her hand had grown warm. "What else do you remember? Is Lily there? Or the Dark One?"

He shook his head and opened his eyes. "I can't explain it, but I feel like someone is watching out for her," he said. "I don't know how this makes any sense. I've never dreamed of anyone besides Tobias, the three of you, and the fifth. Why would I be dreaming of your sister?"

"I don't know," she said, holding back tears. "But maybe it's another sign that she really is alive, like Lily said."

"Maybe it's good that none of us could sleep," Noah said. "We need to decide what we're going to do, because once we get back to Tank's, we might not have a chance to talk in private. So, this is our chance. No one has to go to New York if they don't want to go. You can stay with Tank, where it's safe, and there will be no hard feelings. But I think we all know that we have a greater responsibility here than just surviving."

"I never asked for that responsibility," Karmen said, sitting up taller. "Why can't we just stay safe and let someone else deal with it all?"

Parrish squeezed her friend's hand. She was starting to understand that despite Karmen's words, she didn't actually intend to sit back and do nothing. She was just afraid.

Parrish was afraid, too, but that didn't change what they needed to do.

"Maybe you did ask for it," Parrish said. "In another lifetime. I think at some point, a very long time ago, we chose this for ourselves. I think we gave up everything to do this, and now it's our job to see it through."

Karmen swiped at a tear falling down her cheek.

"Well, I want a do-over," she said, a small laugh simultaneously joining her tears.

"I don't think we're going to get that," Parrish said. "But maybe whatever sacrifice we made all those years ago can still mean something."

She met Noah's eyes across the darkness of the room, and his expression and understanding nearly took her breath away. Yes, they had given up everything to be here, and now it was time to make good on whatever promise they'd made when they first came to this world.

"Okay, so where do we start?" Crash asked.

Parrish leaned forward and placed the fatalis stone in the

center of their makeshift circle. Four of its five sides were clearly lit from within by some type of magical power.

"We start with this," she said. "Somehow, this is what started it all, and I have a feeling that in order to end it, we're going to need to figure out exactly what this stone is all about."

Noah placed his hand in hers, and she squeezed him back. They were in this together. All of them.

Karmen's arm was still looped with hers, and she reached out to take Crash's hand.

Crash, in turn, reached out toward Noah, a gesture of commitment and friendship that ran deeper than anything the four of them had ever known before.

But it was so much more than that, because the moment their hands touched and the circle of connection was made, a bright light burst from the stone in the center.

For a brief moment, a vision flashed through Parrish's mind.

A boy with dark skin reaching toward them. The moment she saw his face, Parrish knew him.

He couldn't have been more than ten years old in this lifetime, but she had known him for centuries. He had once been her greatest friend. Her mentor and teacher.

And she had seen him recently in a dream, standing on a sun-drenched beach, urging her toward the center of a small island.

This boy was the fifth, and as the vision expanded, she could see that he had not been reaching for her. He'd been reaching for a young girl with a violin cradled between her chin and shoulder.

He'd been reaching for Zoe, and she was very much still alive.

TWO
THE BOY

Having his feet on solid ground again felt strange after an evening of flying across rooftops, but the boy was so happy to have the girl with him now as he landed on the roof of his own building. Being alone for so long had been hard.

He led her into his small apartment while the sky was still dark. Luckily, they had made it home before the sun.

"Thank you for bringing me here," the girl—Zoe—said.

She looked around, her eyes wide as she took in the small, bare apartment. He had a feeling she must have grown up somewhere very different from this, but the boy had never known anything else.

It didn't matter that they'd come from different worlds. All that mattered now was that they were together. Only, Zoe didn't look happy to be there. She looked like she was about to cry.

He reached for her hand, and she let her tears fall.

"I kept thinking that maybe when we got here, your

parents would be here, too. Or your friends. But it's just us now, isn't it?"

He nodded, gripping her hand tighter.

"You must have been alone for a while, too, huh?" she asked.

When he nodded, she took a deep breath and smiled as she wiped the tears from her cheek.

"I'm sorry I'm crying. I don't mean to seem like I'm not grateful, because I am," she said. "I don't know how much longer I would have made it there by myself. I think I was going crazy. I kept hoping my sister would come for me, but she never did."

The boy pointed to the necklace Zoe wore around her neck. An infinity symbol with two different colored stones.

She looked down and touched a hand to the pendant, shaking her head. "What?" she asked. "Oh, my sister? How did you know she gave me this?"

His eyes widened. Her sister. That was why he'd sensed the guardian. This girl was related to her.

He pulled his notebook from his backpack and drew an infinity sign.

Your sister's symbol, he wrote.

Zoe looked at him like he'd lost his mind.

"I don't understand. Parrish doesn't have a symbol," she said. "She just said when she saw this, it made her think of me. See, I was going away on a big trip and Parrish couldn't come. She gave me this before I left. I talked to her once when all this first started, and she said she'd figure out a way to come for me, but that's crazy now. There's no way she could make it all the way here, even if she was still alive."

The boy shook his head in frustration. She didn't understand.

How could he explain what he knew when he had no voice to tell her?

What could he write to make her understand?

Parrish has been my friend for many lifetimes. She's alive.

He carefully wrote the words, and then pushed the notebook toward her, wondering if she would believe him or not.

Her lips parted, and she shook her head.

"A few weeks ago, I would have said you were crazy. There's no way you could have known my sister in another lifetime, but now?" She looked at him, her eyes wide with wonder. "We just flew over a city filled with zombies. I guess anything is possible."

She laughed, and the sound was contagious. He laughed with her, so happy for the sound of her voice in this quiet place that he nearly cried from joy.

"Is she really still alive?" she asked.

The boy took her hand and made sure her eyes were locked on his before he nodded. He placed a finger on the infinity sign she wore around her neck and nodded again, hoping that she understood.

Parrish was alive, and soon, she would come for them both.

———

I t took a few hours for his heart to stop racing and for both of them to settle down in the small apartment. He kept checking the windows to make sure they hadn't been followed, and after a while, once he was sure they were safe, his eyelids began to close on their own.

He'd been awake for such a long time.

The boy pointed to the couch in the living room, put his palms together, and brought them to his face in a gesture that universally meant sleep. Zoe understood right away.

"I'm sure you have to be tired after all that travel," she said. "I'm going to stay up for a while, if that's okay. I feel like all I did back in that hotel was sleep all the time. For some reason, I feel wide awake right now."

The boy pointed to the bedroom and then to the couch. She was his guest, and he wanted to make sure she was comfortable, but he wasn't sure how much longer he'd be able to keep his eyes open.

She pointed to the couch and sat down, patting it with her hands.

"This is fine for me, thanks," she said. "I don't want to take your bed."

He smiled. She was a very sweet girl, and he liked her a lot already.

He pulled out his notebook.

Food in the kitchen if you get hungry.

Stay away from the window.

Stay quiet. Many rotters here.

She read over his notes and nodded her head. "I'll be fine. You get some rest."

He nodded and disappeared into the bedroom, leaving the door cracked in case she needed to call out to him.

He must have fallen asleep within seconds, because he didn't even remember laying down. He had no idea how much time had passed before he woke up, but since the sun was still down, it couldn't have been long.

Still, the sound of music startled him. It was so faint, he

almost couldn't tell at first if it was real, but it was so foreign, some part of his brain must have picked up on it and alerted him.

Either way, her playing was dangerous.

He rushed from the bedroom, his hand outstretched as he reached for Zoe's shoulder. She was turned away from him, her head angled downward.

Time seemed to slow down as his hand reached toward her. It was as if some energy field surrounding her connected him to another place.

His vision blurred, and as his hand made contact with the skin on Zoe's arm, a different scene came into focus.

The guardians were there, sitting in a circle around him.

The connection was brief, only lasting for a moment, but it was enough to let him know he was not alone in this world, anymore.

As his own living room came back into focus, he noticed Zoe standing in front of him, her arms hugging her violin as if it were a doll. Her mouth was open in surprise, her eyes wide.

"What was that?" she asked, blinking back tears as she looked around the room. "Was that Parrish and her friends? I don't understand."

The boy smiled, a sense of peace filling him for the first time since the pandemic began.

The connection had been made. A first step to truly finding each other and putting an end to all of this.

Yes, he said inside his mind, sensing that now, she would be able to hear him.

Zoe's eyes grew even wider, and she gasped, touching a hand to her forehead.

He gently touched her arm and squeezed.

Those were four of the guardians sent here a long time ago to keep this world safe, he said, lifting his hand to see that a strong blue glow emanated from within. *And I am the fifth.*

He used the tip of one glowing finger to draw his sign in the air. A spiral that seemed to hover between them for a moment before it faded and disappeared into the darkness.

The boy smiled.

Finally, the real magic had begun.

THREE
CRASH

When the first light of the sun appeared on the horizon, the group left the safety of their small house and started their journey back to the compound.

They'd spent the early morning hours talking about what had happened with the fatalis stone, the boy they'd all seen in their vision, and what it all had to mean. In the end, the truth was undeniable.

This boy they had seen was the fifth they'd been searching for all this time.

And somehow, he'd gotten to Zoe before the Dark One ever had a chance.

Crash hadn't even realized he'd been dreaming of Parrish's little sister playing her violin, but after seeing her there in that flash moment, he knew it had been her all along.

None of them were exactly sure how it had happened. How had they managed to connect to the fifth's energy strongly enough to actually see him?

They'd spent hours trying to recreate it, but it hadn't happened again.

Crash was sure it had something to do with the fact that they'd all been touching at the same exact moment. The four of them in the house, and miles away in New York City, the boy touching Zoe.

Zoe was the connection.

She had more of a connection with Parrish than even most sisters, since she'd had a bone marrow transplant a few years ago. After hours of talking through the possibilities, that was the best they could figure.

Somehow, that transplant had given Zoe some of Parrish's powers. Maybe not enough to allow her to fight zombies with a glowing blue light or make her tears turn to ice, but maybe it was enough to give her a more natural immunity to the virus.

And to allow the fifth to sense her presence.

So, he'd found Zoe first, like some miracle of fate, and in the early morning hours, they'd somehow completed a circle of connection that allowed them all to see and sense each other.

It had also managed to unlock a piece of the magic inside the fatalis stone.

Every single one of them felt a new power surge through them the moment the fifth appeared, and after the brutal attack and betrayal the day before, it had given them all hope and the energy to move forward.

So, they'd spent the rest of the morning making their plans to go to New York.

Making the journey was unavoidable now.

It had gone from a suicide mission to save a small child to a necessary part of their hope of saving the world.

They had no idea what they would face once they got

there, but it was going to take everything they had just to survive it. Rescuing Zoe and meeting up with the fifth would take a miracle.

But then again, crazier things had happened.

Only, despite their hours of talking and planning, there were a few things Crash had decided to keep to himself.

Details about the dreams he'd been having lately. Or more appropriately, nightmares.

He'd hoped at first they were just dreams. Meaningless and random.

He should have known better.

There were tough times ahead.

For all of them.

The walk back to the bridge and, finally, to the Humvee waiting on the other side, was miraculously quiet.

Too quiet.

The lack of rotters wandering around left Crash feeling seriously on edge.

"What's with the silence?" he asked when they were safely back in the truck.

Noah joined him in the front, while the two girls climbed into the back.

It still felt weird to be one person short, and he wasn't looking forward to having to lie to Tank about what had happened to Lily.

"I have a theory," Noah said.

"Let's hear it," Crash said, grateful that the Humvee started right up and pulled away from the bridge easily.

"It was unusually quiet all the way to the hospital yesterday, too, right?" Noah asked. "I think Lily must have already commanded all the rotters in the area to go and wait for us there. We already know that Tank and his crew cleared out a ton of Z's from this area. I think Lily drew what was left in the neighborhood, which means that now there's no one left. Probably for miles."

"Do you think Lily was able to actually talk to those things before we even got to the hospital?" Parrish asked, leaning forward, her eyes wide. "I never saw her leave the compound, and I don't think anyone would have let her out alone. How did she do it?"

"She has some kind of mental ability," Karmen said. "Like mine. I could feel it that time she helped me with that big group back near Baltimore."

"Whoever she is, she has some of the Dark One's power, I think," Crash said. "She's working for her, and she's able to not only communicate with all the zombies in an area, but she's also able to take normal Z's and turn them into those super-crazy ones we've met along the way. She was the one I saw on the infrared that night on the rooftop in D.C., creating those zombie assassins, and she had that whole hospital ambush set up before we ever stepped foot out of the compound yesterday."

"So, then why help us?" Parrish asked. "Why give us the stone or tell us about Zoe? Why explain the truth about the Dark One?"

Crash shrugged. "Maybe in the end, she felt guilty about betraying us. Maybe she had regrets."

"Well, that or she's just setting up the next trap," Karmen said. "We were dumb enough to trust her the first time. I don't think we should make the same mistake twice."

The girl had a point.

If it hadn't been for Karmen speaking up about her suspicions, they might have walked into that trap yesterday with no clue what they were getting into.

"Luckily you were smart enough to realize something was wrong," he said, catching her eye in the rearview.

"I should have said something sooner," she said, looking away. "I didn't tell you guys this earlier, but back when we were still at Crash's place, I accidentally opened Lily's backpack. It was dark, and I thought it was mine, but she had this weird cape thing in there. I thought it was some kind of theater costume or something. I mean, what kind of person would forgo a fresh pair of underwear to make room for a giant black cape in their bag? I should have known better."

"From now on, maybe we should make a pact," Parrish said. "Whenever one of us comes across something strange or out of place, even if it seems insignificant at the time, we tell each other about it. Just in case."

"Yeah," Noah said. "Our best chance of survival now is being able to trust each other and work together. There can be no secrets."

Crash cleared his throat and nodded, shifting a bit in his seat.

He was all for a truth pact when it came to pointing out suspicions or weird things happening around them, but there were some things he'd rather keep to himself, even now.

Like the thing he'd seen in his dreams last night before he woke up in a cold sweat.

He shuddered now just thinking about it.

Sure, he'd considered telling them all about it while they were up talking, but in the end, he'd decided that his darkest visions were his burden to carry. No one else needed to know what they were really up against.

Besides, he didn't think anything would change Parrish's mind about New York. Not even a scary dream from a guy whose dreams almost always came true.

And if he was being honest, he didn't want to upset Karmen. She was tougher than she looked, but he felt a growing need to protect her and keep her safe.

Not that he'd ever admit that to her, of course.

"Well, that was the easiest drive of all time," Noah said, shaking his head as the compound appeared around the corner.

"You don't hear me complaining," Crash said. "Hopefully, your theory is correct, and it's just a case of cleared-out rotters."

Noah muttered, and Crash got the distinct feeling the guy didn't even believe in his own theory.

Oh well, they were safe now. This compound was probably the safest place on the east coast right now.

The guard at the gate jumped up so fast when the Humvee came into view, he nearly dropped his gun. He said something into his walkie and practically ran out of the guardhouse, waving them forward.

Crash slowed down as the guard yanked the fence open.

"You have no idea how happy I am to see you guys back here so soon," he said. "Stephen's taken a turn for the worst. I don't think anyone's expecting him to make it through the day. Please tell me you got the meds."

He said it more as a question than anything else, his expression tense.

The long-term survival of this entire compound likely depended on the medicines and supplies they'd managed to get from the hospital.

"We got 'em," Crash said.

The guard visibly relaxed his shoulders and sighed as he waved them through the gate. Crash pulled through quickly, and everyone jumped out of the truck, their packs all loaded down with supplies.

Crash's muscles burned from carrying several heavy bags all morning, but his bags weighed almost nothing compared to Noah's. It was only thanks to his amazing strength that they'd made it this far with everything. That guy could carry five times what anyone else could, but they had to be careful not to let anyone here know that.

Luckily, several men ran out from the compound to help them unload it all.

"Is this all medicine?" a guy named Quintin asked, his eyes wide as he took in the defibrillator and eight packed bags full of medical supplies and IV's.

"Most of it," Parrish said. "We grabbed as much as we could carry."

"The antibiotics are in my bag," Crash said. "I'll head straight to Stephen's room. You guys can take the rest of that to Tank and see where he wants to store it all."

"I'll join you as soon as I drop this stuff off," Noah whispered as they crossed paths. "Maybe I can enhance the healing without anyone noticing now that we have the meds."

Crash raced through the halls as fast as he could. Everyone he passed moved out of his way with a look of shock and admiration. He got the distinct feeling no one had expected them to come back.

Ever.

And could he really blame them? To everyone else, they just looked like a group of regular teenagers—mostly girls—

heading into a place groups of armed men hadn't been able to clear.

Crash smiled to himself.

They obviously didn't know the strength of the girls he had with him.

He finally pushed through to the area Tank and his wife, Kaya, had set up as the medical wing of the compound.

Stephen's wife, Cheryl, was standing in the hallway talking to Kaya. She was crying softly.

A terrible knot formed in Crash's stomach.

We can't be too late.

"I've got it," he shouted. "I've got the medicine. Is he—?"

Cheryl's eyes widened, and her mouth fell open in a sob.

"Oh, thank God," she said. "Maybe there's still a chance."

Her hands trembled as she pressed them against her growing belly. Kaya took the bag of penicillin from Crash's outstretched hands and ran into the makeshift hospital room.

Crash followed her in and stood with Stephen's wife at the end of the bed as Kaya inserted the IV and got everything flowing. The dude did not look good, but these meds were his best chance now.

Unless Noah was right.

Now that they had medication flowing through this guy's veins, a little extra healing might just be chalked up to the miracle of pharmaceuticals.

He kept one eye on the hallway, hoping to see Noah turn the corner. Unfortunately, Kaya seemed to want them all out of the room to give Stephen some space and extra rest.

Crash hated to point out that the guy was so out of it, he likely had no idea if anyone was in the room or not. A few extra visitors weren't going to disturb him, but Kaya wanted the room clear, which meant they had to go.

She was pretty much the boss around here.

They were all being ushered into the hallway when Noah finally appeared around the corner.

His eyes carried the question Crash had asked when he first got here.

"He's still alive," Crash said, meeting his friend's eyes. "Barely. He's got the IV going, but I don't know if it's going to be enough."

"All we can do now is wait and see," Kaya said. "Hopefully you all made it back just in time."

Noah and Crash shared a look. They needed to get Noah back in that room.

"I'd like to see him, if I could," Noah said, slightly stumbling over his words. "I know he needs his rest, and I promise I won't be in there long, but I just want to check on him."

Kaya's brow came together in a frown. "I don't think that's a good idea. He's been through so much."

Cheryl shook her head.

"For goodness sake, Kaya, look at them. They're exhausted. They obviously risked everything to get back here as fast as they could. The least we can do is honor a small request to see him."

She placed a hand on Noah's arm.

"I know you guys haven't been here long enough to get to know Stephen, but the fact that you all agreed to do this just to help him means the world to me. If you want to see him and say a few words, I think he would appreciate it."

Crash let out a nervous breath and nodded to Noah, opening the door and motioning for him to go inside.

Luckily, the two women stayed out in the hallway while Noah went over to the bed. With a quick look at Crash, Noah placed his hands on Stephen's arm and closed his eyes.

He half expected to see a glow of blue light surround the place where Noah touched the guy, but the only light in the room was coming from a heart monitor beside the bed. Still, Crash could feel the energy shift in the room.

He just hoped it was enough to save the guy.

It was funny how much it suddenly mattered to him that this stranger pulled through. They didn't really know him at all, but the fact that this guy had a baby on the way made Crash anxious to see him live.

Enough families had been destroyed or torn apart during the past few months. It would be nice to see a family growing despite the destruction everywhere else. The idea of it filled him with hope.

After a couple minutes, though, Noah pulled away, slightly out of breath. Crash searched his eyes, but Noah just shrugged. He didn't seem to know if it had even worked.

Crash nodded toward the door. They had done everything they could now, and Kaya was right. Nothing left but to wait.

Tank was waiting in the hallway with Kaya. He clapped a hand on Crash's shoulder as they left the room.

"I can't thank you enough, man," he said. " I saw what you guys brought back, and I almost can't believe it. That's enough medicine and supplies to last us for a long time, if we're careful. I don't know how we can ever thank you, other than to tell you you're all welcome to stay here for as long as you want."

Crash swallowed. God knows, he wished they could stay here forever, but that didn't seem to be in the cards.

"There is something I think you can help us with, if you

have a few minutes," he said. He glanced at Kaya. "No offense to you, Kaya, but if you don't mind, I'd love to talk to Tank for a few minutes alone."

She smiled and squeezed Tank's hand. "No offense taken," she said. "Besides, I've been up all night with Stephen. I'm going to leave someone else to watch over him for a while, so I can get a little bit of rest."

She raised up on tiptoes to plant a kiss on Tank's cheek, nodded to Crash and Noah, and disappeared around the corner toward the main wing.

"What's up?" Tank asked, brow furrowed. "Is this about the girl you lost? Jason told me one of your friends didn't come back with you. The quiet girl. I'm sorry, I can't remember her name."

"Lily," Crash said, trying to make his face look sad, despite his anger toward the girl. He could, at least, be sad about her betrayal and the fact that the fifth was still out there alone. "She didn't make it, Tank. The hospital was so much worse than we imagined."

"Oh, shit, I'm sorry," he said, his eyes darkening. "And here you are trying to make sure one of our guys is doing okay. How are you and your friends all holding up? I know how it feels to lose someone you love."

"We all know that type of loss now," Noah said. "We hadn't known her very long, but for a while, we thought of her like family. I think we're all still in shock about it."

Tank nodded.

"There's been too much loss," he said, glancing at Stephen's room. "Hopefully her sacrifice can make a difference here today. There's no doubt all that medicine is going to save a lot of lives."

"Let's hope so," Crash said. "While he's resting, though, is there someplace you and I could go to talk? In private?"

"Of course," he said. "But are you sure you don't want to rest up and get a shower first? No offense, but you boys look like hell."

"I don't doubt that," Crash said with a laugh. "And while the idea of a shower is just about the best thing I've heard all day, there's something we've got to do that can't wait. We could use all the help we can get."

Tank studied him for a second, then finally nodded.

"Come with me back to my office," he said. "No one will bother us there."

Crash turned to Noah. "Go get Parrish," he said. "She'll want to be part of this conversation."

Noah nodded and jogged back down the hallway.

Tank started heading the opposite way back to his office, and as they passed by Stephen's door, Crash couldn't help but look in on the guy.

His wife sat in a large chair next to his bed, her eyes closed and her hands resting against her belly. Stephen was still asleep, but Crash could have sworn that even though only a few minutes had passed since they'd started up the IV, Stephen's breathing had already evened out and the color had started to return to his cheeks.

"You coming?" Tank asked.

With a smile, Crash closed the door and followed Tank down the hallway.

He had a feeling that despite everything else that had gone wrong in the past few months, this was one time when everything was going to be alright.

FOUR
PARRISH

Parrish headed toward Tank's office, and as she walked through the compound, everyone turned to stare or stopped to say thank you. Word of what they'd done had traveled quickly.

It was obvious most people had thought their trip to the hospital was more of a suicide mission than anything else, and they were probably shocked to know a group of teens had survived it.

Parrish normally might have been annoyed at the fact that they'd sent them out never expecting them to return, but the truth was she was glad they could do it. The five—four—of them were obviously more capable than anyone here knew. If it hadn't been for Lily and her betrayal, the trip would have been easy.

No one here, despite their looks of surprise and awe, had any clue what they had just been through yesterday, or how close they had all come to dying.

And Parrish had a feeling deep down that if the four of them died, it wouldn't matter how many compounds there were like this in the world or how safe they all seemed to think they were. Eventually, the witch Lily had called the Dark One was going to have enough power to break free, and this entire world—perhaps all of humanity—would be over.

The weight of that realization made every step feel heavy.

She agreed with Karmen. She hadn't asked for this kind of responsibility. At least not in this lifetime. And she wanted to save Zoe more than anything else.

But the fate of this entire world rested on their shoulders. That truth was starting to become more obvious by the day. How could they ignore it?

They simply couldn't, and no matter how tired or scared that made her feel, she knew they still had a long way to go before this was over.

She knocked on the door to Tank's office, and he told her to come in. Both he and Crash were sitting by the desk, waiting for her.

"Where are Karmen and Noah?" Crash asked. "Didn't they want to come?"

Parrish shook her head. "All Karmen cares about right now is getting the zombie guts off her arms," she said. "And I don't know about Noah. He said he had something to take care of."

He'd seemed a bit anxious to her, but she didn't have time to stop and question him. She'd have to catch up with him later.

Crash waved her over toward the desk where he'd set up a few chairs and opened up a large paper map of roads in the area.

"Okay, so now that you're both here, are you guys going to tell me just what crazy shit you're thinking of doing?" Tank asked. "Because in my mind, if you're wanting to do anything but stay here and put your feet up for a while, you're stupid."

"I guess we're stupid, then," Parrish said with a smile as she took a seat in the chair opposite Tank. "What did Crash tell you so far?"

"Nothing, except that he wanted to know if I had a map of Philly and surrounding areas," he said. "What's this all about?"

"I'm just going to put this bluntly," she said, already anticipating this guy's reaction. "We need to get into New York City as fast as possible. What do you know about the state of the roads between here and there? And what about the bridges leading onto the island of Manhattan? Is any of it passable? Are the bridges still standing? Has anyone come this way who fled from that area that we could talk to?"

Tank sat back slowly in his chair, his jaw hanging slightly open. At first, he didn't say anything at all. He just looked at Parrish like she had just completely lost her mind.

Whatever he'd imagined they were up to, it apparently had not even touched the crazy that was NYC.

"I don't think I heard you right," he said finally. "Because it sounded like you said Manhattan."

"I did. We have to get up there as soon as possible," she said. "What do you know about it?"

Tank's eyes widened.

"Are you kidding me?" he asked, voiced raised.

He stood up and paced the floor behind his desk.

"It's a death trap. You think that hospital was bad? Whatever you guys faced there is going to be nothing—and I mean child's play—compared to what you'll find in Manhattan, if you could even hope to step foot on that island in the first place. The government quarantined that area, shut off all the bridges and access roads early on. No one in or out, which means a hell of a lot of people dead in a very small area. Any survivors might have been able to hold out for a few days or even weeks with enough supplies and a strong barricade, but there's no hope for anyone stuck on that island, because there's no way for them to get out. That whole area is lost for good."

"There are survivors," Parrish said, having to almost force a lump out of her throat to say it. She'd pretty much given up on ever seeing her sister again, but Lily had given her hope.

The vision they'd had early this morning had made it real. Zoe was alive and hiding out somewhere on or near the island of Manhattan.

"Not anyone you're going to be able to help," Tank said, glancing over at Crash, as if he expected his friend to talk some sense into her. "Maybe if you could get hold of a helicopter or something, you could have a chance of landing on one of the buildings up there and rescuing someone, but trying to make your way through the city by foot? It's impossible. We're talking about thousands of undead. Maybe even millions. You'll never survive it."

Parrish swallowed back her fear, a wave of nausea coming over her. She wanted to steady her voice before she responded. Luckily, Crash stepped in before she had to.

"Then, where can we get a helicopter?" Crash asked, as if it was no big deal to find one and learn how to fly it.

Parrish smiled.

At least he was all in on going with her to rescue Zoe, but at this point, I think they all realized there was more to NYC than just Zoe. If she really had somehow hooked up with the fifth, everyone's fate depended on them reuniting as soon as possible.

Destiny had been leading them with a heavy hand since the very beginning. They were in this now, one way or the other, no matter the danger.

"Look, I know how crazy this sounds, but we're going to New York City," Parrish said, scooting her chair forward so she could get a better look at the large map spread across the table. "My sister is there, and we know she's alive. We know the risks, but we have to at least try to get to her. She's only ten years old, and she's managed to survive this long. I know we can get her out of there if we're smart about it, but we need to figure out the best and fastest way into Manhattan. If you have any ideas, we'd love to hear them, but we don't have time for you to try to talk us out of it."

"And we're going to need to take some of your firepower with us, if we can," Crash said. "Or get your help on where we can pick up some more of our own on the way up there. We have a decent amount of supplies, but we're going to need more."

Tank studied them each in turn, as if trying to tell, once and for all, whether they were playing some kind of joke on him.

"I can't believe you're really thinking of doing this, but if you insist on trying, I'll do what I can to help," he said, finally, sitting back down in his chair. "It's the least I can do after what you've done for us. I hate now that I asked you to do something so dangerous for us right after you got here, and now you're going to leave again, but you have to understand that we didn't have anyone else who could go out there."

"Don't feel bad about it. It's not like you forced us to go,"

Parrish said. "We did it because we wanted to help. Now, help us get to Manhattan."

He took a deep breath and ran a hand over his bald head as he studied the map.

"Well, you aren't going to get there driving," he said. "Like I told you, all the bridges are blocked off by military barricades with no one left to let you through. Not that you could get to the bridges in that Hummer anyway."

"Why not?" Crash asked.

"I-95 is a parking lot of dead cars and pileups," he said. "We had a few guys try to make it up that way to retrieve some family, but once they got about five miles outside of Philly, they said the roads were impassable. They had to switch to back roads, and even then, most of those were clogged up and useless. There are fires, pileups, traffic jams everywhere. Just too many damn people. Trying to get a Humvee through that mess would be impossible."

"Did they get to their family okay?" Parrish asked.

For a moment, nausea nearly overwhelmed her, but she managed to hold it at bay. She was just exhausted.

"They did, and they got everyone, including a few young kids, back here safely, but it took them over a week. They had to take most of it on foot," he said. "If it's that bad around here, it's going to be a nightmare up through New York. The toll roads and tunnels? You'll never make it."

"Walking all the way from here to New York would take us days," Crash said. "And that's only if we could walk ten hours a day without stopping."

"That's not an option, either," Parrish said, her heart racing. "We need to get up there tomorrow. What else can we do? Do you think we could really find a helicopter around here? How hard would it be to learn to fly that?"

Tank laughed.

"I was joking about a helicopter. Even if you could find a helo nearby, it would take one of you weeks to learn how to fly," he said. "But the real hardship would be figuring out how and where to land that beast. It's not going to be easy, especially if half the rooftops of the city are filled with rotters, which is a good possibility. You have no idea what you're going to find when you get up there, and it's not like it'll be easy to refuel."

Parrish groaned. She hadn't thought about all that. She had no doubt Crash could learn to fly it in seconds, but unless they could land directly on the roof of the Four Seasons, they'd end up having to fight their way through a crowded, dark skyscraper and through the streets, anyway.

Of course, Zoe might not be at the Four Seasons, anymore. How, exactly, were they going to find her if she'd left and gone somewhere else?

A helicopter wasn't going to work, but there had to be a solution.

"Not our best option, then," she said. "What else could we do that would be fast and relatively safe?"

She stared at the map, trying to figure out what they could do that wouldn't take them days on foot. Lily had a head start for sure, and she also had abilities none of them fully understood. There was no doubt in Parrish's mind that Lily was already in New York.

Somehow, though, Zoe had gotten away just in time. She couldn't still be at the hotel, then. The fifth would have taken her somewhere safe, and how far could two small children get on their own, anyway?

She racked her mind for any solution, trying to think outside the box. They would keep working on their attempt to recreate the vision they'd had. Maybe, if they could strengthen it enough, they might even be able to talk to Zoe or the fifth. Warn them about what was coming or find out exactly where they were inside the city.

They couldn't rely on that, though.

For now, they had to assume they'd be able to sense their connection once they were all inside the city together.

They just had to get there, first.

The roads were packed too much for a Humvee to get through, but what about something smaller?

"Motorcycles," she said, sitting up. She didn't know if it was the dumbest idea she'd had, or the smartest. "What if we could find some motorcycles and weave around the cars and pileups? Do you think that would get us through the traffic jams?"

Tank raised an eyebrow and considered it. "That could work. You might opt for dirt bikes or something that can go off-road. Something small but powerful," he said. "That will definitely get you there faster than walking. With a small enough bike, you should be able to maneuver through a lot of the traffic, but what's going to stop you is those tunnels."

He pointed to a location on the map.

"Those could be packed all the way through from one side to the other with no idea how many rotters are trapped inside. It's risky. You'd have to get out and walk from there."

It was a start. She leaned over the map, wondering where

they could get their hands on four dirt bikes when Crash stood up and shouted.

"I've got it," he said. "I feel stupid for not seeing it sooner, but it makes complete sense."

"What?" she asked, hoping he really did have a brilliant idea in that head of his.

"Water," he said, sitting back down and pointing to the swath of blue on the map. "We go east to the water, then we can take a boat all the way to Manhattan. It is an island, after all, and there aren't going to be any zombies or fifty car pileups on the water."

She wanted to stand up and dance for joy.

Yes!

Why hadn't that occurred to her sooner? She'd been so wrapped up in thinking about the roads that the idea of taking a boat had never entered her mind.

"That's brilliant," she said, feeling almost giddy with excitement. They would be able to zip up to Manhattan in no time with a nice speed boat. "Now, we just have to figure out where to find a boat and where to dock on the island. This is going to shave off so much time, though, and it'll be the safest way to travel as long as the weather's good."

"Thank you," Crash said, winking. "I bet we'll have our choice of amazing boats at any marina along the coast."

"Do any of you kids know how to navigate a boat?" Tank asked. "Not exactly as tricky as a helicopter, but it's still going to take some skill to get up to New York if none of you have ever captained a boat."

"Karmen's family has a boat," Parrish said. "They used to take us skiing on the lake in the summer when I was little. I've seen Karmen drive it before. She knows what to do."

That little nugget of information seemed to surprise Tank, and a little hint of admiration crossed Crash's features, too. Parrish was pretty sure there was more going on between Crash and Karmen than either of them had let on just yet, and she loved it. Karmen needed a guy like Crash to keep her grounded.

And it was obvious Crash had a huge crush on her.

Parrish smiled. Maybe someday this whole thing would be over and the four of them could double-date. Stranger things had happened, right? Besides, she had to hold onto some type of hope that things could eventually go back to normal.

Otherwise, what were they doing all of this for, anyway?

"Then, water it is," Tank said. "I agree that's your best bet. The safest route to the water is avoiding the highway and taking all the backroads toward the coast. If I were you, I'd head out toward someplace like Brick Township or Toms River."

"What about this place?" Crash asked, pointing to a spot on the map labeled Windward Beach Park. "Have you ever been there?"

"A couple times with my brother," Tank said. "You'll definitely find a good selection of boats to choose from up there, and you'll have an easy trip up to Manhattan from there. I think it's a good spot to aim for."

"How long to get there, you think?" Parrish asked.

"In normal circumstances, it would take about an hour and a half to drive over there," Tank said. "With this mess and all the detours and possible dangers along the way, I'd say maybe six hours? And that's possibly underestimating. If you take the Humvee, maybe days if you end up stuck and having to walk part of the way."

Hope stirred in her heart. If they could find some bikes, they could be there by dark if they left soon.

"And from there, how long of a boat ride up to the city?"

Tank cleared his throat. "I've never made that trip, myself, but if I had to guess from eyeballing it, I'd say an hour tops."

She nearly cried out in excitement. Seven hours to get to Manhattan on a bad day? This was a dream. They could leave in an hour or two, find a place along the coast for the night, and then make their way into Manhattan at first light.

If they could find a place to dock somewhat close to the Four Seasons, they might even make it to Zoe before nightfall. Her sister had to be hiding somewhere nearby.

Parrish still had no real idea how they were going to get through massive throngs of rotters in the city, not to mention whatever super zombies Lily and the Dark One had waiting for them, but they would take it one step at a time.

Plus, they still had the rest of the trip today to work through some ideas. Crash seemed to be pretty good at coming up with battle plans, and they could talk or think while they rode out to the coast.

It was just too bad they couldn't take the Humvee and the machine guns into the city with them, but maybe they could find similar weapons once they were there. Tank had said there was a strong military presence in New York in the beginning before things got overrun, which made sense being the most populated city in the US. Maybe there were still some tanks around the city they could get their hands on.

Even without fuel, Crash could probably get them running with his power.

Of course, she would take every last rotter down with her

sword if she had to. She wouldn't stop until Zoe was safe at her side.

"Okay, so we have the beginning of a plan," she said, following the route to the coast with her fingertip.

"What's next?" Crash asked.

Parrish looked to Tank, an eyebrow raised.

"Got any maps of Manhattan?"

FIVE

NOAH

Noah Vincent smiled at everyone he passed in the hallway on his way back to his room, but when they tried to stop and chat about what had happened at the hospital, he waved them away and made an excuse about wanting to get cleaned up.

The truth was, he was barely keeping it together.

With every second that passed, he felt worse and worse.

By the time he reached his room, he guessed his fever was over a hundred and three. His whole body shivered, and he had started to sweat. He prayed Karmen wasn't in there, because he didn't want to explain what he was feeling to anyone else until he'd worked out just how bad it really was.

Luckily, the room the four of them shared was empty except for their bags and belongings.

He locked the door and quickly stripped down to his underwear. The smell of blood on his clothes made him queasy. But the instant he was half-naked, he could no longer control his shivering.

He crawled into bed and pulled the blanket up to his chin.

Within minutes, he was so hot, his forehead dripped with sweat.

Damn. He never should have tried to heal that guy, Stephen. He'd known something was wrong when he started using his magic on the illness. It felt different from the times he'd healed a small wound.

With this, it was almost like he'd been pulling the sickness and infection out of the guy's body...and into his own.

Without Noah's magic, though, Stephen would have been dead by nightfall. The infection had gotten so bad even the strongest antibiotics couldn't save him. Noah had known that much the second he touched him.

Maybe that was why he kept going, even though he'd felt the sickness oozing into him. If Stephen died after all they'd been through to bring these meds back to him, it would just make everything feel so pointless.

What were they fighting for, anyway, if not for families like Stephen's to go on and rebuild this world, someday?

No one knew at this point just how many had died across the globe, but based on the number of survivors they'd seen since they first left their homes, Noah had a feeling more than half the world's population was gone.

And that was being optimistic.

How many more would have to die because he and his friends didn't know what the hell they were doing?

If they had been sent here to protect this world in case the Dark One awakened someday, why hadn't they been able to remember everything? Why couldn't they figure out how to stop her?

What if they never did? Would all of humanity be lost?

Noah pulled the thin blanket tighter around his trembling body. Damn. His mind was spinning. If he didn't pull himself together, his thoughts would only get darker.

As much as he wanted to just lie here and try to get some rest, he had a feeling that the more he gave into it, the more the sickness would take over.

Just how much of it had he taken on?

Reluctantly, he peeled the blanket off his moist skin and sat up, clutching the edge of the mattress until the room stopped spinning around him.

He laughed to keep from crying.

And he'd thought he was invincible.

Noah made it about three steps toward the door before he collapsed in a heap on the floor.

SIX

KARMEN

Karmen stood on the rooftop of the compound, staring out over the neighboring houses and wondering if things could ever go back to normal.

She groaned and shook her head. That was the dumbest thing she could think, though, wasn't it? The greater part of the world's population was walking around trying to eat people.

That wasn't exactly the kind of thing the world was likely to ever recover from.

Even if they did manage to put an end to this witch person who started the virus in the first place, they would have to kill every rotter and clean up the world before they were all safe again. And how many people would be left at that point?

Enough to start over?

And after what they'd already seen from Lily, what were the chances they could survive the Dark One, much less actually defeat her and her army of rotters?

It was impossible.

Parrish had said they'd made a choice a long time ago, in

another life, to come to this world and protect them from the Dark One in case she ever went free.

But the thing no one had mentioned yet was why, if they were so strong and capable, had they failed to kill this Dark One all those years ago? Why lock her away and seal her power? Why not just kill her if she was so dangerous?

This had been the question on Karmen's mind since last night, even though she hadn't dared speak it out loud.

There was only one answer to that question, anyway.

The only reason they wouldn't have killed her back then was that they couldn't. And that was with their full memories and power.

What exactly did they think they were going to do against her now when they had no real clue what their true abilities were or how to effectively use them?

They needed more time. They needed someone to teach them what to do. Karmen was sure she had only scratched the surface of her powers.

Yes, she could somehow reach into people's minds and command them in some way, but she had a feeling she could do more than that if she really tried. Like listen to their thoughts, maybe.

Or see inside their dreams.

That's what that witch had done, right? Lily? She'd seen inside Crash's dreams.

Well, maybe Karmen could do that, too.

And she wanted more time to play around with those abilities before they went charging into a city full of those dead things. Ugh. It sucked that Zoe was trapped in New York, of all places.

Why couldn't she have been playing her violin in Cincinnati? Or Nashville? Somewhere with less than a million people living there?

Better than Vienna or Paris, where they'd have almost no hope of reaching her, but it still sucked.

Karmen understood why they had to get up there to find Zoe and the fifth before the Dark One could find them, but that didn't mean she had to like it.

If the others thought a handful of super zombies were difficult to defeat and that they'd barely survived the hospital, what did they think they were going to face in Manhattan?

A million regular rotters. Hundreds, maybe thousands of super zombies. If Lily was really creating them herself, and she was up there now with at least a full day's head start, she would have plenty of time to create an army of them and place them all around the city.

They were never going to get through all that, and Lily knew it.

But Lily also knew that Parrish wouldn't be able to resist going after Zoe.

Karmen shook her head and plopped herself down on a concrete block at the edge of the roof. Could she seriously blame Parrish, though?

If she'd had a younger sister, she would have protected that little girl more fiercely than anyone could imagine. There was no way she would have ever let her father mess with her little sister the way he had done with Karmen. She would have killed him first.

So, she could kind of understand how Parrish felt.

Karmen's stomach twisted as she thought of what they were about to face. There was no avoiding it, really. They had to get to New York, find Zoe, and meet up with the fifth. They had discussed it all morning before the sun came up, and no matter how much she hated it, she knew they had to go.

A single male guard was up on the roof with her, pacing from one side of the rooftop to the other, looking out for any sign of unusual activity. He'd passed by Karmen's perch at the edge of the roof multiple times, but this time, he stopped in his tracks and cursed loudly.

She looked up, prepared to tell him to watch his language, but the second she saw the sheer terror on his face, she shut her mouth and followed his gaze.

Karmen scrambled to her feet and backed away from the edge of the roof.

An army of rotters stumbled down the streets. It wasn't just one or two. It was hundreds. Thousands, maybe. Elbow to elbow coming from every visible street in this direction.

"No. No, no, no," the guard muttered.

He seemed to be frozen in his tracks, just staring ahead with his mouth open.

"Sound the alarm," Karmen shouted, waving a hand in front of the guy's face. "There's no time to waste here. We have to move now."

The guy didn't move. A tear rolled down his cheek, and he looked like he was contemplating dropping to the ground and rolling into the fetal position.

Some lookout he turned out to be.

If he didn't get everyone to their stations right away, they were going to be in some major trouble.

No wonder the freaking neighborhoods had been so quiet all morning on their drive back. Hadn't they learned their lesson with this crap yesterday on their way over to the hospital?

An abnormal lack of rotter activity did not mean they weren't there. It meant they were somewhere you couldn't see them, assembling for a massive attack.

She wouldn't forget it again.

Karmen closed her eyes and focused her energy, reaching into the guard's mind with as calm a tone as she could muster, considering the circumstances.

It's going to be okay. Sound the alarm and call for help. Get moving now.

The moment she thought the word "now", the guard seemed to wake up. He ran over toward the siren Karmen had seen them cranking when the group first got there, but instead of turning the hand crank, he reached for a walkie hidden there in a bag beneath it.

The walkie had a strip of red electrical tape around it.

"Code red," he said clearly. "All hands on deck. We have a horde approaching from the South..."

He turned in a circle to survey the area and stopped abruptly, dropping the walkie to the ground. The hard plastic side broke into several pieces that scattered across the ground at his feet.

Loud static responded from the broken walkie, but Karmen couldn't hear what the person on the other side was saying. She picked it up and pressed the button on the side, hoping whoever was there could at least still hear her.

"Major horde approaching the compound from all directions," she shouted. "Get your asses to your stations. Now."

More static responded, so Karmen did the only thing she could think of doing. She had no idea if it would work, but at this point, she had to at least try.

She gripped the walkie in her hand and focused her attention on whoever nearby might be tuned into this frequency.

We are being attacked. Thousands of rotters from all directions. Move as fast as you can. Spread the word.

The guard near her still hadn't moved at all, but she didn't have time to sit up here and babysit him. She needed to find her friends as fast as possible.

The group here was about to get the shock of their lives when they saw the real way she and her friends fought, but if they had any hope of survival, none of them could hold back.

A terrifying thought crossed her mind, and with a growing knot in her stomach, she turned to look at the group of rotters once again. She couldn't quite see them clearly from here. It just looked like a mass of putrid bodies, but she remembered seeing the guy next to her looking through a set of fancy binocular thingies a few times.

She turned to him and was about to ask him to hand them over, but he had totally lost it. His entire body trembled, and his wide eyes made him look insane.

"This can't be happening," he said. *"We cleared all these areas. We'll never survive this. We're all going to die."*

Something about the way he looked seemed strange to Karmen at first, but she immediately realized what it was.

Those last words hadn't been spoken out loud. For the first time, Karmen had actually been able to hear what someone else was thinking.

Goosebumps broke out all over her arms.

"We'll be fine," she said, patting him on the shoulder and sending a wave of calm energy into his mind. "Call everyone in. This is what you've been training for. And hand me those binoculars."

He nodded, inhaled a ragged breath, and then handed her the military-grade binoculars he'd had clipped to his belt.

The door to the roof pushed open, and a group of armed men and women rushed out, the fear in their eyes turning to sheer terror as they saw the number of rotters headed their way.

But these guys had no idea what terror was yet.

With trembling hands, Karmen brought the binoculars up to her eyes and searched the ocean of rotters, looking for one thing.

Glowing red eyes.

SEVEN

PARRISH

P arrish marked three potential docking sites with
pennies from a dish on Tank's desk. No one would
likely be using this kind of money again for a very
long time. If ever. It felt foreign in her hand.

"Where, exactly, is your sister hiding out?" Tank asked.
"And you still haven't explained to me how you know for sure
she's alive. None of the phones have been working for a long
time."

"Her last known location was the Four Seasons," Parrish
said, not really wanting to have to explain more than that.
"She's likely still close to there."

Tank opened his mouth to protest, but she cut him off.

"Look, I know you think we're taking a huge risk here, but I
don't think I have the energy to explain to you how we know or
why it's so important that we go," she said. "I would appreciate
it if you would just trust that we know what we're doing and
let it go."

Tank raised his eyebrows and looked at Crash, who just shrugged.

"Okay," Tank said. "I'll take your word for it, and if you really want me to, I'll stop trying to talk you out of it. You have to understand just how hard it is for me to think about you kids voluntarily walking into such a terrible situation. I'd rather you stayed here, where you're safe."

As if to contradict his argument, though, a walkie on his desk with a strip of red tape across it lit up. "Code red," the man on the other side said. "All hands on deck. We have a horde approaching—"

Tank picked up the walkie and pressed the button.

"Jonathan, say again," he said. "How many can you see?

There was no response. Just static.

Tank repeated himself, but he didn't wait for more information to come through. He grabbed a set of rifles leaning against the wall behind him and handed one to Crash.

"Let's get to the roof," he said.

Parrish and Crash shared a look.

This was not good. And by not good, it was potentially catastrophic.

Had their actions at the hospital brought the wrath of the Dark One down on this small compound of survivors? Parrish would never forgive herself if the families sheltered here died today.

Static burst out of the walkie, but it was too jumbled to really hear. It sounded like a female voice this time, but Parrish only caught a few words like "horde", "compound", and "stations".

"Damn this thing," Tank yelled, throwing it to the ground. "We have to get up there."

He took a few steps and then stopped all of a sudden, placing a hand to his temple. He shook his head, confused.

"What is it?" Parrish asked. "Are you okay?"

Tank took a deep breath and looked into her eyes. "I don't know," he said. "The weirdest thing. Like someone was talking directly into my mind. What the hell is happening here today?"

Parrish exchanged another look with Crash.

"Karmen," he said. "She must be up on the roof. Come on."

But Parrish only took a handful of steps before she heard Karmen's voice in her own mind. Tank was right. It was definitely weird to hear someone else's voice in her head. It was almost like she was wearing headphones and talking on the phone, but it was even clearer than that.

Like Karmen had opened a direct line into her brain.

Neat trick, but when the hell had she learned to do that?

It's bad, you guys. Maybe thousands. Some have red eyes. Meet me in our room as fast as possible. Already on my way there.

Crash grabbed Parrish's arm.

"Did you hear her, too?" he asked.

"What are you doing?" Tank shouted over his shoulder. "Get to the roof, and tell everyone you see on the way to grab their weapons and get to their stations."

He disappeared around the corner, but Parrish and Crash didn't follow him.

"I heard," she said. "Let's get to the room."

They both took off running in the opposite direction from Tank, heading back toward the sleeping quarters. Parrish prayed Noah was in the room, or that wherever he was, he heard Karmen, too.

Parrish had no idea how long Karmen had been able to do something like that, but the girl had basically opened a party line into their brains.

That would come in handy. If they survived whatever the heck was going on outside.

Another horde? Red-eyed super zombies?

It had been less than twenty-four hours since they'd fought the last group of zombies at the hospital. The Dark One wasn't giving them any breathing room, that's for sure.

But this time, she was going after more than just the four of them. She was going after an entire compound full of innocent families.

"What's our strategy?" she said to Crash as they ran through the hallways. "We aren't going to be able to hide our abilities if we really want to save these people."

"Damn, I didn't think of that," he said. "But you're right. I just hope it's going to be enough. Karmen said there were maybe thousands of rotters out there. I mean, I know she can be prone to exaggeration and drama sometimes, but I doubt she'd overestimate this kind of thing."

"I don't think so, either," Parrish said, a knot of fear forming in her stomach. This was bad. "The group here can probably handle a good deal of the normal ones with the weapons they have, but if one of those super zombies breaks through the fence or scales the walls they built here, they could take out half the compound before anyone knew what was happening. These people are defenseless against zombies with powers."

"We can't let that happen," he said just as they got to the room.

But when Parrish turned the knob, it wouldn't budge.

She backed up to check the room number, but it was definitely the right room.

She tried the door again, but it was locked. She pounded on the door.

"Noah? Are you in there?" she asked. "Open the door. There's a horde outside the walls."

When there was no response, something inside Parrish twisted. What was going on here?

Karmen came running down the hallway, her eyes wide. "It actually worked, didn't it?" she asked. "What are you both doing out here? Let's get inside and come up with a plan before it's too late."

"The door's locked," Crash said.

"Is Noah in there?" Karmen asked.

"We don't know," Parrish said. "Did you try to reach him with your mind earlier?"

"I tried to connect with all of you," she said.

"Can you tell if he's in there?" Parrish asked.

Why wasn't he answering the door? And why would he have locked it in the first place?

Maybe he just wasn't in there at all. Maybe he was on his way here now, and he'd just locked the door behind him to keep their stuff safe.

That had to be it.

Only, she didn't think that was it. She knew he was in that room, and that something was wrong. She could feel it.

"We have to break it down," she shouted, suddenly feeling that they didn't have much time. "Crash, help me."

Together, they both walked as far away from the door as they could and then counted to three. In sync, they both rammed the side of their bodies into the door.

Thankfully, these rooms were not designed to be all that secure. No one who built this place ever expected it to be a safe zone against a zombie horde or anything like that, so there was just a normal doorknob and lock, like you'd see in any house or office building.

The door opened, and both she and Crash had to catch themselves before they ran into the set of bunk beds against the wall on the other side of the room.

To her horror, Noah was curled up on the floor, shivering.

No, shivering was not a strong enough word to describe it. He was shaking uncontrollably.

Parrish dropped to the floor at his side.

"Noah, can you hear me?" she asked.

She placed a hand on his arm to try to get him to open his eyes, but the moment her skin touched his, her panic ratcheted up a notch.

"He's burning up," she said. "Crash, grab a washcloth and water bottle from my bag."

"We don't have time for this," Karmen said. "He has to wake up. How did he even get sick?"

Parrish shook him a little less gently this time, and he didn't even attempt to open his eyes. Was he in some kind of coma?

When had this happened? She'd just seen him an hour or so ago when he'd told her to go to Tank's office. He seemed fine then. How had he gotten so sick in just an hour?

Her entire body went stiff with fear.

"Do you think it's possible he's been bitten?" she asked.

Noah had apparently taken most of his clothes off before he climbed into bed, so it made it easier for her to search for any kind of bite.

"There's not a scratch on him," she said. "I don't understand. What could have happened to him?"

Crash handed her a cool, wet washcloth, and she pressed it against his forehead.

"Stephen," he said, sitting down on one of the other beds. "He helped to heal Stephen, earlier. The guy was so far gone, everyone was sure he was going to die. Even with the antibiotics, it wasn't looking good. But Noah stepped in. Did his healing thing. Maybe something got into his system."

Parrish tried to calm her mind, but it was racing a mile a minute.

They had a horde of zombies closing in on this place, with God knows how many super zombies in the mix. Zoe and the fifth were alive and trapped somewhere in New York with the Dark One and Lily searching for them.

And now Noah had contracted some kind of potentially fatal illness from trying to heal a guy they'd never spoken to before and already risked their lives to save.

It was not a great day.

"I hate to break it to you, but we don't have time to deal with him right now," Karmen said. "Let him stay in here and rest if he has to, but we've got a horde to deal with."

"He might die if we don't deal with this right now. A battle out there could last hours. I can't just leave him like this."

"If we don't leave him, we might all die," Karmen shouted.

Parrish shook her head. This was not a choice she was prepared to make. She needed to take it one thing at a time.

Everyone kept looking to her to be the leader here, but she didn't have all the answers, either.

She was tired of having it all put on her shoulders. She just wasn't cut out for it.

"Then you come up with a plan," she said to Karmen. "I'm going to try to wake him up, so you can either help me, or you can get out."

She saw Karmen and Crash exchange worried glances, but she honestly didn't have time or energy to think about them. She just needed Noah to wake up so they could go out and fight. She needed him by her side right now.

Somewhere inside her mind, she realized how ridiculous that was. There was no way Noah was going to be fighting with them right now, even if they could wake him up.

Still, she had to know he was okay.

She took the water bottle Crash had partially used on the washcloth and poured it on Noah's face and neck.

Finally, she got at least some kind of reaction from him, then. He still didn't open his eyes, but his body shifted on the floor a little bit. That was something, at least.

"Here, let me try," Karmen said, pushing Parrish to the side.

Normally, Parrish would have been pissed to be pushed like that, but right now, she was just glad someone else was willing to help.

"I'm going to see if I can snag some of those antibiotics from the storage room," Crash said. "I'll be right back."

He left the room, and the second he opened the door, Parrish got a glimpse of the chaos that had quickly erupted within the compound. Word of the horde had spread to everyone, and they all seemed to be running down the hallways, guns in hand.

Parrish just prayed they could hold off whatever was coming long enough to get Noah up and moving.

She watched, helpless, as Karmen put both her hands on Noah's head.

She stood there for what seemed like ages, even though it had probably only been a few seconds. She needed to do something, but what? She couldn't leave his side. She just couldn't.

Instead, she sat down beside him and took his hands in hers.

Like a miracle, Noah opened his eyes.

"Where are we?" he asked, and Parrish nearly cried from joy at the sound of his voice. "Back in the room?"

She threw her arms around him.

"I was so scared you were lost to us," she whispered in his ear. "I don't know that I could live without you."

He hugged her back, but she could tell he was weak.

"I'm sorry," he said. "I vaguely remember laying down in here and thinking I needed to get up and get moving, but I must have laid back down. How long have I been in here?"

"Only about an hour," she told him. "But we don't have any time to waste."

She told him about the horde and the red-eyed super zombies.

"They're not that far away," Karmen said. "I think they must have been gathering together most of the night and the morning, which is why we didn't see any last night in the neighborhood or on the trip back here today. They were waiting for the right moment to attack."

"What?" Noah asked, bringing a hand to his forehead. "I

don't think my brain is fully working yet. We're being attacked?"

"Yes," Karmen said. "If we don't get out there right now to help, this whole place will fall. There are children in this compound. Families. Those zombies are here because of us, you guys. We're the ones who have to deal with this."

"Okay, so let's figure it out, then," Parrish said, standing to pace the room as Noah pulled on his jeans and a fresh t-shirt. "Karmen, your best vantage point might be back up on the roof. Control and hold back as many of those things as you can."

"I can try," she said. "But I don't even know if my mind control magic will work on them when they're so obviously being controlled by the Dark One. How am I going to override her commands?"

"I don't know, but you can at least try. If it doesn't work, you grab a gun and adapt," Parrish said. She touched Noah's shoulder. "Do you think you can hold a gun? Or are you feeling too weak?"

He ran a hand through his hair.

"I honestly don't know right now," he said. "I feel like I've been hit by a bus. It hurts just to lift my arm over my head."

Parrish sighed in frustration.

"So, that's basically a no," she said, searching her mind for solutions. "Then, if you can at least walk, get out to the Humvee. Crash has that gun on the roof that he used that first night he helped save us from the rotters in D.C.. If you can at least pull the trigger, you should be able to use that without having to use your strength to hold it up."

Noah nodded. "I'll do my best."

He went to stand and then quickly sat back down, clutching his forehead.

Parrish didn't have much hope that he'd be of any help right now but Karmen was right. They had to get moving. They'd wasted too much time already.

Crash burst through the door and then slammed it behind him again. To Parrish's relief, he carried some kind of IV and needle.

"Anyone know how to find a vein and insert an IV?" he asked.

"I can do it," Karmen said. "Hand it to me."

Parrish had no idea why Karmen would know how to insert an IV line, but she actually got it done surprisingly fast.

"Wow, good job," Parrish said. "Where'd you learn to do that?"

"Can we please focus on the plan?" Karmen asked, crossing her arms over her chest. "The fight is ramping up out there, or hadn't you noticed the sound of all that gunfire and explosives?"

She was right. It sounded like a war zone out there.

"Okay, then, Karmen on the roof trying to control and hold back as many as possible," Parrish said. "If you can, see if you can get them to attack each other or turn and go the other way."

"I'll see what I can do," Karmen said.

Parrish was surprised Kamen hadn't argued with her instructions. She'd never just taken orders from Parrish before, but there was a first time for everything.

"Crash, help Noah out to the Humvee. Identify the weakest points of entry like that front gate and the spot in the back where they were still working on the steel walls," she said.

"Do everything you can to protect those weak points. If we don't let them get in, maybe we can pick them off one by one outside the walls."

"Where will you be?" Noah asked.

Parrish shook her head. He wasn't going to approve of this, but she'd already thought through it from various angles in her mind since the walkie first warned them of an attack.

"I'm going out the front gate, and I'm going to hunt down every one of the super zombies and put an end to this attack before anyone else gets hurt."

She didn't wait to see what anyone else had to say. Karmen was right. They had already lost too much time, but now that Parrish knew Noah was going to live and that he was being taken care of, she had to switch her focus to the battle ahead.

As she grabbed her sword and ran out the door, she wondered if the super zombies coming for them now meant Lily was still close by, or if she was already in New York searching for Zoe.

Wherever she was, Parrish hoped she was suffering.

EIGHT

THE WITCH

The witch dreamed of fire only to open her eyes
to ice.

She was surrounded by it. Even her own eyelids
were frosted over, and the cold had seeped so deep into her
bones, everything ached.

It wasn't good for a fire witch to be left in the cold.

On instinct, the witch reached for her fire magic, hoping to
conjure a simple flame to warm the space.

Nothing would come, though. She'd been here too long,
cut off from source.

It was dark in here, wherever she was, but there was
enough light coming in from a block of translucent ice on the
wall for her to at least tell that she was trapped inside some
kind of bare, square room.

No furniture filled the room. No sign of another person.
Just a cold floor that felt slick and icy to the touch and four icy
walls surrounding her.

When she placed her palm on the ice to get traction so she

could stand, the frozen cold of it nearly burned her.

"Hello," she said, her voice so weak she hardly recognized herself.

She cleared her throat and tried to swallow, but she hadn't had anything to drink in so long, it hurt to even try.

How long had she been trapped in this place? And who had brought her here?

She struggled to recall where she'd been before this. What was the last thing she could remember?

Zoe's hotel room.

The symbol of air drawn on the window.

Telling the Dark One that somehow, the fifth had found Zoe before she did.

The memories rushed back with a vengeance now, and the witch gasped. Why couldn't she have left them locked away in a dark place in her mind where she might never see or think of them again?

Hours of torture and pain, repeated over and over again without relief.

And just when she'd thought, mercifully, it was finally over, the horror had started again.

Punishment for her betrayal. For giving the stone to Parrish. For allowing them to give her a name.

The pain was meant to make the witch sorry for what she had done.

Instead, it had made her sorry she'd chosen the wrong side and betrayed the only friends she'd ever had.

There was nothing to be done about that now, though. There was no turning back from her bad choices. Now, the only thing she wished for more than home was death.

When she'd lost consciousness, the Dark One must have had her brought here.

But where, exactly, was this place?

Despite the tenderness of her wounds, she managed to push herself up to a sitting position before finally, after several minutes of pain and determination, finding the strength to stand..

Her shoes had been stripped from her, so that she had to stand on the icy floor in bare feet. She winced through the pain of the cold's burn and walked to the block of ice that provided the room's only light.

She lifted onto tiptoes to look through the clear block of ice, but it was too thick and distorted to see what lay beyond it. A shadow moved across her vision, though, and she backed away.

A cold room was nothing compared to what she'd endured at the hands of the Dark One. She didn't dare do anything to invite that kind of wrath again.

The witch looked down at her burned and deformed skin, then brought a trembling hand to her once-beautiful face. It now matched the horror of the rest of her body.

An icy tear fell onto her fingertips, and she lowered her hand, wishing again for the mercy of death.

She used to hate her life before she came to this world, believing there could be nothing worse than the way the Council of Fire treated her. They ignored her and refused to teach or train her properly. They refused to even give her a name, saying someone like her didn't deserve one.

They did that to all the young girls like her. Orphans brought in from the outerlands.

The witch had believed life with the Council was the worst horror she could ever endure.

Now, though, she could see every blessing. Every moment of joy.

She closed her eyes and imagined the young ones entrusted to her care over the years. The tiniest babes cradled in her arms. Watching them learn to walk and coo. Witnessing their first smiles or kissing their heads when they cried at night.

The witch had always done what she could to protect as many of the young ones as possible from the suffering she'd endured. She held them and whispered loving words in their ears when the Council wasn't watching.

She'd given many of them names. Nothing she'd ever spoken out loud, but names she'd carried in her heart.

Instead of seeing the blessing and joy they had brought to her life, though, she'd focused on the unfairness and heartache when one of her wards was given a real name and a real home.

Her own longing had filled her with anger every time a child was adopted and given a life apart from the Council.

The witch had hated that life, believing there was nothing more in the world she wanted than to have power over all of them. She wanted a chance to make them all regret just how poorly they'd treated her for all those years.

But now, beauty and power stripped from her, the witch could finally see how foolish she had been.

Now that it was too late, she wanted nothing more than to go back to her old life.

Or her life with Parrish and the others.

Why had she ever left them? Why had she betrayed them?

She collapsed onto the floor, tucking her legs and skirt under her body as she prayed for some relief from the cold.

She needed to block those thoughts from her mind. It was too late now, anyway.

"Feeling sorry for yourself?" the Dark One asked.

A shadow crossed the room in front of her, and the witch slid backwards until she hit the wall behind her.

Her body shook in fear.

She didn't dare answer the question. She had no idea what she was expected to say, and she was so tired of getting it wrong.

The witch searched the room for the source of the voice, but there was nothing more than shadows here. She knew better, though. The Dark One often hid in the shadows. Watching.

"You had such promise when you first appeared in this world," the voice said again. It echoed off the icy walls.

"I'm sorry, Mistress," the witch said. The tears she wanted to cry earlier came freely now, so cold they stuck to her cheeks like icicles. "Please forgive me."

The Dark One stepped forward now, her image shadowy and unclear, like a mirage.

"Stand up, girl," she said sternly.

A sob escaped the witch's lips.

Not again. I cannot survive this again.

"You are weak," the Dark One spat. "Not like my Parrish. She was always the strongest. She would have done great things at my side, but she betrayed me, just like you. Why is loyalty so difficult to foster in young ones?"

The witch looked up, surprised. "Your Parrish? What does that mean?"

The Dark One waved a shadowy hand in front of her face and paced the floor. Well, more like hovered over the floor. She didn't seem to actually be there at all, and the witch wondered how she was doing that. Had she escaped her own icy prison already? Or was this merely a projection?

Maybe none of this was real.

"That was so long ago, it no longer matters," the Dark One said, a hint of sadness in her voice. "I have come to know betrayal so intimately, I have learned to use it to my advantage. But I would give anything to have someone strong like her on my side now. You have the potential to be strong, but you are too weak-minded. Perhaps, if I had raised you from birth, things might have been different."

The witch lowered her head, hopelessness flowing through her like a dark river.

This was the end, then. The Dark One would consume her power and her life force, and it would all be over.

The witch realized now that she did not really want to die. She still hadn't made anything of her life.

She would die a failure.

The witch collapsed at the shadow's feet, and was immediately yanked upward until her own feet dangled far above the icy floor.

An invisible power pushed her back against the wall, and despite her instincts, she knew better now than to resist. Resistance only made the torture worse and last longer.

Instead, she gritted her teeth and braced herself for whatever was to come next.

To her surprise, the Dark One smiled.

"There," she said. "A little of that strength I was after. Perhaps I have yet underestimated your resolve and inner fire. Perhaps you are of some use to me moving forward. I'll have to do something about your loyalty, however."

The Dark One's shadow moved in close as a dark purple energy began to swirl around the witch's feet.

Terrified, she kept her chin up, even as her breath came faster and her heart pounded in her chest. She bit down on her lower lip until she tasted blood, but she did not flinch or try to move away.

Whatever was to become of her now, it was out of her hands.

"I have one last job for you," the Dark One said. "One last opportunity to prove yourself as a loyal servant. And to go along with this chance, I will also show you a small glimpse of my power."

The necromancer flicked a finger upward, and the purple energy swirling on the floor snaked up the witch's body, its light growing until it nearly blinded her.

She braced herself for the pain, but what came instead was something she never expected.

Healing.

For the first time in hours, she experienced not only relief, but true bliss, as if the sun had finally chosen to shine on her cold, shriveled body. She blossomed like a flower inside its light.

Her burned skin smoothed out and regained its youthful glow. The warmth of her fire returned to her core. And...

Something else. A flash of blinding light inside her skull, disorienting but not exactly painful.

When the light released her, she fell to her knees.

"How?" the witch cried, running her hands along her perfect skin. She had been so sure she was ruined forever. Gratitude flowed through her like oceans.

Where before she was sure she had felt something close to

hatred for the necromancer standing before her, now she felt nothing but love and adoration.

In fact, she couldn't imagine feeling anything less than love and absolute devotion to the Dark One. It filled her with purpose.

"I am a necromancer," the Dark One said. "In one hand, I control death and can inflict unimaginable pain, but in my other hand, I also hold life. Rebirth. As easily as I have given it, I can also take it away."

The Dark One studied her, looking deeply into her eyes before she smiled.

"But we won't have any more of your foolishness, will we? You see it now, don't you? The beauty of your devotion?"

"I do," she whispered, knowing she had been given a great gift. A second chance. Love filled her heart. "I will not disappoint you again, Mistress."

The Dark One leaned close to her ear and placed a shadowy hand on her back.

"It's all falling into place, and soon, I will go free. The question, my dear, is whether you will still be at my side when I do. Now stand up and get to work. I have given your four guardian friends something to distract them for a while. I need you to find the child. Zoe is the key to everything now."

The Dark One placed a hand on the witch's forehead, forcing her eyes to close.

When she opened them a moment later, she found herself lying in a patch of sunlight in the grass, the tall buildings of the city of New York rising against the early afternoon sky.

NINE

CRASH

This is insane.

Crash paced the room, willing the IV in Noah's arm to dump its medicine faster.

Every second that passed was another second they could be out there, fighting to make sure no one lost their lives.

"How are you feeling?" he asked.

Noah flexed his arm and nodded. "Better," he said. "If you guys hadn't shown up, I'm not sure what would have happened. The infection just started to take over. Do you have any idea how Stephen's doing?"

Crash shook his head. "I have no idea, but it won't matter anyway if those zombies break through the barriers," he said. "How much longer do you think you need with that?"

He motioned toward the IV, which was still half-full.

"I'll just bring it with me," Noah said, standing but careful to keep the IV above his arm. "I can feel the medicine fighting the infection, and I think I've worked out a way to speed up the process."

"Let's hope so," Crash muttered.

He felt stupid leading Noah toward the Humvee. The guy was sick and attached to a freaking IV for god's sake. He was likely to be more of a liability than anything else at this point, but as long as he could still aim and shoot, Crash just had to get him to the Hummer.

With minimal effort, they should be able to take out hundreds of rotters pretty quickly.

What concerned him, though, was that when Karmen had been describing it to them back in the room, she'd said it looked like an ocean without an end.

So, how many were there? And would a few hundred be enough to even make a dent in what they were facing?

Once the rotters broke through into the camp, it was over, anyway. They could retreat, put as many people on the roof as possible, and barricade the doors, but with the super zombies, all it would take was one that could scale walls to pretty much wipe out the rest of the survivors.

Damn.

How could they really be facing this so quickly after they got back from the hospital?

The Dark One wasn't letting up, that was for sure.

Which made him terrified of what they might face if they ever actually did make it to New York, but he couldn't exactly worry about that now, could he?

Right now, they needed to make sure everyone here was safe and that the four of them lived through it.

He had no idea what might happen to their mission to save the world if one of the five guardians died. Was it game over at that point?

Crash was pretty sure that the man in his dreams from

time to time—Tobias—was supposed to be here to train them and take them to the island if it came to this.

How would things have been different if Lily had come through with him and killed him? None of this would have happened.

But what was done was done, and it wasn't going to do Crash any good to start worrying about it now. Instead, he pushed forward, navigating through the halls until they had finally reached the front of the building.

He'd been so focused on getting to the Humvee that he hadn't properly prepared himself for what he would see when he pushed through the door to step outside. In his mind, the rotters were still ambling down the street toward them, and they would have a little time before they were right up close and personal.

The reality of it, though, was that there were already a hundred of those things pressing against the fence and the makeshift steel walls of the barricade, doing everything in their power to claw through.

Just the collective weight of them pressing forward was enough to make the wall bow and bend.

"Oh my God," Noah said.

"This is bad, man," Crash said, breaking out in a run toward the truck.

Beside him, Noah ripped the IV from his arm and threw the needle and bag onto the ground. Crash wasn't sure if he'd finished the medicine or just decided he couldn't afford to mess with it anymore, but either way, Noah was running faster now and apparently feeling much better.

He outran Crash and practically leaped onto the top of the Hummer, placing himself behind the machine gun setup.

Crash reached out to the truck with his mind, starting it up before he even got there.

All around them, members of the makeshift militia that had been living here in relative safety, emptied their guns into the massive crowd of rotters piling against the weakest point—the front gate.

"I can't shoot with all these people in the way," Noah said.

Crash grabbed the CB radio cord and pressed the button on the side. He'd rigged this thing up to a megaphone system a long time ago, but he'd never had an occasion to use it. Well, there was a first for everything.

"Move out of the way," he shouted. "Get to a higher vantage point, if you can. We'll take care of these."

The men and women who'd been fighting at the gate stepped aside quickly, no one doubting their authority, thankfully. Instead, they looked grateful for some kind of leadership or plan.

Their eyes were filled with fear, and he couldn't blame them.

He was sure his own eyes looked the same.

"Blast 'em, Noah," he said, and a split second later, the machine gun sprayed bullets into the crowd pressing against the fence.

With Noah in control, though, it wasn't like when Crash had just randomly shot into the crowd and hit a few by default. This time, each bullet seemed to land a direct headshot. How Noah was controlling each bullet individually when they were coming out so fast, Crash had no idea, but he wasn't complaining about it, that's for sure.

"Hell, yeah," he said, thumping the roof as he watched

almost a hundred zombies at the gate fall dead in a matter of seconds.

This was going to be a piece of cake.

In fact, they might be able to essentially build a barrier of dead rotters that would keep the others from pressing forward. Or, at least, that's how he saw it going in his mind as he reached for his own weapon.

Only, as he stepped out to add his own bullets to the barrage, he caught a glimpse of something terrifying climbing over the mass of dead bodies piling at the gate.

A pair of red, glowing eyes.

And then another set crawling up behind that one.

And another.

Until five red-eyed super z's, each hunched over and crawling on all fours like dogs were lined up on top of the bodies, staring directly at him.

TEN

KARMEN

The roof was a madhouse.

People threw grenades over the side of the steel barricade, while others lined up in a straight line across all edges of the rooftop, using whatever long-range weapons they had available to shoot down rotters as they approached.

The problem was there didn't seem to be an end to the parade of zombies pouring through the side streets in this neighborhood. It was just one endless stream of them, so no matter how many they killed, more appeared to take their places.

Dead bodies piled up at the barricade and new zombies began to claw their way on top of them, creating a kind of ladder that was slowly scaling the wall.

Karmen ran over to Tank, who was standing by a type of command center of walkies and crates of ammo where people were continually running over for refills.

"Do you see what's happening here?" she asked.

"Stand aside or grab a gun," he shouted, dismissing her and giving orders to a group of women who'd just appeared with shotguns from below.

Karmen gritted her teeth, but she did her best to hold back her temper.

"Tank, you need to see this, or it's about to get ugly," she said, following him to another station.

He barked out another set of orders, and then briefly turned to her.

"Can't you see I'm dealing with this attack as best I can?" he said. "I don't have time to sit here and talk strategy with a teenager, so if you'll excuse me."

Karmen took a deep breath as he walked away from her again.

It wasn't like it was all that unusual for adults—and men in particular—to dismiss her as just another dumb blonde. Or a stupid teen girl who couldn't possibly have something important or helpful to say.

Most of her life, she'd been treated like a decoration, there to be seen and not heard.

And she'd built her life around that in some ways, making sure she looked exactly the way she needed in order to get people's attention. But she wasn't stupid. And if Tank couldn't see what was really happening with the pileups of bodies out there, he was going to lose more than just his temper.

She took another deep breath and closed her eyes.

She focused solely on Tank in that moment, making sure she could feel a connection to him. Since he was just right there a few steps away, it was fast and easy to connect to his mind, but she could feel the frantic energy inside him. Getting through that was going to be a bit tougher.

In a way, she could sense the volume of noise in his head the way you could see it on a phone or computer screen. She imagined herself turning it up or down.

She couldn't exactly hear his thoughts, but she could sense their nature.

Fear was the loudest noise in his head, but he was keeping it together, coming up with strategy, too. Being a real leader.

Carefully, she turned down the volume of his fear and placed a message of her own inside his mind.

Look at the bodies around the barriers. The others are climbing them like a ladder. They'll get over the top of it in ten minutes if we don't start thinking this through.

Tank stopped and shook his head for a moment, but then he looked up, finally noticing what was going on with the rotters who died right by the steel walls.

He cursed and immediately pulled a group of friends over. He pointed to the walls, and gradually raised his hand higher and higher.

Karmen breathed a sigh of relief. She had no idea what they were going to do about it, but at least they were aware of the threat.

Having the power to reach inside people's mind was becoming a pretty handy skill to have, but now that they were working on a solution to the pile-up thing, she needed to start working on a plan to get some of these rotters to turn around or fight each other.

Reaching inside the mind of one rotter or person was easy enough for her now. Reaching into multiple people's minds took a little more concentration and effort.

But the only time she'd attempted a large crowd was that

day on the road when they'd gotten surrounded by the rotters fleeing the fires in Baltimore.

Back then, she wasn't even sure if she could do it or not, but Lily had helped her somehow. Touched her and focused her mind.

Karmen was fairly certain that Lily's powers were similar to her own. Some kind of mind control and manipulation, maybe.

She tried to remember exactly how it had felt when she'd reached out to an entire group of those things. That power was inside of her. She didn't need Lily's or anyone else to tell her that. What she needed was to figure out the mechanics of how it all worked.

Looking out at the seemingly endless wave of rotters coming toward them, she wasn't even sure she knew where to start or how big of a group to hope for.

Whatever she did, if it was too big or obvious, was going to throw Tank and his buddies for a loop. She was certain of that.

Parrish and the others seemed to realize that they probably wouldn't be able to hide their strange abilities from the people here after today, anyway, so why not just go big?

The best way to test yourself, after all, was under pressure, right?

Karmen surveyed the horde again, searching for one of those things with red, glowing eyes.

If she could turn down the noise inside Tank's brain, then maybe she could do the same thing with one of these rotters. If she could reach inside it and turn down the Dark One's control, maybe she could take over.

She had no doubt one of those special rotters could take out a bunch of the regular ones if it were working on their side.

It didn't take her long to locate one. A beast of a dude with half his face ripped off. He was a little toward the back, but as he made his way to the compound, he merely flung the normal-sized rotters out of his way, like they were dust-bunnies.

You'll do nicely, she thought.

She stretched out a hand, giving herself over to instinct. After all, even though no one had properly trained them on how to use their abilities, some part of her had to remember.

She focused on the Beast, stretching her magic toward him and sinking it deep inside his mind.

Unlike Tank's mind, this one was mostly empty. There was no strategy to speak of. There was only hunger and a strong, clear desire imprinted on its brain.

Find and infect the guardians.

The fervor behind it made her shiver. This thing wanted them dead with a vengeance, but he was not going to get his way today.

Karmen pushed her power into its mind and turned the Dark One's orders down so soft, the sound of them almost disappeared entirely. Instead, she filled its head with a new thought.

Protect the compound at all costs. Keep the people safe.

The Beast stopped mid-stride, pounded his flat palm against his forehead two or three times, and then shook his head, as if trying to shake her voice out of his mind.

Karmen dug deeper, finding a well of power inside her that she imagined plugging into. She took one deep, centering breath in, and then let it out slowly, imagining her power trav-eling across the top of the zombie horde to reach the Beast. She plugged the other end of that power into his head and tried again.

First, she suppressed the orders from the Dark One, making them as quiet as she possibly could.

Then, she gave her own command, pouring all of her own confidence and passion into it.

Protect the compound at all costs. Keep the people safe.

The Beast pounded his head with his own fists several times and then let out a roar that shook the ground slightly. Everyone on the roof stopped for a moment, searching for the source of the sound.

Someone screamed.

"What is that?"

Karmen ignored the chaos and waited, knowing that she'd either just turned the tide, or doomed them all by pissing that thing off.

When the Beast finally started moving again, though, he grabbed rotters by the skull, one in each hand, and crushed them with a single, easy motion, and dropped them to the ground at his feet. Then, he moved onto the next two he could grab, until a mountain of them lay around him.

Karmen let out the breath she'd been holding.

Somehow, she'd managed to turn the tide at least a little bit. For how long? She didn't know. She had no idea if the Dark One could turn him back to her will in an instant, or if he belonged to Karmen for good, but what she did know was that for now, they had a Beast on their side.

She picked a pair of binoculars off the ground and scanned the crowd again, searching for another set of red eyes.

ELEVEN

PARRISH

Parrish scaled the chain-link fence near the guard's hut, ignoring the men who yelled for her to stop.

They probably thought she was crazy, but she was beyond caring what anyone else thought of her right now. They'd been so careful to keep their powers hidden, too. All that was about to be for nothing, because the way Parrish figured, these zombies were really here for them, right?

So, what better way to make sure the compound stayed safe than to leave it and then let them all know where to find her? If she could at least draw the super zombies away, she could buy the rest of the compound time to deal with the normal ones.

Of course, she probably should have come out here with a better plan than just to wade through an ocean of rotters, searching for red eyes. There were more of them than she'd anticipated, and they were so close together she hardly had any elbow room to even swing her sword.

She had a few tricks up her sleeve when it came to her magic, but she didn't want to have to use it when she was still so close to the compound. Instead, she took her time, carving small pockets of space for herself in the crowd, using whatever means necessary.

Kicks, jabs, punches.

At one point, she even had to use one of the rotters as a shield against a group that pressed in too close for comfort.

She didn't stop moving, even for a split second.

Hands grabbed at her, tugging on her clothing and her braid, but she pressed on, setting her sights on a city bus that had been abandoned and parked at the other end of the street across from the mall.

Parrish had no idea what she would do if she just happened to run into a crazy powerful super zombie somewhere in this throng, but she was in too deep to turn back now.

She really wished she'd had the good sense to change into a pair of jeans and a long-sleeved shirt before she came running out here, but instead she was wearing a pair of black workout shorts and a black tank top, neither one of which provided even minimal protection against these things.

Her entire body was going to be scratched all to hell, but as long as she avoided getting bitten, she would be okay. If Noah recovered okay, she'd get him to heal the scratches, no problem.

A few seconds ago, she'd heard the machine gun start up near the gate, and smiled. That had to be Noah and Crash finally getting their butts in gear and helping out, which meant the gate was covered.

Hopefully, Karmen was on the roof holding some of the others back and helping where she could.

Now, it was up to Parrish to create a disturbance in the

singular focus of the horde. If she could split their attention, with the advantage of higher ground on top of the bus, she should be able to turn the tide, so to speak.

Well, as long as there weren't half a dozen super zombies headed straight for her.

One or two, she could probably handle. Anything more than that, and she'd have to move to Plan B.

Which meant she should probably have been trying to figure out a Plan B as she fought her way through the horde.

The only backup plan she could think of, though, was to run. If things got too bad, she'd try to make it back to the gate, where Crash and Noah could help. In reality, though, if she got cornered by a handful of those things all at once, she'd never make it back to that gate in one piece.

So, no real backup plan. She just had to make Plan A work.

It took nearly fifteen minutes for her to get all the way out to the bus, and along the way, she was sure she'd taken down at least 100 or more rotters. Not a bad workout, that's for sure.

Between yesterday and today, she was going to have some majorly sore muscles. She didn't even want to think about what that would mean for making her way through the horror of New York City, but she'd cross that bridge when she came to it.

A night of good rest would make all the difference.

The only thing that would have been better was if she had access to a huge garden tub full of piping hot water and scented bubble bath. An unlikely dream at this point, but she let the idea of it fuel her as she sliced through the handful of zombies lingering around the bus.

At this point, so many rotters had pushed forward in

waves toward the compound that she'd actually reached the back of the horde. She was grateful, at least, that there was an end to it.

The Dark One—or perhaps Lily—had had all night to gather this ragtag crew of rotters. There could have been thousands in this horde. Instead, she'd brought maybe a thousand in total.

A nightmare, for sure, but it could have been worse.

Parrish was beginning to realize that it could always be worse. Even when you couldn't imagine anything more horrifying than what you were facing at that moment, there was always a next level when it came to the horrors of this new world.

She climbed on top of the bus in two quick leaps, the muscles in her legs and arms burning from non-stop movement. None of the rotters heading toward the compound had followed her out here, which meant she was right about their general directive to attack the compound.

But the super zombies out there?

They had orders to kill the guardians. She had no doubts about that.

She stood there for a moment, surveying the battle scene and the carnage.

From what she could see up here, none of the rotters had managed to break through the steel barricades on this side of the wall. She couldn't quite see what was happening inside the front gate, though. She could see a large pile up of dead zombies near the chain-link fence, but it was at the wrong angle to see the Humvee inside or to tell if the gate had been breached.

She listened for the sound of machine-gun fire, but there

were too many guns and other explosions going off for her to tell from here.

She had to just trust that her friends were holding their own. Besides, she had a feeling they were so connected now that if something terrible happened to them, she would know it.

After all, she was pretty sure she'd sensed Noah's nausea while she was in the office with Tank, even though she hadn't known what it was.

At the time, she thought it was just exhaustion taking hold.

She'd have to ask the others if they had also sensed Noah's distress at all, even in some small way.

The crew on the roof seemed to be making the biggest impact. Thankfully Tank and his group had managed to gather a lot of guns and ammo early on that they'd stockpiled here inside the compound, but they were going to be decimated after this.

It's all our fault.

She pushed the thought aside.

Not because it wasn't true, but because she didn't have the mental space to worry about it right now.

Their ammo stockpile wouldn't matter if no one survived the day.

From the looks of it, after only about fifteen minutes, the militia at the compound had managed to take out about half the rotters in total.

But where were the red-eyed zombies? They had to be out there somewhere, and Parrish was sure they would have sent some who could scale walls or break them down, entirely.

Why was it taking so long for them to make themselves known?

Or had they, by some miracle, already been dealt with by the others?

But no, that didn't seem to be the case.

Parrish's eyes landed on a set of them about twenty feet away. A man and a woman, both about the same height and build.

It was their arms, though, that made them stand out.

They looked more like tentacles, and after watching them for a minute, it looked like they could extend them out pretty far from their bodies. It was possible they were poisonous, as well, because from here, there looked to be some kind of greenish residue coated on them.

Awesome. Perfect time to be in shorts and a tank top.

All she'd wanted was to be free of blood and guts for a little while. So much for that dream.

She scanned toward the other side of the crowd, searching for more. That's when she caught a glimpse of several rotters leaping into the air and over the fence at the front gate.

Her heart skipped a beat. What the hell was that? There were definitely three or more of them, whatever they were.

She thought back to the crouching one they'd faced in D.C. These were probably similar. Regular humans turned into disgusting, dog-like creatures with fangs or scissors for hands.

There were no words for how horrible the Dark One was, using people who had once been fathers, sons, mothers, or daughters, for her own twisted game.

Parrish prayed there was no part of who they used to be still locked away inside of them. Hopefully, they were nothing more than mindless shells of the people they used to be.

She wanted to go to Crash and Noah and help them with the dog-like rotters she'd just seen leaping toward them, but she could do nothing from here. All she could do was continue on with her plan and hope to draw some of the others away.

Not seeing any other potential threats than the couple in front of her, Parrish took a deep, centering breath and solidified her stance, sword drawn.

She focused on the power deep inside, drawing it to the surface until her blade seemed to be engulfed in an icy-blue light. She wasn't exactly sure what she was capable of accomplishing with this magic, but she remembered that very first time she'd cut down the large trench-coat zombie inside the office building the night they met Crash and Lily.

She'd somehow controlled a blast of blue light that was focused to a single point.

Today, though, she was going to try something a bit different, because if she wanted to get their attention, she was going to have to do something big and bold.

Something really freaking dangerous but hopefully also effective.

She played through the move in her mind several times before she was ready, and then she drew her sword back, pouring even more of her power into its blue light.

With a yell, she sliced her sword horizontally across the air, imagining the light spreading out across the sea of rotters still headed for the compound. She kept her intention toward the middle of their bodies, hoping to take down as many of them as possible, and not entirely knowing what it would do to them.

To her surprise, it worked, too.

Every zombie her blue light touched fell to the ground, its bottom half severed from its body.

Including the super zombies.

Only, while the regular zombies who had fallen stayed where they were, the tentacle twins began pulling themselves toward her, their tentacles lengthening and extending over the tops of the other writhing on the ground.

She steadied her sword and readied another blast, but before she had a chance to unleash it, a flash of silver appeared in her peripheral vision.

Parrish didn't even fully have time to process what was happening, but her instincts kicked in before her brain did, her sword gliding through the air toward the figure.

Only, the blade didn't slice through the rotter's flesh like she expected.

Even though she'd landed a direct hit, all she heard was the sound of steel clanging against steel.

The zombie, red-eyed and covered in some kind of silvery metal that acted like a shell or armor over its entire body, had caught the blade of her sword in its left hand. With a strangled cry, Parrish tried to leap back, pulling on her sword with all of her power.

But the rotter wasn't letting her go that easy.

It pulled her sword from her hands with one swift movement and tossed it to the ground with a clatter. Parrish gathered her blue light in her hands and was about to unleash it toward the silver zombie when the thing quickly drew back its metallic fist and punched her in the gut.

Parrish went flying off the top of the bus, landing with a crack on the hard asphalt below, a pair of poisoned tentacles dangerously close.

And getting closer.

She'd been stupid to believe she could handle this all on her own, and now she was going to pay for it with her life.

TWELVE

KARMEN

"What the hell was that?"

Everyone on the roof stopped shooting and ran to the opposite side of the roof. Karmen had just barely caught the flash of blue light in the binoculars, but she didn't have to see it to know what it was.

She stepped onto a milk crate nearby and lifted the binoculars to her eyes, scanning the area for Parrish.

Just as she suspected, the girl was standing on top of a dang bus over a hundred yards away at the back of the horde. What was she trying to pull here?

But then Karmen noticed the sheer number of rotters who'd been grounded by Parrish's magic. She'd somehow used her light magic to sever their legs from their bodies, so even though they were still alive, they couldn't move without dragging themselves forward with their hands.

She'd severely crippled their numbers with one swift move, which was pretty badass, even if Karmen wouldn't have admitted it to her face.

Only, before Karmen could fully appreciate Parrish's use of magic and intelligence, something leapt at the top of the bus from out of nowhere.

Red eyes flashed as a silver-coated zombie yanked Parrish's sword from her hand and hit her so hard, she went flying like a ragdoll to the pavement.

Karmen's stomach churned.

This was bad.

She spun around, seeking out the four super zombies she'd managed to turn to their side so far. She imagined creating a web between them, kind of like a mental group text.

That was the best way she had for making sense of it in her head, anyway.

As soon as she could feel the connection between her own mind and the four of theirs, she gave them a new directive.

Find Parrish. Save her. Destroy everything in your path.

She quickly gave each of them directions for how to find Parrish from where they were standing, and she was relieved when each of them broke out in a run. Well, all of them except the Beast. She wasn't even sure he could run without breaking the ground beneath his feet, but he did manage to move quickly, smashing heads as he made his way around the compound's steel barrier, in front of the gate, and toward Parrish on the other side.

But would it be enough? Karmen wasn't sure she'd be able to get them there fast enough, but she at least had to try.

There was no way she could move fast enough to get down the stairs and over to where Parrish was before whatever that silver thing was got to her, but she could do her best to stop it from here.

To at least buy her some time.

Karmen pushed a few men out of the way so she could get to the edge of the roof on that side. She'd already used up so much of her energy, and she had a feeling using too much of it at once might make her pass out the way Crash had done back at his apartment when he'd been running all those computers and trying to make phone calls to New York, but she couldn't just leave Parrish out there to die.

As much as she liked to give the girl crap, she had really come to love her. In fact, she had a feeling they'd all be totally lost without her.

Karmen focused her mind on the silver rotter standing on top of the bus. She'd become pretty good at tapping into their minds in the past fifteen minutes or so of practicing it over and over again, but this one was different, somehow.

Maybe it was the silver shell around its body? Or maybe this one was just further away?

It could have been any number of things, but no matter how hard she tried, she couldn't seem to connect with this one's mind at all.

That's when she noticed the tentacled zombies quickly crawling their way across the parking lot toward Parrish.

Karmen shuddered. How disgusting could these things get?

There was no telling what they'd do to Parrish once they got close enough to her to wrap those giant tentacles around her, and without her sword, she was practically powerless.

True to form, though, it didn't look like Parrish was giving up anytime soon.

Despite how hard she appeared to have been hit, she stood up quickly and began to gather more blue light in the palms of her hands. She also made a run for her sword.

Sadly, that only seemed to spur the silver rotter to move faster. It jumped down beside the sword and kicked it under the bus, as if toying with her.

Yes, this one definitely had more agency. Karmen wasn't sure if it was truly a mind of its own or if the Dark One had somehow gotten her claws really deeply into this one's mind, but she decided to let Parrish sort that one out.

Instead, she turned her focus on the two tentacled zombies still inching toward Parrish. Their minds should be easier to hack.

This better work.

Parrish's life—and the lives of all the humans left alive in this god-forsaken world—depended on it.

THIRTEEN

CRASH

The dog-like rotters snarled at him as he reached back inside the truck to grab the microphone.

"Everyone out here by the gate, get inside now," he shouted. "Run and barricade the doors with whatever you can find."

Confused, one of the women near the gate holding a shotgun held up her hands in a questioning gesture. Obviously, she hadn't taken his tone of voice seriously.

Instead of trying to calmly and politely explain the situation to her, he hooked his thumb toward the five red-eyed zombies crouched and ready to pounce.

She followed his gesture, squinted in confusion, and then grabbed the man next to her by the arm and told him to move his ass. The dogs seemed to follow the others with their eyes, but they made no move to leap after them. Instead, they trained their eyes on the Hummer.

Which could only mean one thing. These guys had been

specifically looking for them, and they most likely had been given orders to kill or infect on sight.

Crash slammed the door of the Hummer, shutting himself inside for a moment as he crawled through to the back and opened the bench seat he'd taken careful steps to install before the pandemic even began. He'd hidden tons of extra ammo and supplies in there, so he quickly grabbed a couple of grenades, a loaded machine gun, and a hunting knife.

Of course, he had to be careful with the grenades. If he destroyed the gate or the fence itself, there would be hell to pay.

He hooked them onto his belt, anyway, though. Just in case.

He also handed Noah extra ammo for the gun on top of the Hummer, though he had a feeling guns weren't going to be enough against these things.

With the super zombies, there was no real way to know what they were capable of until you were actually fighting them. Then, you had to kind of figure it out on your own. They could have poisonous fangs, stoneskin, or a giant tongue that came out of their mouths and tried to lick you to death.

So, who knew about these guys?

He wasn't going to find out hiding here in the truck like a pansy, though. He'd been a gamer all his life, and this wasn't so much different from that. The first time you fought any major boss in a video game, you had to figure it out for yourself. Find their weaknesses.

He'd been training for this his whole life.

Crash grabbed his AR-15 and threw open the back door just as something heavy hit the truck from the front. Crash stumbled to the ground and turned to see two of the dogs crouching on the hood of the truck, inches away from where Noah stood.

He was pounding them with bullets, and while the impact knocked them back slightly, even direct headshots didn't seem to be making any difference.

Which would have been bad enough, but then the other three dogs decided it was time to join the party. They leaped over the fence, but this time, they landed closer to him.

"Hey, how come you only get two and I got to deal with three of these things?"

Noah laughed. "This Dark One person must not realize who the real boss is out here."

Crash lifted his machine gun into the air. "Oh yeah. Well, we'll see about that."

He emptied his entire clip into the three dogs, pushing them back a little bit. The bullets seemed to just fall away, hitting their mark but leaving almost no trace that they'd hurt these things at all.

He couldn't throw the grenades, and bullets didn't seem to be harming these guys. What else could he do? He backed away slightly as the dog-like rotters growled and snarled at him.

"Got any brilliant ideas?" he asked as Noah left his post and joined him at the back of the Humvee.

"I have a feeling this is about to get up close and personal," Noah said, grabbing his bat from the truck and holding it at the ready. "I'm still not at full strength, but I can try to bash them with this. Primitive, but often effective."

Crash laughed. "I asked for brilliant ideas."

Noah laughed, too, and Crash was grateful to have such a cool guy to spend the end of the world with.

But they wouldn't die today. Crash was certain of that. If his dreams were any indication, they still had a long journey—and a lot tougher battles than this one—to face before this was all over.

If only his dreams had shown him how to fight against rotters who were immune to bullets.

Before he could come up with any great strategy, the three on the ground ran toward them at full speed. Noah reared back and swung with devastating accuracy, hitting all three of them in the head and sending them flying backward.

"Ha," Crash shouted, spraying them with follow-up bullets, just in case. "Take that, dogs."

"Heads up," Noah shouted, raising his arm to shield himself as the other two dogs leapt from the top of the truck and barreled into him.

Crash's heart nearly stopped beating as one of those things dug its teeth into Noah's skin and locked its jaw tight. The dog violently shook its head from side to side, trying to tear Noah apart.

Crash didn't see any sign of blood, though, so he had to hope Noah's stoneskin was still in effect.

The second dog hadn't been as lucky. Noah had its neck in his other hand and seemed to be squeezing the life out of it.

In the meantime, the three Noah had slammed with the bat were making a comeback, and they looked angrier and more determined than ever. With Noah currently occupied, this left the three musketeers over here to Crash.

With guns out of the question and the grenades too dangerous to use, he only had one thing up his sleeve. When they were back at the hospital, he remembered feeling a deep fire ignite inside his body. Somehow, he'd poured pure electricity into a rotter's body.

Of course, at the time, he was severely injured and pinned down, which had his adrenaline going crazy. He could, if needed, convince himself that this situation was about to go down the same path.

He tried to remember what that had felt like to channel so much power through his own fingertips, and as he reached for that same fire, it appeared. Like a tiny little ember that had been smoldering all this time. He had just managed to reconnect with it.

So, now he just had to figure out how to amplify it by a thousand and roast these things.

Nothing like the fear of death to motivate, huh?

He dropped his gun to the ground and held his hands out in front of him, feeling kind of stupid because he had no real idea what he was doing. All feelings of self-consciousness fell away, though, when he curled his fingers inward and sparks danced between them like little cracks of lightning.

"Hell, yeah," he whispered.

He focused all of his energy on that burning ember deep inside, imagining he was pouring fuel onto it, causing it to burn hotter and more intensely.

That intention seemed to do the trick, and the lightning in his fingertips also grew hotter and more controlled.

"Time to test this out," he said.

He pulled his curled fingers back and then shot them forward, straightening his fingers out at the last second and directing the bolt of electricity at the dog nearest to him.

A flash of lightning struck the dog-like zombie, and it

squealed, pulling back and lowering its face to the pavement, dazed and, from the looks of it, slightly singed.

"What the crap was that?" Noah asked, finally ripping the dog-like rotter who'd tried to bite him off his arm. "Did you do that? Or is that something else I need to be watching out for?"

"That was me, man," Crash said, laughing maniacally and holding up his fingers to show Noah the lightning. "How awesome is this?"

Noah's eyes grew wide. "Do it again. Here they come."

Crash cursed and turned his attention to the three dogs again. The one he'd singed had recovered quickly and joined the pack. Now, they were all heading for him.

He had no idea how quickly he could recharge his ability or if he could even get a shot off quickly enough to hit all three. He pulled his hands back toward his body as the rotters leapt off the ground, charging toward him.

With a yell, he put everything he had into the lightning and this time, instead of just a single flash or bolt, he kept pouring his energy into the stream.

A stream of almost rope-like lightning flowed from the fingertips on both hands, combining into a single, thick stream that connected with the head of the rotter he'd hit the first time. Crash kept yelling as he pushed the stream outward, holding onto it for as long as he could, imagining the ember of power inside him being stoked and heated over and over again.

Something shifted in the energy, and all of a sudden, the stream of lightning traveled from the first dog to the second and then the third, like a chain. All three of them fell to the ground, shaking with the force of the electric flow running through their bodies.

Crash held on as long as he could, the energy draining out

of him. He grew light-headed, but he could not let go until those things stopped moving.

"Crash, let it go, man," Noah said, holding a hand toward him, but not daring to actually touch him.

And who knew what might happen if Noah had grabbed his arm. Was Crash's entire body a giant conduit right now?

He wasn't sure, but he had never felt anything more powerful and exhilarating than what he'd just done. He released the stream, but only because he felt like he might pass out otherwise.

With them heading to New York maybe even as soon as tonight, he couldn't afford to completely burn himself out unless it was that or death.

And he prayed that wasn't a choice he was going to have to make today.

He looked around and realized he and Noah had actually managed to kill all five of those things in a matter of minutes. If the Dark One really wanted them to die she was going to have to try a lot harder than that.

Just then, a giant flash of blue light went off in his peripheral vision.

"Parrish," Noah shouted, immediately taking off to climb on top of the Humvee and search for her.

"Wait up," Crash said, following him but taking a quick look behind to make sure those dog rotters weren't getting up. When they didn't move at all, he relaxed and climbed on top of the roof.

He'd just had enough time to take in the carnage of all the rotters wriggling on the ground between them and where Parrish stood on top of a city bus when something bright and fast appeared beside her.

Noah shouted out a warning, but he was too far away and too slow to make a difference.

Parrish swung her sword toward the thing at the last minute, but Crash gasped when the rotter simply reached out and grabbed the blade, pulling it from Parrish's hands and throwing it to the ground.

Within another second, Parrish went flying ten feet onto the pavement below.

Crash didn't wait to see what would happen next. Instead, he grabbed his gun from the ground and followed Noah over the chain-link fence.

FOURTEEN
THE BOY

They're in trouble.

The boy was sitting in the living room with Zoe when he felt a disturbance deep down in his core. Their panic and fear filled his heart, but he could also feel their powers rising inside them.

His own powers buzzed against his skin, and he ached to use them.

He couldn't sit still, so he stood and paced the room, wishing he could figure out exactly how they'd made that connection before. He'd been touching Zoe's arm at the time, and he was sure that was part of it.

Her connection to Parrish was incredibly strong for just being her sibling in this one lifetime, but the boy could almost feel part of Parrish's power flowing through the girl's veins. It was faint, but it was there.

That wasn't supposed to happen when they reset each lifetime. Yes, their bodies held the DNA of the parents they were born from, and they shared that set of DNA with any human relatives or siblings, just like anyone born in this world.

But for the magic he'd created to work properly, there was also a second set of directions inside each of their bodies. It was a delicate reset each time, and every time they were ready to give up their current lifetime and start anew, he was the one to reset them.

It wasn't reincarnation, exactly. Not the way humans here liked to think of it.

It was, in a way, less like being reborn, and more like being rewritten, over and over.

That was part of the reason none of them remembered their past lives. Only the original life remained imprinted on their memories.

It was also one of the reasons he was so much younger now than the rest of them.

He was the one to reset the spell and the seal each time, so he was always the last to be reborn. After a thousand years, it had put him a few years off from the others.

Crash was always the first to go back. Then the other three all at once, which was why they usually lived nearby or found each other first, even if they didn't understand it. They would always be drawn together.

When they'd originally fought against the Dark One, the boy had actually been the oldest of the group. Some from their world had even called him an Ancient.

He was more than a thousand years old before they ever came to this world and had been considered one of the greatest strategists and alchemists ever born.

It was his knowledge that had allowed them to set up their recurring lifetimes here, using the fatalis stone.

He had not created the stone, of course. Only someone with power over both life and death could have created a stone like that, and there was only one person who had ever lived with that kind of power.

Her intention for the stone was very different from the way the boy had used it, though. When the Dark One created it, she had planned to use it to open portals to new worlds, like this one, and then siphon life from any beings there in order to give her and her followers life eternal.

She'd called it the fatalis stone, because it was meant to defy Fate itself. To defy death.

But sooner or later, fate comes for everyone.

The Dark One never understood that. Even now, she still fought for a way out. For a chance, once again, to control her own fate by stealing the lives of others.

The boy was scared that this time, she might actually succeed.

Nothing had gone according to their grand plan here.

Over a thousand years of resetting and rewriting their own minds and powers in order to keep this world sealed away from the Dark One's power. A thousand years of sacrifice as their powers lay dormant.

A thousand years of Tobias hiding the stone and keeping it safe from this world, and him returning it once in their lifetimes so that they might find each other and gather on the island to reset once again.

A thousand years of trying to keep everyone safe, and when they had finally needed to use their powers and the power of the stone, something had gone terribly wrong.

Instead of coming back to train them and reunite them,

Tobias must have been killed. It was the only explanation the boy had been able to come up with. It was the only way the fatalis stone could be here in this world without him.

But none of that mattered now.

All that mattered now was coming together as a group of five and getting to the island to reset the seal on the Dark One's magic before she grew strong enough to break free.

The boy could feel the stone calling to him like a beacon in the darkness.

He could sense that they weren't too far away from him now, but with the state of the world, it was a difficult distance.

He'd been thinking of going to get a map from the bodega down the street. He was pretty sure he'd seen paper maps there for tourists.

But honestly, he didn't have much hope of finding a way for them to get off this island by flying across rooftops. He had learned to go quite a distance when the buildings got sparse in some places, but to get fully out of New York, they'd have to travel across bridges and into areas where there were no tall buildings. Only houses and roads where the rotters would easily get to them.

Of course, he could run faster than any rotter could, so maybe they would be okay.

Maybe they had a better chance of getting out of the city than Parrish and the others did of getting in safely.

If he could just tap into their consciousness the way he'd somehow managed to do yesterday, maybe they could have a conversation about it. He could tell them he and Zoe were together.

Most of all, he longed to talk to his old friends. He knew

they wouldn't remember him the same way he remembered them. That was also part of how the reset worked. He would always be the first to remember, because it was supposed to be his job to activate the stone each time.

Then Crash would dream of them, and they would go about the business of finding each other as quickly as possible.

There was a whole protocol in place, but it was a mess now. The Dark One had somehow managed to mess up all their plans, even from her icy prison inside the earth.

And right now, she was attacking them again.

He'd felt the guardians' distress in the past, but it had never been this clear.

He guessed it was because of the connection they'd shared. It had closed a circuit between them, but it still wasn't enough for them to talk openly to each other the way he could to Zoe.

Still, he had to at least try to give them hope.

To give them a clue into how to use their powers against the Dark One.

"What is it?" Zoe asked, standing up from where they had been sitting together on the floor by the coffee table, putting together a puzzle.

He had loved putting puzzles together with his parents. It was one of their favorite ways to spend a Sunday afternoon, short of walking to the park, and even though he knew now they had only been his parents for a short time in this one lifetime out of hundreds, they had been so good to him.

He had loved them.

And he missed the simplicity of their life before this. They'd never had much when he was growing up, but they'd always had love and that was the most important thing a family could have.

The boy motioned for Zoe to join him on the floor in the middle of the room.

Zoe scratched absently at her left arm and pulled her sleeve down over her hand.

"Are you trying to reach Parrish again?" she asked softly.

He nodded, and she smiled a little.

He sat cross-legged and rested his hands on his knees, palms facing up as if he was about to meditate. Zoe sat across from him and imitated his position, not questioning him but rather following along and understanding what he wanted her to do.

"She's okay, isn't she? Because when you stood up, you looked worried," she said. "You can sense her, can't you? That's how you knew to come find me? You thought I was her?"

He opened his eyes wider. They hadn't really spent any time talking about this, but she had figured it out on her own.

She was smart for someone so young, but he guessed he was, too.

He nodded again and pointed to the infinity sign necklace she wore.

"She saved my life," Zoe said, tears shining in her eyes. "A bone marrow transplant when I was very young. I think that might be why. I always knew she was special, but I couldn't explain it. I don't think she's ever really seen herself that way, but she is special, isn't she? Like you?"

He smiled.

That was why he could sense Parrish's power inside her sister. She was more than just a sibling. She had taken on a piece of Parrish through the transplant.

He wanted to tell her Parrish was the most special, even if

she would never admit that to anyone. She had always been humble.

Or maybe humble wasn't the right word for it.

She had always been blind to her own greatness, and it was one of the only reasons she'd never fully embraced the unlimited power that flowed through her.

Yes, Parrish was special beyond understanding, but until she could see that for herself, her full power would remain locked within.

But if there was ever a time for her to embrace it, it was now. In this lifetime.

They needed her more than she realized.

And right now, she was fighting for her life. He could feel her pain like a punch to the gut.

It wasn't a physical pain for him. More of a sensation of being hit or thrown. But he could feel it clearly now.

Heart racing. Fear pouring through her veins.

If he wanted to reach out to her he was going to need to do it now. There was no time to waste.

He caught Zoe's eyes, hoping she would understand to follow his actions. She nodded, her eyes glued to his face.

He took a long deep breath and slid closer to her until their knees were touching.

He turned his palms down and touched the tips of her fingers with his own. He closed his eyes and focused on the blood flowing through Zoe's veins. He reached out to that feeling inside him that had experienced Parrish's pain and fear. He plugged into it and deepened the connection, breathing into it and allowing it to flow between him and his connection with Zoe.

Finally, a small zing went through his entire body, like a jolt of electricity, and Parrish's face came into clear view in his mind.

He'd done it. They were connected.

FIFTEEN
PARRISH

Parrish scrambled to her feet, doing her best to ignore the pain screaming through her side. She needed to get to her sword, but the moment she made a move toward it, the silver zombie casually jumped down and kicked it under the bus.

Damn.

This one was different, somehow. More intelligent.

Parrish suddenly knew deep in her bones that this one had not been created by Lily and sent here like the others.

This silvery zombie had been carefully crafted by the pure magic of the Dark One.

The thought chilled her, but she didn't have time to sit and think about what that might mean.

She had bought them all some time with her flash of blue energy, but she had a feeling that wouldn't do anything against the metallic outer shell of this zombie.

She did, however, know that it had hurt the two tentacled ones still crawling their way toward her. Only when she turned to face them, they were both completely still, as if they'd been stunned.

She glanced around, her eyes naturally traveling toward the roof.

This had Karmen written all over it, and sure enough, her friend stood at the edge of the rooftop, along with a crowd of survivors from the compound, staring down at Parrish and the rotters she faced now.

Of course, she'd barely even turned her attention away from the silver zombie for a second or two, but that little bit had created an opening. This thing was too fast, and Parrish couldn't seem to get ahead of it.

Silver ran toward her, fist raised again.

Parrish just barely twisted her body around in time to miss the blow, but she took advantage of Silver's momentum, landing a strong kick in its side that threw it against the side of the bus.

The metal on that entire side of the bus caved in as if it had been hit by a freight train.

Parrish's foot and knee pulsed in pain, too, from the hit. Just how strong was this thing?

She needed to put together a better strategy, or this rotter was going to get the best of her. She widened her stance and gathered as much blue light in the palm of her hands as she could manage, increasing its energy with the intention of her mind. The light flickered and then expanded as its intensity grew.

When Silver turned back around to face her, Parrish unleashed the ball of light in a brilliant flash that this time, instead of expanding outward, focused into a single point of intensity.

To her horror, Silver simply lifted its hand in front of the light and absorbed it. The light went out, doing no damage to the rotter at all.

Parrish stumbled backward, feeling more afraid than she had at the hospital yesterday. She'd put everything she had into that spell, and it had done absolutely nothing to this thing. It just kept coming for her.

She thought of running away, but where could she go?

This thing was obviously faster than she was, and with its power, there would be no place inside to hide from it. She'd only end up getting everyone else killed, too.

She needed to find a weak spot in this thing's defenses. Everyone and everything had a weak spot somewhere.

And she wanted to get her sword back. Even if it couldn't slice through whatever armor this zombie wore, it made her feel more focused and in control of her power.

She held her ground, then, paying attention to every micro-movement the zombie made as it studied her. Finally, when it ran forward, Parrish was able to shift her balance at the last minute, stepping out of the way of the zombie.

Silver obviously had been expecting her to try to kick it again, which was maybe why it had come to her the same way they had last time. It wanted to use her own movements against her.

But Parrish didn't try to kick it this time.

Instead she ran and slid under the bus, grabbing her sword and quickly crawling out the other side.

She had moved with great speed, but it wasn't enough.

As soon as she stood up on the other side, Silver was there waiting for her.

There was nothing she could do fast enough to try to save herself.

Silver reached out with both hands and grabbed her by the neck, its skin cold as steel and equally as hard.

Parrish didn't have enough room between herself and Silver to even attempt an attack with her sword, and the way this rotter was squeezing her neck, she knew she'd run out of air fast if it didn't break the bones in her throat first.

She dropped her sword and clawed at Silver's hands, trying to gain any leverage she could to pull them apart.

She couldn't breathe.

Since she was on the other side of the bus, there was nothing Karmen could do to help her either. Karmen wouldn't be able to see what was happening over here, and without line of sight, it would definitely be harder for her to get inside this thing's mind.

So, what could she possibly do?

Her feet dangled at least a full foot off the ground, so she kicked backwards against the side of the bus, hoping to at least pull this thing off balance. Silver didn't budge, though, no matter how hard she kicked and protested.

Instead, the silver rotter just looked at her. No emotion on its face or in its eyes. It had a job to do, plain and simple, and once it was done, she had no doubt it would go after the rest of them, too.

She couldn't fail them all like that.

So she did the one last thing she could think of. She wrapped her fingers around the fatalis stone and asked for help.

She had no idea the true power of this stone or even what it was meant to be used for. In her dreams, she had seen the fifth use it on the island to retrieve or reset their memories but other than that, she wasn't sure how to use it.

But she sensed in that moment that it could help her at least communicate and connect with the others. To ask them to come help her.

Because she understood now that even though she wanted to take this burden on by herself sometimes, they were so much stronger as a group. She never should have come out there by herself.

Please, she said in her mind. *If you can hear me, I'm on the other side of the bus. A strong zombie made of silver or steel has me trapped. I can't breathe.*

I'm coming for you, Noah responded immediately. *Just hold on.*

At the sound of his voice, Parrish felt renewed. She reached into the stone for more power and then pressed her hand against the rotter's silvery arm, pouring as much of her icy cold light into it as she could.

Frost built up on the outside of its armor, but it didn't let up on its grip.

She was running out of air, praying she could hold on until Noah got to her.

But then, after Noah's voice faded from her mind, there was another.

Parrish?

Tears welled in her eyes, and hope flooded her heart.

Zoe, is that you? Are you safe?

Hearing her sister's voice was like feeling the sun on her face after a long winter.

We're safe, and I miss you. But I need you to listen to me.

The boy here says to use your fire, not your ice. I don't know what that means, but he said you can melt metal.

Parrish gripped the fatalis stone tighter.

In all the craziness after the hospital, she hadn't even thought about the moment her hand had practically burst into flames. She'd been so used to using ice as her main power that she still wasn't even sure how she'd created flames.

From what she could tell, everyone in their group—even Lily—had powers that were based in either ice or fire.

No one else seemed to be able to control both, but somehow she had done it.

Parrish stared at her hands and focused everything inside her to this one, singular image. A hand covered in flames.

The instant the thought took hold inside her, a flame appeared, covering the hand that gripped the silver zombie's arm. Remembering what Lily had done to kill the rats in the apartment, Parrish took what was left of her precious breath and blew across the top of the flame, directing it up and down the rotter's body.

Silver screamed and released her, stepping back as the silvery armor melted onto the skin beneath it. Parrish didn't let up. She blew more flames onto the rotter, coaxing them hotter and more powerful. The zombie writhed and kicked and screamed until whatever was left of its life faded away in pain and horror.

It worked, she said to Zoe in her mind. *I can't believe it worked. Tell him thank you.*

But instead of Zoe's voice in response, she heard the boy.

Parrish, watch out.

The moment he said it, a figure moving toward her caught her attention. Hope drained from her face as the sheer power radiating from the zombie woman almost pulled her to her knees. There was no thought of trying to run or fight.

All Parrish could do was watch.

This rotter had been beautiful once, she had no doubt.

Long black hair that, though matted now in parts, still cascaded down her back in curls. Her black dress was partly sheer at the skirt with a tight, leather bodice that reminded Parrish of a corset.

It was the kind of dress Parrish might have chosen for herself if she'd ever been asked to Prom.

The woman barely had any signs of decay on her dark skin, except for an occasional bruise-like mark on her face or arms. Maybe she'd only been dead a short time, though Parrish couldn't imagine why anyone would have been so dressed up during this mess.

The woman's eyes glowed with a deep, amethyst light, and Parrish knew without a doubt that she was, for the first time, standing in the presence of the Dark One.

Not in the flesh.

Not yet.

But it was her, nonetheless.

"I have waited so long to see you again," the Dark One said, coming up so close to her that Parrish could now smell the woman's decay, despite her lingering beauty. Her voice was almost wistful and sad. "You don't remember me, though, do you? All these centuries dreaming of my revenge, and you don't even know who I am."

"I know some of it," Parrish said. "I know you're the one who started all of this. The one who killed all these innocent people."

The Dark One shrugged, as if that had been nothing at all.

"You're the one who brought me here to this pitiful world." She glanced around. "Doesn't seem like your little plan has worked out all that well, after all."

The fight inside Parrish told her to run. Or to lift her sword or gather some of her power into her hands. But she couldn't. The power of the Dark One's presence held her to the spot, her knees trembling.

With what confidence she could manage, Parrish squared her shoulders and lifted her chin. "We've kept you in prison for centuries, haven't we? I wouldn't say we've done such a bad job."

The Dark One smiled through the woman's eyes and face, and Parrish wondered how it must have felt for her to be locked away alone for so long with no power. No one to talk to.

She obviously enjoyed having some of her freedom back.

Parrish hadn't realized the Dark One could take such direct control of a zombie, but she wasn't entirely surprised, either. With every new death and awakening, she grew in power. There were likely over a billion deaths worldwide now. Maybe more.

What more would it take for the Dark One to go free? Did everyone have to die? Or was she on the brink of freedom, even now?

And if this was how her power felt when she was using a dead human as a vessel, what would it be like to face her in person?

Parrish sucked in a ragged breath.

"You used to love me, though you'll never remember it now," the Dark One said. "You were once like a daughter to me. You were a lot like me, in fact."

Parrish lifted her chin. There was no way she'd ever loved this woman. "I don't believe you."

"It doesn't matter what you believe." The Dark One leaned against the side of the bus, so close Parrish had to turn her head slightly to see her face. "It's practically over now, anyway. I have almost everything I need to retake what was stolen."

Parrish wanted to move, but at the same time, she wasn't entirely sure she had control of herself.

The magic surrounding the Dark One was both intoxicating and terrifying at the same time.

"Then why show up here, if you're so close?" Parrish asked. "Just to see me one last time before you kill me?"

The woman studied her and laughed.

"I don't want to kill you," she said. "Not here. That would be too easy for you."

Parrish glanced at her, confused.

"Too easy for me?"

The Dark One's eyes flashed, and she leaned in closer, running a jagged fingernail across Parrish's cheek.

"I want you to suffer for a thousand years, the way you made me suffer," she said, almost growling low in her throat. "I want you to watch everything you've ever loved be taken from you, including the home you once adored and cannot even remember. I will force you to remember, and then I will kill everyone who aided you or opposed me in any way, including the Guardian's Council."

Parrish recognized that term from one of her dreams of the old man, Tobias. He was part of the Guardian's Council.

"I've had a thousand years to plan my revenge on you and the world who betrayed me and denied my gifts," the Dark

One said. "And I will not let you die in a brief flash of pain. I will torture you in a million twisted ways you could never imagine. I will make you beg for death. I will bring you to its merciful edge, and then I will give you life so that I can do it all again."

Parrish's lip trembled slightly, but she kept her head held high. As long as she wasn't going to die here and now, she could endure whatever she had to so that she could fight back against this horrible monster of a woman and all the pain she had brought to this world.

"I will hunt you down first and kill you before I'll let that happen," Parrish said, daring to look the Dark One in the eye.

The woman laughed.

"That's the strength I was looking for," the Dark One said. "Even though you cannot remember your true self yet, you are strong to your very core. I have always loved that about you."

"We beat you once. We can do it again, with or without our memories," she said.

"If you had beaten me, we wouldn't be standing here now," the woman said. "Between the five of you with all your power and knowledge, you couldn't figure it out, and you've gotten no closer to the truth after all these years of rebirth or reset or whatever it is your ancient one likes to call it.

She leaned in and whispered.

"You did not beat me, Parrish. You enraged me, and the entire universe will suffer for it. I promise you that."

"No. We won't make that same mistake again," Parrish said. "This time, we won't lock you away. We'll kill you. That's my promise."

"I cannot die," the Dark One said, leaning closer. "But I can kill. And I'll start with your sister. I have her now, in fact.

She plays her violin so beautifully, it seems to weep in her arms. Such an innocent girl. I will enjoy introducing her to unimaginable pain in your presence."

The Dark One kicked at the hunk of melted metal near her feet.

"Maybe I will turn her into one of my toys and send her after you. Let you kill her a second time. Won't that be fun?"

Parrish laughed.

"You're a liar. You don't have my sister," she said. "She got away from you, and you'll never find her now."

Surprise flashed in the Dark One's eyes for a brief moment, but her surprise quickly turned to rage. She gripped Parrish's jaw in her hand.

"You obviously don't understand," the Dark One said. "I am death, and eventually, everyone belongs to me. Even you."

A thick wooden bat came down on the woman's head with a crack, and the light in her eyes went out as she fell to the ground in a broken heap.

At the same time, a giant beast of a man appeared around the other side of the bus.

Parrish grabbed her sword and held it toward the beast, but Karmen ran around the corner after it, her hand raised.

"Stop," she said. "He's mine for now. We still need him."

"Yours?" Parrish asked, her body trembling.

Her best friends stood around her, all staring down at the lifeless woman in the black dress.

"Was that her?" Noah asked.

"Yes," Parrish said. "That was her."

"She's growing stronger by the day," Karmen said.

Parrish looked around at their group.

Noah seemed to have regained his strength in record time.

Crash had lightning crackling between his fingertips.

Karmen had tamed a beast with her mind.

Parrish could control both ice and fire with a single thought.

And the boy? He'd just saved her life from hundreds of miles away.

She held the fatalis stone out for them to see, the five symbols all glowing brightly.

"So are we," she said with a smile. "So are we."

PART TWO
THE BEACH

SIXTEEN

THE WITCH

The witch wandered the streets of the city just before sunset, the edges of her black skirt trailing across the asphalt. All around her, rotters who had hidden inside during the heat of the day stumbled into the cooler evening air.

If she had been a normal human, they would have been feasting on her bones by now, but the rotters she passed hardly noticed her at all. They staggered past, moaning low and keeping their distance.

She could sense them all around the city, as if she'd somehow been plugged into the power of their deaths. Millions by now. All commanded by her Mistress.

Ever since she'd been blessed by the Dark One inside the ice cave, the witch could feel nothing but adoration and awe for what her Mistress had created here. How had she ever dreamed of betrayal? Of choosing anything but love and loyalty?

A scene flashed before her. Unimaginable pain and torture. Burned skin.

She winced but quickly pushed those images down. Something took their place, like a soothing balm being placed on a deep wound.

In seconds, she had no memory of the pain at all, and everything inside her was back to love.

For a moment, some part of her wanted to fight against it, recognizing deep down that whatever magic the Dark One had cast on her was taking her over, erasing her emotions or maybe poisoning her.

The same way the Dark One had taken over all these humans.

With her new perspective, the witch had a greater sense now of how that power worked. It was an exchange of sorts.

The virus had worked like a siphon, draining the life-power of every infected human and transferring it to the Dark One. In return, as her powers grew, she reversed the process, letting a small trickle of her own power flow back into these dead humans.

The magic not only allowed the necromancer to control them. It also allowed her to see through them. To be them. To connect them up like a hive mind in order to increase her power even more.

It was chilling and elegant. Why wouldn't the witch want to be a part of that exchange? She was lucky to be included in the Dark One's plans, even if it meant losing a piece of herself along the way.

No one in the Council of Fire had ever displayed an ounce of power this great when the witch was growing up. They pretended to know so much, but compared to the power witnessed here, they were nothing.

What would it be like to re-enter that world as the top ally of the most powerful necromancer to ever live?

The women of the Council would throw themselves at her feet and tremble when she spoke. They would beg to be commanded by her and mourn for the way they had treated her.

But I will never be loved.

That tender part beneath the surface—the part that still belonged to her own soul—wanted to weep at the thought of never being loved. It made her stop for a moment, wondering where in the world she'd just been headed.

But then a voice whispered inside her mind.

What good is love? Another way to make you weak and vulnerable. Another chance for someone to hurt you. Isn't it more powerful to be feared? To be followed?

The witch closed her eyes, listening to the voice that sounded like her own but did not belong to her. The sound seemed to wrap itself around her doubt and squeeze it out of existence.

She felt every drop of resistance evaporate, and suddenly her mission was clear to her once again.

Yes, I want to be feared. Powerful.

All she'd ever wanted was respect and a chance to prove her power, and she'd almost ruined it all. She'd almost given it up, and for what? Friendship?

The witch gathered flames on her fingertips and watched them dance. Her power had grown since her time inside the ice. A gift from the Dark One?

Always. Her entire life was a gift at this point.

And all she had to do to keep it was one final task.

Find the girl and, if possible, kill the fifth.

In a city with infinite places to hide, that might have been impossible for some. But the witch was a tracker. It was her business to find things.

She brought her fingertips together, forming a single flame between them, then focused her mind on the image of that spiral symbol she'd seen on the window of the Four Seasons.

Zoe, a normal human girl, might be difficult to find, but she was with the fifth now, and he'd been using his magic.

She tuned into his power, like tuning into a specific frequency.

When she caught the edge of it, she leaned in, pouring more of her energy into the search.

For now, she could only sense the slight pull. It had been too many hours since he'd used magic, but the residue of it was still out there. And it wouldn't be long before he cast again.

He wouldn't be able to help himself.

And bit by bit, the witch would inch closer to him until both he and the girl belonged to her.

The witch crouched low to the ground, opened her palm, and blew over the top of the flame in her hand. The fire jumped to the blacktop and travelled forward like an arrow before it turned north on second avenue.

She smiled.

This was going to be a piece of cake.

SEVENTEEN

PARRISH

By the time the sun had set, the last of the rotters had been killed and hauled away.

Parrish did one last walk around the entire compound to make sure they hadn't missed one or failed to see a spot in the fence or metal sheets that had been compromised.

The entire compound was lucky to still be standing, and Parrish had half a mind to leave tonight just so they didn't risk bringing on another attack before dawn.

She had no doubt the Dark One only zerged this place because of them. Coming here had put the whole community at risk, but to be honest, she wasn't sure she had the energy to leave even if they needed to.

She'd never been so exhausted in her life.

And her fatigue wasn't just physical. She was tired to her core in every way. Tired of trying to figure out why they'd been given these powers. Tired of worrying about Zoe and how they were going to save her and the entire world at the same time.

Tired of being slapped in the face by new information that didn't fully make sense.

Her brain was constantly working, putting pieces of the puzzle together, but never quite seeing the entire picture.

The Dark One could have killed her today, but she didn't. She said she'd once loved Parrish like a daughter.

Was that true?

Why couldn't she remember any of that?

She found it hard to believe she'd ever been close to someone so evil and terrible. Maybe the Dark One was just trying to mess with her mind.

If so, it worked.

Parrish couldn't get the whole encounter out of her head, but she didn't have time to keep going over and over it. They needed to make a plan for how they were going to get to New York.

"We need to be heading toward the coast by noon at the absolute latest," Parrish said when she got back to the room.

She collapsed on the bed beside Noah, and he motioned for her to rest her legs across his lap. When she did, he massaged her sore calves, and she could have sworn he must have put some of his healing power into his hands.

She felt better instantly, and she was so grateful he seemed to be feeling okay. Finding him passed out on the floor had nearly scared her to death. How he'd recovered so quickly, she still didn't fully understand.

But none of them understood their powers, did they? The Dark One sure seemed to know what she was doing, but the group in this room was clueless with a capital C. How they'd made it this far was a miracle.

"I know you want to leave early, but we can't push

ourselves past our limit, either," Crash said. "I don't know about you all, but every part of my body hurts. Unless lover boy over there wants to give us all massages tonight, I'm going to need some rest before we can even dream about Manhattan."

Noah patted the bed beside him. "You're next," he said, giving Crash a wink.

To Parrish's surprise, though, Karmen was the one who got up and started massaging Crash's shoulders. That was quite a change in attitude from even just a few days ago. Something was definitely brewing there, and Parrish wished she could remember everything about who they used to be before all of this. Had they all been close in the world they came from?

Had they loved each other?

Her hand reached for the fatalis stone hanging around her neck. When they'd gotten back into the compound earlier, she'd wrapped it with a piece of leather and decided to wear it closer to her heart. It was her only link to Zoe now, and she wanted it where it would rest against her skin at all times.

This stone was also the key to the island. To their memories.

They needed to get to Zoe and the fifth, and then they had to get to that island. It was obvious the Dark One didn't want them to go there, so it had to be important.

"We'll just have to play it by ear and see how it goes," Crash said. "It's totally possible we'll get to the water in just a few hours, if we can find our way through the traffic and we don't run into much trouble along the way."

"Can we please get some food before we start speculating about tomorrow's trip?" Karmen said, clutching her stomach.

"As much as I love hearing you both talk endlessly about things we can't control, I am starving."

"Wait," Parrish said, clutching the fatalis stone in her hand. "We have to try to contact Zoe and the fifth. I don't fully understand how or why they can talk to us through this stone, but we need to make some kind of plan. Figure out exactly where they are and how we're going to get to them."

"Can't we do that after we eat?" Karmen asked, pouting. "They're probably just sitting around some New York apartment, doing nothing. They can wait."

Parrish gave her a look, and Karmen rolled her eyes but didn't argue. Instead, they all moved to the floor and sat down the same way they had the other night when they'd first heard the boy's voice.

They touched hands, but nothing happened.

"Zoe? Can you hear me?" she asked out loud. "Is anyone there?"

They all waited quietly, but again, there was no answer.

"Anyone else feel like we're in middle school trying to do a seance at a Halloween party or something?" Karmen asked, laughing.

Parrish had to admit, Karmen was right.

Well, she didn't have to admit it out loud, but yeah. It was a strange feeling to try to be contacting someone they'd never actually met through a stone none of them understood how to use. They still didn't even know the fifth's name.

They kept trying to make contact for ten minutes or so, but everyone else seemed to be losing patience.

Noah was the one who finally convinced her to try again later.

"We'll figure it out," he said. "But you heard them both earlier today when we weren't sitting around like this, right?"

She nodded. "Yeah, I was holding onto the stone when I heard their voices in my head."

"So we don't necessarily need to be touching each other or sitting together," Crash said. "Maybe it has something to do with what the fifth is doing where he is."

"Maybe," Parrish said. She just wished there were some better answers to what was really going on with them.

"Maybe he can reach out to you as long as you're touching the stone," Noah said. "You should keep it somewhere it's always touching your skin."

"Put it in your bra," Karmen said. "Plenty of room in there."

Parrish kicked her friend's foot.

"That's why I wrapped it with this piece of leather. So I can wear it like a necklace," she said.

"I bet as long as you're touching it in some way, he can contact you when he needs to," Noah said. "When he does, we can all sit down and come up with a plan to find them and bring them out of the city. Sound good?"

"Sounds good to me," Karmen said, standing. "Now, can we please get some food?"

"Let's go," Parrish said, tucking the cool purple stone inside her shirt and standing to join the others. "We can work out our plans when we get back tonight before bed."

They left the small room they all shared and headed toward the dining hall.

"It's going to take some time to get the bikes and everything, too," Parrish said as they walked, anxiety already making her stomach ill.

There were so many pieces that needed to come together quickly in order for this to work. But they'd made it this far. Zoe and the fifth were still alive, despite the Dark One's power.

All they could do was keep moving forward with hope, facing each challenge as it came.

"I already have an idea where we can get some bikes," Crash said. "There's a dealership only about fifteen miles from here, and I think we can get there easily in the Humvee in the morning. If we have the energy to load up a few things tonight, maybe we can be out of here by nine."

"Sounds good to me, I—"

Parrish was cut off by the sound of applause as they entered the mess hall. Everyone was on their feet, cheering.

Parrish's face grew warm, and she ducked slightly behind Noah. She didn't know how to react or respond to this kind of attention. Zoe had gotten all the attention growing up, and though Parrish had resented her sister for that, she realized now she never really wanted the applause.

All she'd really wanted back then was for her parents to love her just as she was.

Besides, the praise and applause made her feel guilty. The rotters never would have come here like that if it hadn't been for them.

She wasn't going to complain, though. These people had been through a lot today, and it was a miracle no one had died. Parrish still wasn't sure how they'd managed to pull that off, but she was so grateful.

Kaya came over to say a few words and then showed them to a special table near the front that had been decorated with a beautiful tablecloth and a basket of fresh flowers.

But it wasn't the decor that had Parrish's mouth watering. The table was loaded up with foods she hadn't seen, smelled, or tasted in what felt like an eternity. Steak, baked potatoes, pizza, fresh vegetables, fruit, and a bowl of actual ice cream and cake for dessert.

Her shyness suddenly disappeared as she saw the spread. She couldn't believe it.

Food like this was worth more than gold these days. She'd assumed this kind of feast was extinct forever.

"Looks like you guys have been holding out on us this whole time," Crash said with a wink.

Everyone around them laughed, easing the tension a bit.

"This is too much," she said to Tank and Kaya as they came around to the front of the table. "We don't deserve all this. You should give it to the kids or something."

"Go ahead, have a seat everyone, and settle down to eat," Tank said.

He turned to the group of teens and put his arm around his wife.

"We're more than happy to offer this to you," Kaya said. "We save this food in the freezer for all our groups that go out on dangerous missions like what you all did yesterday, so don't go worrying that this was just for you."

Parrish smiled and sat down. Kaya had a way about her that made everyone feel welcome and safe. Tank was a lucky guy.

"The entire compound is going to benefit from what your group brought to us this morning, and I know we wouldn't have survived the attack this afternoon if it hadn't been for the four of you." Tank leaned in closer, lowering his voice. "I still don't understand exactly what you did out there, but after the dead started walking around eating people, I stopped questioning things so much."

"Thank you for this," Noah said, sitting down across from her and motioning for everyone else to join them. "I haven't seen food that looks this good in a long time. I feel bad eating it in front of everyone else."

"They're used to it," Kaya said with a laugh, and several people around them chuckled in agreement. "Like I said, we serve this to everyone who goes out on big missions. We won't be able to do it forever, but as long as we are able, we'll do what we can to say thank you to those who go out of their way for the rest of us."

"I don't know how to thank you for what you've done," Cheryl said. She stepped forward, one hand on her belly.

"How's Stephen feeling?" Noah asked.

"It's a miracle how far he's come in just a few hours," she said. "This morning, I honestly didn't think he was going to make it, and now, he's sitting up and talking. He even asked if he could walk here himself to say thank you, but we told him he wasn't allowed to get out of bed just yet. He said he's feeling better than he has in a long time. If you guys hadn't gotten back when you did, I don't know what I would have done."

She wiped tears from her face.

Parrish and Noah exchanged glances across the table.

No one here would ever know just what they had done for Stephen and his family. And at least now they knew Noah wasn't quite as invincible as they originally thought.

"We were glad to do it," Noah said.

"Are you sure you won't stay?" Cheryl asked. "We could really use your help keeping this place running."

Parrish shook her head.

"We can't stay," she said. "But if we are able to find my sister and bring her out of the city, we'll do our best to come back. At least for a little while."

"You're always welcome here," Tank said, but a slight cough and a strange look toward his wife told Parrish that maybe he didn't entirely mean that.

There was no doubt the attack earlier had shaken everyone up. They were doing their best to act normal, but Parrish could tell they had questions they were afraid to ask.

She couldn't blame them, really.

"Okay, you guys, let's leave them in peace to enjoy their meal before their ice cream melts," Kaya said.

"Was I not supposed to eat that first?" Crash asked, looking up from his empty dessert bowl.

Parrish pressed her lips together to hide a smile. She wanted to eat hers, too, but she couldn't stop looking at that gooey slice of pizza.

She actually moaned as she took her first, glorious bite.

"Oh, how I've missed you," she said.

"Did you just speak words of love to your pizza?" Karmen asked, raising an eyebrow.

"Yes, I did," Parrish said, laughing. "Me and pizza go way back."

Karmen smiled and shook her head.

"You're crazy," she said, taking a bite of a ripe strawberry. "But oh my gosh, that's good."

They ate together, laughing and joking as they enjoyed the amazing food, and when they were done, they thanked everyone and said their goodbyes.

Many people tried to convince them to stay, and Parrish nodded and told them that she hoped they'd be back soon. She knew they wouldn't, though. They had a bigger role to play in the days ahead, and she had a feeling it would cost them all their lives before it was over.

Even if they managed to rescue Zoe and unite with the fifth, there was a battle coming. Something bigger than Manhattan. It would be a battle for the whole world, and possibly for worlds beyond.

Today had been a small taste of it, but mostly the battle here had taught her just how unprepared they were to face the Dark One's power. Maybe they'd been strong enough to capture her a thousand years ago, but now?

They were weak and vulnerable, and they were running out of time.

We have to get to the island.

Parrish reached up to touch the fatalis.

One step at a time.

Tomorrow, they would head to the coast, and in a few short days, they would be reunited with the fifth and with her sister.

Then they could go to the island.

There was still time to save this world.

She had to believe it was true, and as they walked back to their room and settled down to sleep, she sent up a prayer to whoever might be listening that by this time tomorrow night or the next, her sister would be safely at her side.

C rash said goodbye to Tank and Kaya just before nine the next morning. The couple had prepared a hot breakfast for them and a large backpack full of food.

Tank had asked him a dozen questions about the magical powers he'd seen them use and the hyped-up rotters with red eyes, but Crash didn't want to scare the guy too badly.

"It's a long story, old friend," he said. "I'll tell you what, if we survive it, I'll come back and tell you the whole thing over a game of chess. Deal?"

Tank shook his head.

"Do I have any choice in the matter?"

"Not really," Crash said.

"I figured as much," Tank said. "Just be careful out there. I've seen a lot of things in my life that scared me, but nothing compares to yesterday."

"After we're gone, I hope you'll never see that kind of thing again," Crash said. "I'm sorry to think we brought that danger here to your group, but I promise we'll do everything we can to make sure you all stay safe, okay?"

Tank nodded. "You know, when all this first started, I figured it was just a freak thing. Something like in the movies. Terrible virus causes some kind of mutation and the whole world goes crazy. Seeing what I saw yesterday, though, has me thinking there's a lot more to this story than any of us ever realized. You and your group. You're a part of this, aren't you?"

"We didn't start it, but I hope we're going to be the ones to end it," Crash said. "That's why we can't stay here. There's work to do."

Tank seemed to take it all in for a moment before finally clapping his hand hard against Crash's back.

"Before you go, come pick out whatever you want from the armory, too. Whatever you think you can carry," he said. "It's all yours."

That was one offer he simply couldn't turn down.

Crash was like a kid in a candy shop inside that place.

In the end, he only chose two guns and some extra ammo for himself. He also grabbed a hunting knife for Zoe and the smallest pistol he could find for the fifth. Crash hoped it wouldn't come down to a couple of kids having to face the kinds of zombies they'd faced so far on their trip, but he wanted to make sure they had at least something to protect themselves if it came down to it.

There were so many other weapons he'd wanted to take, but carrying a bunch of guns while riding on a dirt bike was too impractical. It had truly hurt his heart to leave them all behind.

In a way, it had hurt everyone to leave the compound behind.

He could see it in their expressions as they drove through the gate, leaving safety behind them. It seemed stupid to head straight into the heart of hell like this, but it felt strangely powerful, too.

It felt like destiny.

Crash had been dreaming of this plague and the fallout it would cause for months before it actually began, and no matter how devastating it was, it was all exactly as it was meant to be.

And despite the danger they were speeding toward, there was still hope.

There was still a chance they could end all of this. But the only way to do it was to keep moving toward the danger, not hiding from it.

Crash kept his eyes on the road as things got more and more congested. According to satellite pictures and what Tank had told them, once they got about thirty miles from the city, the roads became parking lot graveyards.

They were going to need alternate means of transportation soon.

Leaving his beloved Humvee behind was definitely going to hurt, but it couldn't be helped.

He just hoped they could make it to the bike shop before the roads got too bad.

They still hadn't made contact with the fifth again yet, but as long as they were heading toward the coast, they'd be ready to head into the city as soon as the fifth was ready for them.

Crash kept his eyes on the satellite, and sure enough, about fifteen minutes into their trip, he saw exactly what he'd been looking for. He pulled off the road, waking up a sleeping Karmen in the back of the truck.

"Hey, what the hell," she said. She sounded pissed, even though he'd told her it would be a short ride.

"Time to say goodbye to the Humvee," he called back.

The website for this place claimed they sold everything from dirt bikes to golf carts to four wheelers. Crash just hoped there was some good merchandise still available, because from the looks of the outside, this place had been raided pretty hard a long time ago.

"I still don't understand why we have to ride motorcycles," Karmen said, yawning.

"We'll never make it to the water in this thing," Crash said. "Things are already getting congested, and all the roads leading both north and east on my satellite are packed with random pile ups and impassable traffic jams. We need to be more mobile and able to dodge cars and wreckage if we're going to make it to the waterfront today. If we can find four usable bikes inside, I think I can power all of them even if there's no fuel."

"Wait just a minute," Karmen said, sitting up wide awake. "You expect me to ride on my own? Are you insane? I've never done this before."

"It will be fine," Noah said, always the patient one. "I'll help you find a good one, or you can ride with me, if you want."

"I still don't see why we can't at least try to use this heap of metal we're in right now?" she argued.

Crash guessed she was still pretty upset about the fact that they'd had to leave her Beast behind. They'd managed to lock him up last night so he couldn't hurt anyone, but by morning, his body had already been massively corroded by whatever acidic power had been running through his veins. The Dark One's magic was toxic, it seemed, even to the undead.

Besides, there was no way they were getting that thing to the coast and on a boat, although they did try to figure out a safe way to do it. Having a guy like that on their side would have come in handy in the city.

If they'd had more time, maybe they could have built some kind of cage for it that they could have hauled behind the truck, but even then, they would have never gotten the whole thing through traffic.

It didn't matter, anyway, though. The guy was probably a pile of goo by now. Karmen would have to find a new pet in Manhattan.

Crash was sure she'd have her pick of super zombies once they got there.

"The Hummer's gotten us through plenty of traffic jams so far," she said. "Besides, the Z's can't bite through metal. On a motorcycle, we'll just be out in the open. Zombie food. We can just go around anything we find, right? This thing can go off-road."

"The areas we're going to are worse than anything we've seen so far," Crash said.

Karmen continued to protest, but Crash wasn't in the mood to spar with her. They had some stressful crap coming up, and his body was still sore from the past two fights.

He didn't have a speck of energy to spare.

From the look on Parrish's face, she felt the same way. He caught her eye and motioned toward the building. She nodded, opened her door, and stepped outside.

"What kind of bike is best, you think?" she asked. "You guys said to find a dirt bike or something that can do well off-road, but I honestly have no idea what to look for."

"Let's get inside and see what they have left," he said.

"Looks like we aren't the first ones here. Probably people looking for a way out of the city when they either didn't have access to a car or, like us, couldn't get through the traffic."

The front door of the large warehouse was already open, and Crash pulled out one of the industrial-sized flashlights Tank had given him. He switched it on and banged it against the door frame a couple times.

"What are you doing?" Parrish asked.

He smiled. "Calling the Z's out of the darkness," he said. "If they're in there, I'd rather fight them out here than get caught off guard by one of them inside."

Karmen placed a hand on his arm, and he nearly jumped from surprise at her touch. "Why don't you just turn on the overhead lights, electro-boy?"

She batted her eyelashes at him, and his cheeks flushed from embarrassment.

"I was trying to save my power as much as possible today," he said. "We don't know what we're going to face in the city, but I have a feeling it's going to be much worse than that hospital. I only have so much juice in me before I pass out, remember? Do you really think we should waste it on this trash heap when we have flashlights?"

She frowned and shrugged. "I guess I didn't think of it that way."

He turned and patted her shoulder.

"It's okay. I know you aren't used to using your brain."

He quickly backed out of the way before she hit him, and he ended up stumbling into the warehouse and nearly falling into a rotter who was somehow stuck between the wall and a giant cardboard display of some racecar driver.

He cursed as the zombie's fingers raked across his neck.

Before he had a chance to fully react, the rotter's head rolled off its shoulders and onto the floor.

Parrish stood there, sword in the air.

"Thanks," he said.

"That's what you get for saying ugly things about my brain," Karmen said, sticking her tongue out at him.

God, that woman drove him crazy in a million different ways he wasn't even sure he had words for yet.

How could he be so turned on and so annoyed by the same person?

Was this what love was all about?

"I promise I'll be nicer to your brain in the future," he said, throwing a glance back at the dead zombie that had almost meant the last of him in a moment of stupidity.

Flirting could be deadly in this world. He'd do well to remember that and stop being an idiot.

"Okay, on second thought, I'm going to turn these lights on for a few minutes. Grab what you want or need as quickly as possible, and let's get the hell out of here," he said.

He focused on the hum of energy always buzzing on the edge of his consciousness, and he easily located the power source in the room and flipped the lights on. The inside of the warehouse erupted in bright white light.

He quickly pointed toward the back, where a row of bikes and four-wheelers were still undisturbed.

"Looks like the front of this place was picked clean, but no one was brave enough to go all the way into the back," he said. "We got lucky, ladies and gents. Take your pick."

They raced back toward the bikes, where Parrish and Karmen quickly claimed a couple of smaller dirt bikes.

Karmen's was banded with pink stripes, while Parrish chose a sleek black one with matte paint.

Crash stepped over to a row of larger bikes. "This is more my type," he said, rubbing his hands together.

"Are you sure you can handle one of these bad boys?" Noah joked, poking him in the ribs.

"Oh I can handle it," Crash said, straddling the bike. "It's that girl over there I can't handle much more of."

"Who? Karmen? I thought you guys were getting along pretty well these days." Noah looked over at the girls and Crash followed his gaze.

"It's not that we aren't getting along," Crash said. Then, under his breath, he added, "It's that I like her too much for my own good."

Noah laughed, and Crash shook his head.

"Stupid, I know. There are times when I feel like we have a real connection, but then I look at her. A girl like that could never go for a guy like me."

Noah shrugged.

"Don't sell yourself short," he said, clapping him on the shoulder. "Besides, we're like literally two of the last guys on earth, and I happen to be spoken for."

Crash laughed. "That's super encouraging, dude. Thanks for the vote of confidence."

The guys tried out a couple of options before they each settled on their ride of choice.

"We should get outside and load up. I know Parrish is anxious to get moving," he said.

Noah hung back for a second, his expression darkening.

Crash turned back to him, concerned. "Everything okay, man?"

Noah sighed. "What are the chances we're going to be able to survive this trip into New York?" he asked. "I was all for going in, but now that we're actually on the way, I'm scared man."

"You got to stop thinking like that," Crash put his arm around his friend. "Yesterday just has you shook. We're alive right now, against all the odds. Don't you think that means something? We're here for a reason. If anyone can make it through this, it's us. It's our destiny. Can't you feel that?"

As he said it, though, Crash thought of the nightmares he'd been having lately. He still hadn't told anyone about them, but each day brought them a little closer to hell on earth.

Knowing that wouldn't help them, though. And no matter what they were facing, they couldn't give up.

Fate was knocking on their door, now, and there was no turning back.

They made their way out of the warehouse together to meet up with the girls.

Thirty minutes later, the four of them had loaded up all the supplies they could carry and started the next leg of their journey on their new motorcycles.

NINETEEN

NOAH

The journey toward the waterfront park was not an easy one.

The roads were completely blocked in some places, and they ended up having to maneuver their way around the wreckage in creative ways. They even rode into some wooded areas and down steep hills in some cases.

They came across fires, rotters wandering between cars and others trapped inside, and horrible wrecks that had spread debris and body parts across the entire road. They were only about twenty miles into their journey when Noah was over-come by a sick feeling in his stomach.

At first, he thought maybe it was just a reaction to the stench of rotting flesh on this stretch of road. There was a particularly bad stretch of highway where at least sixty cars had piled up in a horrible accident no highway crew would ever show up to clear away.

They'd had to bike way out into a field to avoid it, but the smell of all the bodies stuck in cars lingered for miles.

Shouldn't his stomach have settled down by now?

They'd passed that wreck a good five miles back, and all he could smell now was the heat coming off the asphalt.

He really hoped it wasn't some kind of lingering effect of the infection he'd taken on. It seemed to be completely out of his system after he pushed the antibiotics through.

And he was fairly certain it wasn't something he ate. All he'd had that day was an MRE they'd gotten from Tank back in Philly, and he said those things wouldn't go bad for years. He hoped he wasn't coming down with something.

Talk about bad timing for a stomach flu.

On their new bikes, the group was actually making decent time.

Crash had definitely been right about the bikes. The stretch of road they were on now was a relatively clear, straight shot, but they'd been through some rough patches the Hummer never could have gotten through.

They would have ended up on foot by now if they didn't have these bikes.

For the last few miles, they'd been riding in a straight line.

Crash up front, then Karmen, Parrish, and Noah in the back. Every once in a while, they had to swerve around some debris, but overall they'd been flying through.

They pulled around a couple of abandoned cars and hit a clear stretch of road, and all of a sudden, dread and sickness rolled through Noah's stomach with a vengeance.

He wobbled slightly on his bike and considered telling them he needed to pull over. Parrish wanted to be at the park by four, so he didn't want to slow anyone down and set them all back, but his stomach was not cooperating.

Inside his helmet, he could hardly breathe. It was so hot.

He had the overwhelming urge to pull it off and toss it aside.

He was going to be sick.

Noah slowed his bike to a crawl, set his feet down on the hot pavement, and yanked the helmet off his head.

Everything around him faded to these dull black and grey tones, but when he looked ahead at Parrish, her figure seemed to be outlined in a bluish haze. Noah blinked his eyes several times.

Was he having some kind of heat stroke?

The events of the next few seconds happened for him in slow motion.

Crash and Karmen zipped around a truck and narrowly avoided a box of sports drinks scattered across the road beside it, but Parrish didn't see them fast enough.

Her front wheel struck one of the bottles, and her bike jerked to the side.

Parrish lost control, and Noah reached forward as she skid across the blacktop, strengthening the light of the haze that surrounded her.

The light stretched between them like a rope.

He wasn't sure how he did it. His only thought was of keeping her safe.

When she stopped sliding, though, the blue light he'd stretched toward her snapped back at him, and he cried out in agony.

His calf burned. Quickly, he threw the kickstand up on his bike and rolled up his jeans. Part of his skin had been ripped off, and he was bleeding.

He limped toward Parrish, but Crash and Karmen had

already parked their bikes and rushed to her side by the time Noah got to her.

"Are you okay?" he asked.

She pulled her helmet off and her long, black hair tumbled down her back. She was obviously a bit shaken.

Her black jeans were ripped to shreds, but her leg seemed perfectly fine.

"I don't understand it. I could feel the pressure of the road scraping on my leg, but there's not a single mark, and it doesn't hurt. I should be in a lot of pain right now."

"There's not even a scratch." Crash examined her leg and shook his head. "How is that possible? With that kind of a fall, you should have a huge burn or a strawberry on your leg."

"Her jeans must have kept her safe," Karmen said with a shrug. "Cool. Looks like your bike is okay too. You got lucky."

Parrish's eyes were glued to his leg, though.

"Noah, what happened?"

She quickly stood up and rushed over to him.

"Noah, are you okay?"

He stared at the long stretch of burned skin on his own leg, still trying to understand what he'd just done.

Parrish came around beside him and then lifted a hand to cover her mouth. She ran to grab her first aid kit and brought it over to him.

"Sit down," she said. "This is going to hurt for a second."

He did as she asked and winced when she sprayed something cold on his leg.

"I don't understand," she said as she applied some ointment and wrapped his leg in a clean bandage. "How did you get hurt? Did you crash, too?"

His eyesight had gone back to normal, but his mind was

still spinning. He wasn't even sure how to explain to them what had just happened.

"I didn't crash, but I saw it coming before it even happened," he said, realizing again just how wrong he had been about his abilities. He wasn't invincible at all.

Not when he was helping someone else.

He was going to have to be more careful from now on, but there was one thing he was glad about.

He reached up and ran a finger along Parrish's cheek.

If he could see it coming, he could protect her and keep her from getting hurt.

"I think I just became your shield."

TWENTY
PARRISH

Parrish Sorrows kept her eyes glued to the road for the rest of the trip.

She was lucky her bike hadn't been too damaged to ride, but from the looks of it, Noah's leg had suffered most of the injury intended for her.

And just how the hell had he done that? Listening to him talk about it, it sounded like he'd had some kind of premonition before it happened. Like he'd known it was coming.

That was new.

She wanted to hear him tell the story again, because she wanted to understand just what he'd done and how it worked, but they needed to keep moving. When they stopped for the night, she'd get him to tell her more.

Between the illness he'd drawn out of Stephen's body and the injury today, Noah was looking a lot more vulnerable than any of them had originally thought. He'd seemed invincible, and for some reason, it really upset her to know that he wasn't.

Of course, Noah seemed thrilled about it. He said he'd be

able to shield her and save her life, but what did that mean for him? She didn't want him getting hurt, either.

She needed to be more careful.

No more wrecks. All they had to do today was get to the coast, and they would be one step closer to finishing this.

Crash had been using Karmen's old, shattered iPhone to navigate through the area. It still amazed her how easily he could connect his brain and energy up to a phone that had zero battery left and a network that was likely not in service anymore, but there he was.

He read the screen like the world was normal again, and Parrish suddenly wished for the weirdness of social media. She'd never been on it much, but she'd had a few friends on Discord and over on Instagram who she'd come to know pretty well, even though she'd never met them in real life.

Were any of those people even still alive?

And if they were, would she ever have a way to contact them again?

She couldn't imagine a world where things were back to normal. Even if they got rid of the zombies, she had a feeling this world was changed forever.

As if to punctuate her thought, a massive, hundred-car pileup came into view just over the top of a hill. The groups like this were the worst, because there were always people trapped inside their cars. Most of them had either turned or been partially eaten by those who had.

The stench of places like this was almost more than she could bear, and she'd gotten used to carrying a scarf with her so she could wrap it around her nose and mouth whenever they got close to one.

It helped, even if it didn't totally eliminate the smell, altogether.

They also needed to be careful when they were going through and around these large pile ups. Rotters were stuck in their cars, but there were always roamers, too.

Luckily, there weren't any super zombies in their path. As long as they could steer clear of those guys for a while, they would be okay.

Parrish was still rattled by the ones she'd fought back at Tank's.

She'd never expected the Dark One to attack the compound the way she had, but at least no one had been hurt. By the time they left, Stephen was doing better, too. It looked like he would make a full recovery.

So, all in all, they'd been extremely lucky.

Or was it more than just luck?

The Dark One could have killed them all if she'd wanted to. Parrish had no doubt about that. Before the others had arrived, she'd been completely incapacitated there for a while.

And yet, the Dark One let her live.

Supposedly to torture her even worse in the coming days, but something about that didn't quite sit right with Parrish.

She wanted to talk it through with the others, but it was way too difficult to talk on these bikes. They were too spread out, and the wind and road noise were just too loud. When they got settled somewhere for the night, though, she wanted to bring it up.

For now, she kept her attention on the road.

What had seemed like a smooth and easy start had quickly turned into a nightmare trip.

Hundred-car pile ups that required an hour or more of detour just to get around, even on motorcycles, small hordes of rotters they couldn't avoid no matter how hard they tried, and at one point, even a small band of survivors that needed their help.

When they finally made it to the beach-side town where Crash had decided to stop, the sun was already beginning to set. So much for her hopes of getting there in just a few hours and heading into the city today. There was no way they were going to New York City after dark.

Crash had said this town would likely be deserted, and he was right. The town was pretty small, so the low population before the virus seemed to also mean low zombie population post-virus.

The group pulled their bikes over to the side of the road to figure out what they would do for the night.

"What do you think?" Parrish asked, looking mostly to Crash.

He'd been the one to navigate so far, and she trusted his opinion on what was best.

"If we'd gotten here earlier, I was going to suggest scoping out the boats and finding one big enough to hang out in for the night." He looked around and then shook his head. "It's already getting dark, though. I don't think we have enough time to search for the perfect one and make sure we have enough supplies for the night. Much less find working bathrooms and such."

Karmen cleared her throat, and Parrish looked at her, wondering what annoying opinion or complaint she was going to share this time.

"I know my ideas are not always the most popular ones, but here's how I see it," she began. "Just down this road, I saw some beachfront mansions. I'm talking about ten-million-dollar,   we-could-never-have-owned-a-house-like-this-in-our-dreams, kind of houses. And I'm guessing the owners of these homes are either deceased or moved on by now for the most part. I was just thinking that since we might all die tomorrow, it would be nice to live a single night in luxury and peace."

Parrish wanted to agree with her, because the sound of a gorgeous, luxury mansion on the beach with a really nice bed sounded amazing. But at the same time, there were dangers in a big house.

She opened her mouth to protest, but Karmen held up a hand first.

"Don't even tell me the houses are too big or too dangerous," Karmen said. "You're the one leading us all into the city of death, so I don't want to hear it."

Noah tried to hide a smile, and Parrish smacked his arm.

"What?" he said, laughing. "She's got a point."

"Come on," Karmen said in a pleading, sing-song voice. "This is my one last wish. I'm begging you."

Parrish looked to Crash, and he shrugged.

"It's safer to get inside than be out here in the dark trying to make a decision," he said. "We can go in together and clear it out, block the doors, and do what we need to do."

Parrish sighed. "Okay, Karmen. Take your pick. We'll follow you."

Karmen's eyes widened, and she clapped her hands together, raising her shoulders. "I can't believe we're actually going to do what I want to do. This is so awesome! Follow me. I know just the one."

She led them to a large, modern home with floor-to-ceiling windows all the way around and some kind of fancy modern arch at the top. At least they could basically see through the house, so it was easy to tell there was no one home.

It looked to be deserted but clean.

Like most cities they'd passed through, the power seemed to be permanently off, but with Crash in their group, that didn't matter as much as it could have.

They didn't want him lighting up this house like a Christmas tree and announcing their presence, but they also didn't want a small horde sneaking up on them.

While Crash and Karmen searched through the garage and the downstairs rooms, Noah and Parrish went through the bedrooms and bathrooms upstairs, just in case.

From the looks of it, no one had even squatted here or looted this place. It was completely clean and organized, which felt strangely unsettling to Parrish.

It was too much like normal life for her taste. She didn't want to be reminded of how things used to be, but Karmen was right. It was a beautiful, wildest-dreams kind of house.

Parrish led the way, her sword raised with a soft blue light emanating from the blade. Noah had a gun in each hand, both new and courtesy of Tank's armory.

"Did you ever dream you'd be such a natural with a gun?" Parrish asked.

"I never had any desire to shoot a gun in my life before this, but now it feels like I might as well have grown up with a pistol in my hand," he said. "It's weird."

"Weird is the new black," she said, laughing. "Nothing's going to be normal ever again."

"I suppose not, but there are perks to this new life, too," Noah said, giving her a look that made her cheeks warm.

He took out a flashlight and shone it into one of the

bedrooms. When they were sure it was clear, he shut the door and moved on to the next room.

"Wow, look at the view from this room," she said when he opened the door.

This was obviously the master suite, and whoever had built this house pulled out all the stops.

Iron chandelier, a large canopied king-size bed, and a limitless view of the Atlantic from the large balcony.

While Noah checked for zombies, she stepped outside to take in the view of the beautiful sunset.

For as far as she could see, there were no rotters in sight. Just waves and sand. It was so peaceful, it nearly took her breath away.

It was like the world had no idea it was dying.

"Isn't this beautiful?"

Noah came to stand beside her, leaning on the railing as they watched the waves crash against the shore.

"You're beautiful," he said.

She was about to tell him that was the cheesiest transition she'd ever heard in her life, but when she glanced over at him, the expression in his eyes made her knees weak.

She'd never imagined herself as the kind of girl who wanted a guy to bring out the romance, but here she was, practically swooning.

He reached for her hand and pulled her closer, causing her heart to beat faster.

How many lifetimes had they found each other? How many years had they spent together over all this time?

And how much more time would they have?

Was it too much to pray that when this was all over, they

could have just one more lifetime together? One last chance to get it right and to have peace?

Her eyes fluttered closed as his lips dipped toward hers, but just before they kissed, a gunshot sounded downstairs.

Without hesitation, they both drew their weapons and ran.

TWENTY-ONE

KARMEN

K armen screamed and turned away as the rotter's body fell to the floor, its dark blood oozing across the hardwoods.

"That was a close one," Crash said, lowering his gun. "Are you okay?"

"I'm fine," she said, her heart racing. She'd been stupid, stepping into the massive closet without checking it for rotters first.

The house had been completely empty so far, and she'd just assumed no one was home. Besides, what kind of person locked themselves in the closet?

Maybe someone else had locked this woman in the closet when she'd turned. There was no way to know now, but if it hadn't been for Crash, Karmen might have been rotter food just then.

He never seemed to be too far away these days, and she'd never been more grateful.

"Thank you for that," she said, touching his arm.

His eyes widened slightly at her touch, and she'd have been lying if she said his expression hadn't just sent butterflies fluttering in her stomach.

She kind of wanted to see where things might go between them, but when Noah and Parrish appeared in the doorway to the bedroom, she quickly took her hand off Crash's arm.

She wasn't exactly sure why, except that she didn't think she was ready for the whole world to know how she was feeling for the guy.

And right now, her whole world was standing in this room.

"What happened?"

"Everything okay?" Noah asked.

"We're fine," Crash said. "Just a rotter trapped in the closet. It jumped out at us."

"Well, the sound of that gunshot should bring any others out if they're in here," Parrish said. "From the looks of it, though, this whole neighborhood is pretty quiet."

Karmen shifted uncomfortably.

"That's not exactly a good thing," she said. "The trip to the hospital. The trip back to the compound yesterday. Everything was quiet and look what happened. There might be a huge horde gathering just down the street, waiting to attack as soon as we let our guard down."

Noah nodded. "Good point. So, how do we protect ourselves?""

"Well, seeing how we picked a house with nothing but windows everywhere, it's going to be hard to set up much of a defense, but at least we'll be able to see them coming," Parrish said.

That was actually the reason Karmen had picked this

house in the first place, besides the fact that it was absolutely gorgeous and modern.

No amount of furniture pushed in front of a door was going to barricade them or keep them safe if a horde was waiting to attack, but if they could clearly see what was all around them, they'd at least avoid being surprised when it happened.

Or at least that was her theory.

Someone was going to have to stay up and keep watch, though, and she hoped it wasn't her. She was so tired, she was afraid she might fall asleep standing up.

"Did you clear the upstairs?" she asked. "Is there anything else we need to do tonight? Or can we get some rest?"

"After we eat," Crash said.

"And after we try again to contact the fifth and my sister," Parrish said.

Karmen sighed.

She was pretty hungry, but nothing compared to how exhausted she felt. Part of that probably had to do with just how scared she was about the idea of actually going into New York City.

They'd been talking about it ever since before they left their neighborhood back in Virginia, but being out here on the coast like this, a simple boat-ride away, made it all too real.

"We should talk about our plan, too," Parrish said. "And about where our current abilities are."

"What do you mean?" Crash asked as they all headed back into the main room of the house.

"I mean, what's changed since we first made contact with the fifth," Parrish said. "All our powers have grown some or shifted, haven't they? Karmen, how did you figure out you could turn those rotters to our side? That was awesome, by the way."

Karmen blushed, and then tried to hide it by looking out toward the sea.

Man, it was beautiful here.

It was a shame the sun was setting, because she would have killed for an hour out on that beach. To her delight, there was a beautiful pool out back, though. She wondered if she could talk Crash into a swim.

"Karmen?" Parrish asked.

She cleared her throat, bringing her attention back to the conversation and doing everything she could to stop thinking about a late-night swim with the guy standing next to her.

"Oh, well, you know I've been able to put my own will or my own thoughts into someone else's head in the past, right? Like if I wanted someone to stop coming toward me or to move over, I could put that thought or suggestion into their mind," she said. "But when I was standing up on the roof with that guard and I first saw the horde coming, I realized I was also able to hear his thoughts."

"Uhh," Crash said, running a hand through his hair. "Please tell me you haven't been trying to listen to my thoughts, because that shit is private."

"I haven't," she said, then narrowed her eyes at him. "Not yet, anyway."

"Threat acknowledged," he muttered.

"Could you hear the thoughts of the super zombies?" Noah asked.

"They had no thoughts," she said, motioning for them to all take a seat in the living room. She was way too tired to be standing up if they didn't have to. "Not of their own, anyway.

It seemed like their only thoughts were the orders the Dark One had put into their heads. Basically, she'd told them to seek us out and kill us."

"No surprise there," Parrish said.

"Or maybe it was to seek us out and infect us, but what's the difference," Karmen muttered.

But Noah's head snapped up.

"Wait, infect us?" he asked. "Which was it? Can you remember the exact thought in their heads?"

Karmen shrugged, not sure why it mattered. Noah appeared to think it did, though.

She thought back to the attack on the compound yesterday, trying to remember the exact orders she'd heard repeated in the rotters' minds.

"Find and infect the guardians," she said. "That was it. Why? Do you think there's a difference?"

Noah sat down on the couch. "I don't know, but it seems like nothing the Dark One does is random. Everything has a purpose. Besides…"

His voice trailed off and he looked at Parrish, then shook his head.

"It's okay," Parrish said. "You can say it out loud, because I've been thinking about it ever since the Dark One first trapped me there by the bus."

"What?" Karmen asked, feeling frustrated. "I don't have any clue what you guys are talking about."

Noah sighed. "The Dark One could have killed Parrish yesterday. Easy." He looked to Parrish and placed a hand on her leg. "No offense."

"None taken. It's true," Parrish said. "I couldn't even think to move or fight back. Just being in the presence of such power had me like a deer in headlights. She could have snapped my neck or set me on fire. Who knows. But she didn't. She just threatened me. Said she wanted me to suffer."

"Maybe it's the truth," Karmen said.

"Maybe," Noah said. "But what about Lily? She was right there with us while we slept. She could have killed us any time she wanted, but she didn't. Instead, she kept arranging these rotter attacks."

Karmen nodded. This was something that had been on her mind a lot since the hospital, and she was glad he had finally brought it up.

"Yeah, why not just slit our throats in our sleep?" Karmen asked, her stomach turning at the thought of how vulnerable they'd all been while Lily had been traveling with them. She'd slept right next to the enemy and hadn't even known it. "If the Dark One was so keen to see us dead, why didn't she have Lily slit our throats? Or poison our food? There were so many opportunities in Crash's apartment alone, but instead of killing us, she sent rats? Terrifying, sure, but not deadly."

"Yeah, and it was Lily who killed those rats, anyway," Crash said, shuddering at the memory. "I know that apartment wasn't much, but it was home and I had a lot of good times there. I'll never get that burned rat smell out of my mind."

It wasn't a fond memory for Karmen, either. She'd had one crawling in her hair, and it was the grossest feeling of her life.

"She summoned an army of zombie rats, and then killed them all. Why?" Karmen asked.

"To earn our trust," Noah said.

"Okay, but why did she need it?" Karmen asked. "If the goal was really to kill us all, she didn't need us to trust her. She just needed an opportunity to kill or infect us, which she had plenty of right there in that apartment."

Everyone was quiet for a minute, and Karmen thought about that apartment and what Lily must have been thinking when she brought those rats there. She obviously hadn't intended to kill them.

Sure, she wanted them to trust her, but they already did at that point. Or at least, she hadn't given them any reason not to trust her.

So, why the rats?

Karmen felt she was on the verge of understanding something very important, but it wasn't fully coming together in her mind just yet.

Crash brought over one of the backpacks and spread some food out on the coffee table, along with four fresh bottles of water.

"Thanks," Karmen said, taking a long drink of water.

"So, you're thinking there's some reason the Dark One doesn't want us dead?" Crash asked.

"I'm thinking she wants us dead in a very specific way, maybe," Noah said. "Maybe infecting us gives her more power. What was it Lily said back at the hospital again? About how the Dark One's power works?"

Parrish looked down at her hands for a moment, as if trying to recall the exact words.

"With each death, the Dark One grows stronger. That's what Lily said."

"So, when someone dies from the virus, the Dark One takes their life force," Karmen said. "That's why she wants us infected. She wants to take our powers away."

"Maybe that's the only way she can go free," Parrish said.

"So, why not infect you yesterday?" Karmen asked. "If she had you right there, why not just bite you or whatever? Why would Lily kill the rats? It doesn't fully make sense to me."

Parrish shook her head. "I don't know, but every day, we unravel a little more of this mystery. I feel like we're so close to finally figuring it all out."

"Karmen, tell us how your powers worked again. You were saying you could hear that guard's thoughts, so then what? You turned that power onto the super zombies? What else?" Noah asked.

She took another long drink of water and continued explaining how her powers had progressed and how she'd been able to turn down the volume of the Dark One's orders and replace them with her own, instead.

"That's cool as hell," Crash said, his mouth slightly open in awe.

"It's also extremely powerful," Noah said. "And you turned how many to our side in just ten minutes? Four?"

"Yeah," she said. "There didn't seem to be a limit to how many I could turn, and I could sense my connection to each of them once it was made. I think if they had been turned back to the Dark One's orders, I would have known or sensed it."

"Did you feel lightheaded at all when you were doing it?" Parrish asked. "Or any other indication that you were reaching the limit of your powers?"

She thought about it for a second and shrugged. "Not that I noticed."

Parrish looked impressed, and for some strange reason, that sent a surge of pride through Karmen's body. She'd always been popular, but she'd never really been someone people were impressed with.

Annoyed with was more normal for her.

Jealous of, maybe.

But never impressed or proud of.

She liked the idea of being unique and strong.

"What about everyone else?"

She sat down and chose a selection of snacks from the pile. Not exactly a gourmet meal, but with this view to enjoy, she didn't care.

"We know Noah healed Stephen, but he also took on the illness. So, that's good and bad, both."

"He healed himself faster than expected, though, too," Crash said. "When we first saw you, face down on the floor, I thought you were a dead man."

"Thanks," Noah said, shaking his head. "I've never felt worse in my life, to be honest. I sort of remember trying to stand up, but I don't remember passing out. But once I got the IV meds flowing, I could feel what it was doing inside my body to heal me. I instinctively knew how to speed up my own recovery, so at least that was a bonus."

"And an opportunity to learn," Parrish said. "Because that's the rub, right? We're only progressing in our powers when we're pushed to the brink of death. Not exactly the most nurturing environment. Do or die, so to speak."

Karmen hadn't thought of it that way before, but Parrish was right. Other than Crash, most of them had only learned they had powers when they were pushed to the limit or threatened with death if they didn't use them.

"So, basically, New York City should mean we'll either realize our greatest potential, or we'll all die trying," she said, half joking, half terrified she was right.

"I wish we had more time," Noah said, not laughing at her

joke. "Maybe with some thought, we could have created some training or practice scenarios."

"We don't have that luxury, though," Parrish said, turning the fatalis stone in her hand. "We still haven't heard from Zoe and the fifth, but at this point, we're just an hour or so away from the city by boat. If we can figure out where they are and come up with a plan, we could be there before noon tomorrow."

"Yeah, but if they're safe where they are and the Dark One hasn't found them, as long as they stay put and in hiding, we could take all the time we need," Karmen said, already knowing as she said it that wouldn't be a popular option.

"Every day we wait to get this stone to the island is a day the whole world suffers," Parrish said.

Karmen was about to say something else about the trip into the city when Parrish's eyes grew wide. She pulled the fatalis stone from beneath the collar of her shirt and placed it on the table.

"This is it," Parrish said. "Take hands."

Karmen's heart raced as the four of them joined hands and the fifth—a young boy she knew in her soul was once one of her closest friends—appeared before them.

TWENTY-TWO

THE BOY

I t was time.

The boy could feel how close the others were. They must have been traveling all day to get to the coast. He'd been tracking their fear and anxiety. At this point, he was so connected to their energy, he could even feel when one of them was hurt.

Noah, the healer of their group, had somehow taken on an injury earlier in the day. Nothing life threatening, but it was bad enough to have caused him considerable pain.

But other than their fear, the traveling guardians had stayed out of any real danger all day.

Still, the boy had wanted to wait until they were settled and safe to contact them.

Zoe had been waiting nervously all day, too. She kept asking him if he could tell where Parrish was and whether she was coming to get her or not. She wanted to talk to her sister and make sure she had gotten out of the encounter with the Dark One.

No matter how many times he reassured her that Parrish was okay and was already making her way to the coast, Zoe didn't seem to trust it.

He couldn't blame her, really. They'd all been through so much, and Zoe had experienced the added torture of having to hear her own father turning into one of those things in the other room.

Late last night, when they'd been up talking about their lives and what they'd been through since the virus started, Zoe had told him that she'd spent the entire time in that hotel room worried that her father would break out of that room at any moment and kill her.

"I've been having nightmares about it again," she'd confessed to him late last night, pulling her arms tight around her body. "As if it had really happened. As if my own father had killed me."

She hid her head in her arms and shivered.

It was enough to make the boy cry.

How did a ten-year-old girl ever really recover from that kind of trauma?

Seeing her sister again was the only thing she cared about anymore, and he was determined to help make that happen.

Besides, the survival of this entire world depended on him reuniting with Parrish and the others and getting to that island.

Now that they had finally connected to each other and completed the circle between them all, the boy's memories had been coming back more and more. His powers, too.

He hadn't had a chance to really test it, but he had a feeling he could fly a lot further now, even without rooftops. He was pretty sure he could change the weather a great deal, too. He'd played around with it a little bit this afternoon, and it hadn't taken much concentration to turn a relatively sunny, cloudless day into a stormy grey afternoon.

He had to be careful with that, though. The Dark One would be able to sense his magic the same way he could now sense the presence of his friends as they got closer.

Too much time using his powers would allow her to pinpoint their location, and that would ruin everything.

New York City was bad enough when you were just a normal human trying to survive.

Surviving when you were a specific, sought-after target of the Dark One was impossible. At least for now.

Once the five of them got together, things would be different.

Which is why he wanted to talk to them tonight, when they were calm and safe and able to really listen to what he had to say.

He wasn't sure if they would listen to him, seeing how he was just a kid in their eyes, but he had to trust that some part of them understood he was the eldest of their group. And the most experienced.

He motioned for Zoe to join him on the floor of the small apartment.

Anxious, her knee bounced as she sat down across from him. She scratched her arm and bit her lip.

He took a deep breath and then nodded for her to do the same. If they were going to make a stable connection with the others, he needed their combined energy to be calm and stable, too.

They might not get many opportunities beyond tonight to have a conversation like this and make their plan, so he wanted to make sure everything was perfect.

Relax. It's going to be okay.

He could tell that Zoe heard him in her head. She nodded and stopped her fidgeting, finally calming down enough for them to reach out to the others.

He held both hands out to her and she carefully placed her small hands in his.

Together, they both took deep breaths and closed their eyes.

With his mind and power, he reached out to the guardians. To Parrish specifically, at first, because he could feel that she held the stone. But then, to all of them as a connection was created, like threads being woven together.

And then, with a jolt, he was transported. His body was still sitting in the small New York apartment, but his spirit or essence was there with them in a house on the beach in Jersey, not far away.

"*Hello, old friends,*" he said, smiling. Coming into their presence again was like coming home after a long absence. It was like finding peace for the first time after centuries of war.

Like finding his voice for the first time in several lifetimes, its magic having been drained away from resetting the spell over and over again.

And then, as he studied the faces of his dear friends—the first ones he had ever come to love like family—he suddenly remembered his name.

Somehow, he'd forgotten it when all of this started, but now, it was here. It was a part of him.

"*I am so glad to see you all again,*" he said, his voice more like an ancient wise man than a ten-year-old boy. "*You've been searching for me for a long time. The fifth. The boy. But my real name is David.*"

TWENTY-THREE

PARRISH

The boy—David—sat in the center of the circle. He was both there and not there. His image was transparent, but their connection to him was the best it had been yet.

Parrish had only gotten a glimpse of him the first time they had connected to his energy. He had been there with them only for a second.

When she'd connected with him and Zoe yesterday, she'd only heard their voices in her head.

Tonight, though, she could see him as if he were sitting there with them now.

The boy had black skin and short, black hair. His eyes were brown and bright, and in them, she could see both strength and wisdom far beyond his years.

He smiled at them like he knew them.

She had a feeling he saw them as they had once been, rather than as they were now.

When she studied him, she could also see a little bit of the man who had been on the island with her in her dreams. He'd been much older then, with thick dreadlocks falling over his shoulders and creases near the corners of his eyes, but it was him.

"David," she said, his name sounding right on her lips. "Is Zoe with you?"

He nodded. *"She's holding my hands right now,"* he said. *"She's the only reason I could connect with you like this. She told me about your bone marrow transplant. I think she has some of your magic inside her."*

"That's how you found her, isn't it? Did you know there was a witch who was coming for her? To take her to the Dark One?" she asked.

She had no idea how much he could see or what he remembered about all of them. He'd been alone this whole time, and yet he'd known who they were.

David shook his head, the first sign of fear showing in his expression. It was the first time he'd looked like a child since he'd appeared to them.

"It's hard to explain, but some part of me knew I had limited time. Who is she? Is she human? Or one of the Dark One's zombies?"

"Her name is Lily," Parrish said. "And she's human, but she's not from this world."

She explained to him how they'd found the witch inside the closet, at first believing it was him.

The story seemed to put something into place for him, and he nodded, as if understanding something he'd questioned for a long time.

"I knew the Dark One was looking for her and that she was alone, but I didn't realize it was your sister," he said, smil-

ing. *"I thought it was you. I could feel your magic inside of her."*

"Thank you so much for getting her out of there," Parrish said, choking a little on her words and trying not to cry.

She wanted to ask if Zoe could appear to her the way he was, but she didn't know for sure how much time they might have together. Would the connection hold for as long as they wanted? Or would their ability to connect fade over time? Or drain their power?

She wasn't sure how it worked, and she wanted to make sure they used the time wisely.

"Please, tell my sister I love her," she said.

He smiled again.

David had the kind of smile that could light up the whole room. There was something so beautiful and calm about him. So strong and grounded.

"She can hear you," he said.

"I love you, too," Zoe said softly. *"I miss you."*

Even though Parrish couldn't actually see her right now, just the sound of her voice again brought tears to her eyes. Noah squeezed her hand.

"David, can you tell us where you are in the city?" Crash asked. "We made our way to the coast in New Jersey, and we're planning to take a boat into Manhattan tomorrow. We want to get both of you out of the city, but we're going to need your help."

David shook his head. *"We're not in Manhattan,"* he said. *"We're in the Bronx. Concourse Village. Do you know where that is?"*

David gave them the exact address of his building, but Parrish wasn't sure where that was at all.

"I know where the Bronx is," Crash said, running a hand through his dark hair. "That's going to be a longer trek than we expected. Do you know if the water's clear? Any boats or debris in the East River?"

Parrish had the urge to pull out one of the maps Tank had given her and see where he was talking about. She'd only been to New York City a handful of times, and mostly they had stayed near the opera house in Manhattan. She'd never been to the Bronx, and she wasn't even sure where that was in comparison to the island.

She was worried that if she broke the connection to everyone's hands, though, so she could look at a map, they'd also lose their connection to the fifth.

"*I saw a lot of ships in the river,*" David said, shaking his head. "*It's a mess. Some of the bridges are down, too. Some people were trying to evacuate that way, and it all got overrun. I can scope it out, if you need me to, but I don't think you can use the East River.*"

Crash sighed. "We'll need to pull out a map and take a look around, but tell me. How the hell did you get Zoe all the way to the Bronx without getting overrun by rotters? Isn't the whole city crawling with those things by now?"

Wow. Parrish hadn't even been thinking about that but Crash was right. How had he done that? Was it possible things weren't really as bad as they seemed?

But the boy smiled like he knew a secret no one else knew.

"*It's a long story,*" he said. "*Let's just say we travelled across rooftops and were able to avoid almost all of the rotters. I wish I could tell you the city was better than you think, but it's horrible here. So many are dead. I haven't seen any survivors in a while.*"

"Rooftops?" Parrish whispered.

"You can fly," Karmen said, practically jumping up and breaking their connection.

Parrish barely held onto her hand.

"I can't believe I'd forgotten it, but seeing you again like this tonight," Karmen said. "I remember. David can fly."

Parrish's eyes grew wide. She could hardly believe it, but then again, they all had incredible powers. What an awesome one to have when you were stuck in a huge city, though.

"That's freaking crazy," Crash said. "Can you really?"

David nodded. *"I think so,"* he said. *"It started with me running really fast. I was able to get food and bring it back to the apartment without any of those things catching up with me. But then, when I sensed the guardian close by, I knew I needed to get to Manhattan. I was forced onto the rooftops, but that's when I realized I could do more than run fast. It's hard to explain, but I can control the air. I can ride it, like a bird. At least for a little while."*

Parrish looked again at the symbol on the fatalis stone that represented the fifth. A spiral.

Air.

It made sense.

They all did, in a way.

Lightning for Crash, and he could not only control and communicate with electricity and technology, but now he could also shoot lightning bolts and streams of lightning from his hands.

A cross for Noah. Healing and shielding. Crosshairs for accuracy.

A flame and a rose for Karmen. Beauty and fire. Passion.

Manipulation. Being able to reach inside someone else's mind and control them or hear their thoughts.

Now a spiral for air and flight.

But what did her infinity symbol mean? Parrish thought maybe her symbol should have been a sword or a weapon of some kind.

She knew the infinity sign was for her. Some deep part of her recognized it, but she still wasn't quite sure what it meant.

"So, you flew all the way to Manhattan, picked up Zoe, and then made it all the way back to your apartment in Concourse Village without being detected by the Dark One or the witch we knew as Lily?" Crash asked.

"*I never saw the witch, but I was careful to stay hidden from the eyes of the rotters,*" David said. "*I think if the Dark One saw us, she would have come for us already.*"

"I think she would have, too," Parrish said. "So, for now, we hope and believe she doesn't know where you are. She seems to know where we are, though. Even though we're traveling now, I have a feeling she can sense us or the stone. Or both. If we come to the city, she'll know we're there."

"Lily's probably there now, too." Karmen said. "Maybe that's part of why the Dark One came after us yesterday at the compound. She sent Lily to get Zoe, and it didn't work. She must have been pissed."

"She wanted me to believe she already had Zoe," Parrish said. "I don't think she knew we could communicate, but I guess I let that cat out of the bag. I told her I knew she didn't have my sister and that she didn't know where Zoe was. She seemed surprised by that."

"Well, that's good in a way," Noah said. "It proves she

doesn't know everything, and it shows that we might be able to rattle her if things don't go according to her plans."

"What do you know about the island?" Parrish asked. "Have you been dreaming about it like we have? About getting a purple stone there so we can get our memories back?"

The boy nodded.

"The fatalis stone must go back to the Island of Memories," he said. "Tobias was supposed to lead us all there, but I can't sense him in this world. Do you know what happened to him?"

Parrish explained Lily's confession about killing Tobias when they'd both come through the portal.

"*That's what broke my magical seal,*" David said, shaking his head. "*All that careful planning, destroyed in an instant. We must get to the island to reseal this world from her magic.*"

"What will happen when we get there?" Crash asked. "Do you know or remember?"

Crash had obviously picked up on the same thing Parrish had. David was wiser than any of the rest of them. He remembered things no one else had, even though he'd been alone for longer.

"*I'll explain more when we're together again and have more time to talk,*" David said. "*There's so much to tell you, but you're right about our memories. They will all come back from our first lives once we get to the island. And so will the seal on this world. It will cut off the Dark One's magic, and the virus will end.*"

Parrish gasped and nearly dropped Karmen's hand.

"End?" Parrish asked. "Are you sure?"

"*I'm sure of it,*" he said. "*It won't save the people who are already dead, but the virus itself will be gone. I believe the rotters will all die. I've been trying to remember if there was some way we could still save them with the stone or with our own magic, but I can't think of anything. I'm hoping the island will help me to remember something that can save the dead in this world, but if nothing else, we can still save the people who are left."*

"And the other world?" Karmen asked. "The place where we came from? What do you remember about that?"

"You're not any more patient in this life than your first," David said, laughing. *"I won't have to tell you about that place. You'll remember it for yourself, I promise. Maybe we'll even be able to go back there after all of this is over but for now we need to find each other. We'll be stronger together than we ever could be apart."*

Parrish nodded.

"We're ready to do whatever we need to do," she said. "We can't exactly fly over rooftops, but we should be able to get one of the boats here up to Manhattan. Is the East River the only body of water that goes up near the Bronx?"

"No, there's also the Hudson River," David said. *"But I don't know if there's a clear path through there or not. Like I said, I can check it out tomorrow during the day, if I'm careful. There are less undead out during the day."*

"That will take too long. We need to get together as fast as possible. Besides, it's way too dangerous," Parrish said, panicked at the thought of being away from Zoe for even a few more days. "Now that the Dark One knows you have Zoe, she's going to be looking everywhere for both of you, and she can see through the eyes of any zombie now. She can speak through them and control them individually."

David shuddered.

"*Her powers are growing fast.*"

"That's why we have to move fast, too," Noah said. "Crash, do you think you could pull up some surveillance cameras in the area and get a good look at the Hudson all the way through?"

"Probably," Crash said. "If not, I could definitely pull up some satellite footage and see what it looks like through there."

"If it's clear to take a boat up through the Hudson River, we need to identify a good spot to dock the boat and meet up with you both," Parrish said. "It's probably best to stay in contact, and that way the second we get the boat into the city, you and Zoe head over the rooftops to meet us somewhere in between. The faster we can get together and get back to the boat, the faster we'll be out of the city."

"Plus, once we're in the boat, the Dark One won't be able to reach us," Crash said. "Or at least as far as I can tell, none of those things can swim or are smart enough to drive or navigate their own boats."

"Maybe if she took direct control of one of them, she could chase us that way, but we could face one better than an army," Parrish said.

"We'll have Lily to contend with there, too," Karmen said. "We can't underestimate her, either."

"Good point," Crash said.

"*I think it's smarter for me and Zoe to sneak across rooftops and wait for you near the water,*" David said. "*When you pull up to one of the docks, we can just jump in.*"

"Too dangerous," Parrish said, shaking her head. "I don't want you both out there and exposed for that long, just waiting for us."

"*You said yourself the Dark One could sense your move-*

ments and tell where you were," he said. *"I don't think the same is true for the two of us. As long as we can move undetected, we should be able to get into the boat before the Dark One even realizes we're there."*

"He's got a point," Crash said. "The second we step foot on land, she's going to have a thousand of those things coming after us, and they're not going to stop coming. We'll be fighting the entire way to that apartment. How many blocks are you from the Hudson, in general?"

David seemed to think it over for a while. *"I'm not sure,"* he said. *"We'll have to get over the Harlem River first. That's maybe ten blocks away. Getting over the bridge isn't easy there, but we made it through once already. It would be harder for you than for us."*

Parrish didn't like the sound of this. She didn't want two little kids making the most dangerous part of the trip alone.

"I think once we get over to the other side, it's another fifteen blocks, maybe. It depends what part of Manhattan," David said. *"But if the wind is right, I don't think I'll need to worry about the bridge."*

Well, that got her attention.

"You can just fly over the river without the bridge?" Parrish asked. "Are you sure?"

"I haven't tried it yet, but yes. I think I can do it."

Her heart nearly dropped through her stomach.

He thought he could do it? With her sister on his back or something?

If he hadn't safely gotten her all the way from the Four Seasons to the Bronx without being detected by the Dark One, she wouldn't have trusted him at all.

"How far was it from the hotel to your place?" Parrish

asked. "I just want to get some kind of reference in my head for how dangerous this is going to be. How many blocks?"

He paused again.

"More than eighty, but I'm not sure of the exact distance."

Parrish nearly fainted.

He'd carried Zoe eighty blocks across New York City?

Okay, she needed to shut up and just let him make some decisions about what was best. She obviously had not understood the extent of his abilities.

"Eighty blocks? Man are you serious?" Crash asked. "Damn, okay. Do your thing, boss. We'll meet you at the river. You with me on this, Parrish?"

"It still scares me, but yeah. I'm with you," she said.

David nodded. *"Then, let me ask you for one more thing,"* he said. *"Patience. I understand you are anxious to be reunited with your sister, Parrish, but careful planning will pay off for us in this instance. It's supposed to rain for a few days, too, and I don't think your journey through the water will be as smooth as you'd need it to be. Give me a few days to check out the rivers with my own eyes. We can communicate every evening like this, and Crash and I can work out several routes and plans in case things go wrong."*

Parrish looked to Noah, and he nodded.

She sighed. She did not like the idea of having to wait a few more days, but this was not a stroll through D.C. or Philly. This was New York. David was right. They needed to make as much of a plan as they could.

Besides, a few days would give them time to practice their powers a bit. Test different things and maybe have an actual shot at getting out of there alive.

"Okay," she said, finally. "We'll do it your way."

They spent the next half hour discussing their plan and deciding on a time to talk again tomorrow evening.

"We'll talk to you tomorrow, then," Parrish said. "I love you, Zoe. I'll see you soon."

Tears flooded to the surface as she said it, realizing just how close she was to seeing her sister again.

Please, God, don't let anything take this away from me. Not after everything we've all been through.

"David, promise me you'll keep her safe," she said.

"*I'll do everything in my power,*" he said. "*I promise.*"

"*It's going to be okay,*" Zoe said. "*We'll all be together soon.*"

"*Good night,*" David said. "*Don't give up hope. We've survived worse. Trust me.*"

His image wavered and then disappeared.

Parrish let go of the hands she'd been holding and fell into Noah's arms, unable to contain her tears.

Zoe was truly safe, and it wouldn't be long now until they were all finally reunited.

C rash spread out what was left of his equipment on the kitchen table and booted everything up.

He really should have taken time to look for some better tech along the way.

Between the cracked screen on Karmen's old iPhone and the junky keys on his laptop, he was already missing his sweet rig back in his old apartment.

He'd spent so much time and money building that computer setup, it had broken his heart to leave it behind.

Now, though, there was billions of dollars of useless tech and computer equipment just laying around in people's cars and houses. If it wasn't dark out, he would have been tempted to go around to some of the fancy houses in this neighborhood and see what he could find.

Maybe that's what he'd do tomorrow morning, if he could convince Noah to go along with him. His strength might come in handy if Crash found a few nice systems.

There had actually been a decent computer in one of the

rooms down here, but he didn't feel like going into a bedroom all by himself. He'd spent enough of his life alone in small rooms.

Besides, he was hoping Karmen would stick around and hang out.

"Where are you two lovebirds going?" he asked as Parrish and Noah slipped around the corner toward the stairs.

It wasn't like he really needed to ask, but he did want to make sure they had a plan for who was going to keep watch through the night. He had a lot of research to do, and he wanted to make sure it wasn't all going to fall on his shoulders.

"We're going to try to get some rest for a while," Parrish said. "We'll be in the master bedroom. First door on the left up the stairs."

"I'll be back down in a few hours to take over the watch for a while," Noah said.

Crash lifted his chin. "See ya then. Get some rest."

He cleared his throat and glanced at Karmen, who was going through some fashion and design books in the massive living room. He'd turned on a few of the lights here in the main open living room and kitchen area, and he'd also turned on the lights out front so they could see if anyone was approaching from the road.

So far, though, it was ridiculously quiet.

He wished that was comforting, but these days, quiet was terrifying.

"So, want to help me look at footage of New York?" he asked.

She shook her head and turned a page in the book she was reading. "I think seeing what New York looks like right now is only going to scare the crap out of me," she said. "Besides, I don't know how you're going to see anything from a satellite at night."

"These satellites are always taking pictures," he said, typing in some coordinates and hacking into a few government websites.

He wondered if there was anyone left who was actually still checking this stuff, anymore. Was there any form of government left in the world?

"I should be able to pull up images from earlier today when it was still light outside. I'm also pulling up any surveillance cameras I can find close to where David lives. What are you looking at over there?"

"These pictures all seem so ridiculous now," she said softly, turning another page. "And to think so many of us spent our lives thinking about the perfect outfit to wear for an Instagram photo."

"Yeah. I really wish I hadn't wasted so much time on my modeling career," he said.

She rolled her eyes. "You know what I mean," she said. "A year ago, the person who lived here might have been stressed out for weeks trying to pick the perfect thousand-dollar lamp for that corner."

She waved at some lamp he hadn't even noticed the whole time they'd been here.

Now that she mentioned it, though, it was exactly the kind of lamp he imagined rich people spent their time stressing over. It was weird enough to be cool.

"What a waste of a perfectly good life," she said, closing the book with a thump.

"Not a waste," he said, trying his best to concentrate on the satellite work but finding himself much more interested in the fact that he was alone with the most beautiful girl he'd ever seen in a mansion on the beach.

Not someplace he'd ever expected to be, but definitely not a waste of a life. Not for him, anyway.

She stood and motioned to the windows and view outside where the moonlight reflected on the water.

"I mean, how much time do you think the people who owned this house even spent here?" she asked. "It doesn't really look lived in, does it? More like a vacation home, if I had to guess. Or something they rented out."

He shrugged. He'd never had the money to even dream of buying or renting a place like this, so he had no idea.

"And yet, how many hours did they have to work to afford this place? How much time did they spend worrying over keeping it perfect."

"Who?" he asked. She was talking like she knew these people.

"I don't know," she said. She grabbed a picture frame off a side table near the door and shoved it at him. "These people. They don't even look happy."

Crash studied the couple in the photo, immediately recognizing the woman from the corpse now face-down in the bedroom just a few steps away.

Karmen was right.

They were both smiling in the picture, but neither of them looked happy. They looked like a typical couple going through the motions, living their lives the way everyone expected them to.

"All of this, and they look like they were bored with each other," she said. "If I could, I'd go back in time and tell them they were wasting the one thing that should have mattered more than money."

"What's that?" he asked, curious to hear what she would say.

She shrugged and met his eyes. "Time. Life. I don't know. But whatever it was, they were wasting it."

"I guess we all were," Crash said. "What's that saying? You don't know what you got till it's gone."

She smiled, and her eyes lit up from the inside.

"See, you get me," she said. "I've never had anyone get me before."

"Me either," he said. "Not really."

His work with the satellites was completely forgotten now, and even though it was important, so was this. He could look at the river and the maps in the morning, but he might never have another chance to be with her like this again.

"Do you want to sit out by the pool for a little while?" he asked, his voice catching a little with nerves.

He'd really only ever dated a handful of girls before, and those were mostly girls he'd met online and hung out with a few times. None of them had ever gotten serious, and for the most part, he'd lost interest pretty quickly.

Karmen was different, and it wasn't just because he'd known her before in some other lifetime. He liked her in this lifetime.

"Sure," she said. "Do you think it's safe?"

"Should be," he said. "There's a fence around this whole house, and I haven't seen any rotters around since we got here."

He focused his attention on the lights inside the pool, and they blinked on. It was a beautiful effect, like a greenish-blue lagoon. If the people who'd lived here wasted part of their lives trying to make their pool look perfect, at least someone was left to enjoy it.

Before they walked outside, Crash grabbed his gun, just in case, but he had a feeling they were going to be okay out there.

Karmen was barefoot as she walked outside. She dipped her toes in the water and shivered. There was a light breeze out here tonight, and the temperature had dropped some since the sun went down.

It wasn't cold, exactly, but it was perfect snuggle weather.

"Damn," she said, pulling her arms tightly around her middle. "I was hoping to put my feet in for a while."

"Hold on a second," he said, connecting with the tech inside the pool to see if there was a heating unit.

He would have bet money on there being one, since it would have been dumb to spend millions on a house like this in New Jersey without springing for a heated pool.

It was there, of course, so he switched it on.

"Heated pool. Give it a few minutes, and it'll warm right up," he said. "Hang on."

He ran back into the house and grabbed a blanket off the couch. He put it around Karmen's shoulders, and for a moment, as she lifted her hand to secure it around her body, their fingers touched.

She hadn't pulled away, either, and the way her eyes met his for a long moment made his stomach flip and his heart race.

While they waited for the water to heat up, they sat down on the L-shaped couch by the pool.

"I bet you spent a lot of time in places like this," he said.

She laughed and shook her head. "Never. I mean, my

family went on vacation to the beach a few times, but we never could have gotten a place like this, are you crazy?"

"I see you in places like this," he said. "Like you belong here."

She looked around. "I dreamed of this all my life. Of being the woman in that photo, you know? I thought having a house like this or being married to the right kind of guy would make all the difference," she said. "But mostly, I just wanted to get out of my house and away from my dad. I was counting down the days til senior year and then graduation. Now, looking back, I don't know that I would have made it another year in that house without losing my mind."

"It was that bad?" he asked.

He didn't want to press her on this particular topic. He was pretty sure he already understood the kind of guy Karmen's dad had been. The types of things he'd done to her.

Whenever he thought of it, he wanted to pick up his machine gun and go looking for the dude. Even if he was already dead, Crash wanted to kill him again.

"There aren't words for how bad it was," she said, her voice hitching slightly. "But you don't want to hear about all that."

He wanted to change the subject, to protect her, but he wondered if she somehow needed to let it out and talk about it for once.

"I want to hear about whatever you want to tell me," he said, turning toward her. "Maybe we'll find out we have more in common than we thought."

"How so?" she asked, carefully wiping a finger across her cheek.

"My dad was a piece of shit, too," he said. "He used to beat my mom. She'd go into the hospital and swear she was never coming back. But then, he always convinced her to come home or held something over her head until she felt like she had no choice, like she was some kind of prisoner. He liked to toss me around a bit, too, and I have no doubt it would have gotten a lot worse if Mom hadn't finally gotten me out of there."

"She sounds like a very strong woman," Karmen said.

"She was incredible," he said, closing his eyes and picturing the way she used to read to him every night and push his hair behind his ears just before she kissed his forehead. "Losing her was the worst thing that ever happened to me."

"You were lucky to have someone who loved you like that," she said.

"Everyone deserves to be loved like that," he said.

Tears glistened in her eyes, and she reached for his hand, snuggling up next to him.

This whole time, he'd looked at Karmen like she was stuck up or too good for him. Like she'd never go for a guy like him because he wasn't worthy of her.

But now, in the light of the moon here by the water, he saw her for what she truly was.

A girl who had never once believed she deserved love, yet who needed it more than most.

She wasn't angry or mean or rude. She was just guarded to an extreme, and for good reason. The truth behind those walls she'd built was scary and almost unbelievable. Not the kind of thing you'd have thought a beautiful, rich cheerleader from the perfect preppy neighborhood would have gone through.

He wanted nothing more than to pull her into his arms and take it all away.

Since he couldn't change the past, though, and nearly

everything about their future was uncertain, he did the one thing he knew he could do to help.

He put his arm around her and pulled her closer, no longer afraid to make a move or scared she'd reject him.

Talk about a waste of a life, he thought. Well, he wasn't going to waste another second.

"Tell me about your favorite books," he said. "I saw the way you were eyeing my copy of The Catcher in the Rye. You're a reader like me. So, spill it. Your favorite author, favorite books, favorite characters you would change places with if you could. Tell me everything."

She leaned forward and looked at him skeptically.

"Seriously? We're out here under the moon, sharing our deepest secrets, and you want to hear about my book collection?" she asked.

"Yes, I do," he said. "We've got a few hours until Noah takes over the next watch, and if you're as wide awake as I am, I can't think of any better way to spend it than right here with you, talking about our favorite things. I have a feeling we have more in common than we thought."

"Wow, my favorite," she said. "Are you sure you're up for this, because I don't think there's any way I could possibly pick just one. This could take a while."

"I've got all night," he said.

Their eyes locked, and he saw something there he'd never seen before.

Trust.

A slow smile spread across her beautiful face, and she lay back against him, finally relaxing as she put a hand on his chest.

"Okay," she said. "So let's start with this fantasy series called The Wheel of Time. Have you ever read it?"

"What do I look like?" he asked. "An amateur?"

She laughed, and for the next five hours, they lay there together talking, the heated pool and the state of the world long forgotten, if just for a little while.

Despite all she had been through, Karmen was happy to find the beach could still raise her spirits. She awoke feeling refreshed.

And thinking about Crash.

It had to have been around three in the morning when Noah had found them out by the pool, their bodies tangled together, laughing and talking about things she'd never been free to share with anyone.

He had made all her exhaustion disappear, like she could have stayed up all night talking.

There had been a part of her that wanted to invite him to come back to her room to sleep, if only so they could stay tangled up the way they had been for hours.

But in the end, she'd been too embarrassed.

Or too scared of where things might go.

It wasn't like they could really date each other during the apocalypse, and she didn't want to fall for him only to watch him die.

But she didn't want to think about that this morning.

She'd slept for a full five hours without having to take anything and without having any bad dreams, and she'd woken up to the sound and sight of the ocean. She couldn't have asked for anything more, so when a familiar smell greeted her as she walked into the kitchen, it nearly brought tears to her eyes.

The house they were staying in didn't have power, but there on the kitchen counter, she found a fresh pot of coffee already brewed and waiting for her.

Crash had to have done this, but where was he now?

She beamed but then looked around to make sure no one was watching.

She didn't want it going to his head or anything.

There was no sign of him in the kitchen or living room, so she allowed herself to bask in the joy of actual gourmet coffee, freshly brewed and piping hot.

Mug in hand, she wandered around the empty rooms, taking in the beautiful decor now that it was light enough outside to see it all, and looking for anything they might find useful on their trip.

She couldn't remember the last time she'd been in such a good mood.

What she found in the hall closet put her in an even better mood.

She even felt inspired, for the first time since they'd been quarantined at Noah's house, to get creative and make breakfast for everyone. Ingredients were limited, since there was nothing fresh or cold, but she found enough stuff in the pantry to make it work.

"Time to wake up, sleepy heads," she called, throwing open the door of the master bedroom on the second floor. Her cheery tone surprised even her. "Come on, the sun's up, and we're at the beach!"

A pillow flew toward the door and smacked her in the hip, but she wasn't going to let anything bring her down today.

"There's fresh coffee and breakfast," she said, knowing the food was her secret weapon. She didn't even need to use her magical mind powers to manipulate them. Their stomachs did it for her.

Within minutes, the entire group was sitting at the kitchen table eating fresh cinnamon rolls dripping with cream cheese icing and staring out at the beautiful sunny day outside.

"I have no idea how you did this without a fridge, but I'm not complaining," Noah said. "This is incredible."

Karmen beamed. She had spent a lot of time growing up just playing around in the kitchen as a way to escape. She knew enough about how to bake to come up with some substitutes here and there.

"I was lucky to find some cream cheese icing in the pantry," she said.

She'd also found applesauce, flour, sugar, and yeast. It was hard to make a perfect cinnamon roll without butter, eggs, or milk, but she'd done a pretty good job overall with what she had available.

"I couldn't have done it without Crash turning on the power in the kitchen, though," she said. "Thanks for that."

She held up her second cup of coffee in a kind of salute. It was truly delicious. Hazelnut, her favorite.

Karmen savored it, not knowing when she might ever get another cup of coffee like this again.

Everything she'd ever taken for granted was now a luxury with a ticking clock.

At the table, the others discussed their next move.

"When we get the go-ahead from David, we travel up the coast," Crash said, showing them what he'd discovered last night from the satellites. "Getting up to the bay won't be an issue, but here's where it all gets tricky."

Karmen zoned out and chose to watch the ocean, instead.

She wished more than anything they could just stay here at the beach. They'd only seen a handful of undead since they got to this little seaside town. The houses here were all fully stocked and gorgeous.

There were worse ways to spend the rest of your life.

It wasn't an option, of course. At least not right now, but what about after all this was over? What if they somehow managed to defeat the Dark One, and like the boy said last night, the virus was over?

There were still survivors who could rebuild this world.

Maybe someday, she and Crash could come back to this house and—

She cut off all her own stupid daydream thoughts and turned back to the conversation of routes and maps and rotters.

When there was a short break in the discussion, though, she seized the opportunity to speak.

"I know you guys are all anxious to make the plans and work it all out, but you're ignoring one important thing." They all looked at her questioningly. "Our sanity."

"I'm pretty sure you lost yours a long time ago," Parrish said, laughing.

"Very funny, but I'm talking about all of us. Our mental health is not something we should ignore."

"Karmen, what are you talking about?" Parrish looked

annoyed. "Just tell us what you want, because I know this is leading up to something."

"I'm trying to get a point across," Karmen said, walking toward the big windows. "We've all been super stressed with the fighting and near-death experiences the past few days. We can't just waltz into a city like New York without taking a little break from the death stuff for a little while."

"Just spit it out," Parrish said, dropping her head into her hands.

Karmen smiled.

"I think we should put on some bathing suits and go out to the beach for a few hours," she said. "It's a warm day, it's sunny and beautiful, and we could all use a bit of fun for a change."

There was a short beat of silence as everyone contemplated Karmen's idea. She knew they were tempted. They all needed a little release that didn't include shooting guns or worrying about zombies hiding behind a clothes rack.

"We still have to find a boat and get things ready," Parrish said. "There's a lot of work to do."

"We've got time," Crash said. "I don't think we'll be heading into the city for at least two or three days."

Noah walked over and put his hands on Parrish's shoulders. "Maybe it's not such a bad idea," he said. "It is a beautiful day, and we can't really make any big decisions about the plan until we hear from David and Zoe."

Parrish's shoulders relaxed, and she smiled.

"Too bad I forgot my bikini," she said, rolling her eyes. "But okay. I guess we can spare an hour or so for the beach this morning."

A huge smile spread across Karmen's face. She grabbed the

large beach bag she'd hidden by the couch and lifted it into the air.

"Don't worry, I found bathing suits for all of us," she said. "Let's get changed."

——————

"Race you to the water!"

Karmen laughed as Noah and Crash ran toward the waves. The sun was bright overhead, glittering off the water for miles. She could almost close her eyes and pretend all was right with the world.

Maybe they were just friends, here on a fun, late-summer vacation at the beach. No virus. No Dark One or witches. Just fun in the sun with her best friend and a couple of hot guys.

Next to her, though, Parrish sighed and shook her head.

"Stop worrying," Karmen said. "Just for one hour, try not to act like the weight of the entire world is on your shoulders. You've got to loosen up."

"Not everyone is like you, Karmen." Parrish dug her toes into the warm sand. "And I mean that in the best way. I wish I could just relax and have some fun for a change, but I can't get New York out of my mind."

"You know I wasn't joking about the mental health thing," she said. "If you spend all this time worried about what could go wrong in New York, you're more likely to make a mistake or miss something important. But if you relax and just let loose for a while, you'll think more clearly when it's time to go. I promise."

Parrish studied her.

"How do you know all that?" she asked.

Karmen laughed. "Years of therapy, I guess," she said. "Maybe it wasn't all money down the drain, after all."

Her therapist had actually been really nice and very smart. The woman had known there was more going on at home than Karmen was willing to say, but her father had warned her that if she said a word about their special relationship, he'd tell everyone she was a habitual liar and have her put in some kind of institution.

Looking back on it now, she realized those were just empty threats.

He'd abused her for so long, he'd brainwashed her to believe that even if she spoke up, no one would believe her. That she would end up all alone and ridiculed if she said anything.

So, she kept her mouth shut, even in therapy.

But she'd learned that spending all your time worried or focused on the bad parts of your life only made things worse. Instead, it was better to make the most of the good things when they came.

And today, this morning by the beach, this was a good thing. And she wanted Parrish to enjoy it, too.

"Come on, let's have some fun," she said.

She grabbed Parrish's arm and together they ran down to where the guys were splashing around in the waves. The water was colder than she expected, and she shrieked as it splashed against her legs. Crash laughed and grabbed her around the waist, lifting her high into the air

As the next wave came, he dove into it, carrying Karmen with him. They came up together, laughing and wiping salt water out of their faces.

"Come on, let's swim out past the breaking waves where

the water is calmer. Maybe we can dig with our toes and find sand-dollars," Karmen said, grabbing Parrish and pulling her along in the surf.

All these years, the two of them had been fighting and exchanging harsh words and ugly looks, but now, after all they'd been through together, Karmen was glad Parrish was the one she'd gotten to be with here at the end of the world.

Together, the four of them swam out past the point where the waves broke. Karmen could barely touch the bottom with the tips of her toes, but Crash held onto her, as if she belonged to him. Their bodies kept touching under water, and she had to admit, she didn't hate it.

For half an hour, they jumped and swam out in the ocean, laughing and playing together like old friends without a care in the world. Karmen found a few shells she wanted to keep, and Crash slipped them into the pockets of his swim trunks.

Every once in a while, his arm would casually circle around her waist, sending shivers of excitement up her spine.

She wanted to stay just like this forever, and for a little while, she pretended that they would.

"Holy crap," Crash said, pointing into the distance as his grip around her waist tightened. "Is that a ship?"

Karmen smoothed her wet hair away from her face and squinted into the distance. On the horizon, she could just barely make out the silhouette of a ship. At this range, it was hard to tell exactly how big it was, but she thought maybe it was a cruise ship or some kind of freighter.

"I have binoculars in my bag up on the beach," Noah said, then started swimming back to shore.

By the time they all got back to the beach, the ship had already gotten closer, and from the looks of it, there was

another one not too far behind it. Noah dug through his backpack and pulled out his binoculars.

"We thought we saw lights on the water last night from our
balcony," Parrish said. "Maybe it was these ships."

"Do you see anyone on board?" Crash asked.

"It's definitely a cruise ship," Noah said. "A big one."

"Maybe it's a group of survivors," Parrish said, but Karmen
had a bad feeling about this.

Her stomach twisted, all good vibes of a day on the beach
shifting to discomfort and fear.

"Come on. What are the chances the people on that ship
aren't infected?" Crash asked. "A million to one."

"I remember hearing on the news that they were quaranti-
ning cruise ships when the virus first began," Parrish said.
"Keeping people on the ship for weeks until they knew for sure
no one was sick. Maybe the people on this ship were lucky.
Maybe they heard what was happening on shore and decided
to stay on board."

"I don't see anyone," Noah said, handing off the binoculars
to Crash.

The closer the ship got to them, the more uneasy Karmen
began to feel. Nausea swept over her and she felt chilled,
despite the heat.

What the hell happened to you? Don't come any closer!

A man's voice rang out in her head, and Karmen felt a stab-
bing pain behind her left eye. She winced.

Oh God! What are you doing?! Someone help me!

The voices grew louder. When she closed her eyes against
the pain, an image appeared in her mind, as clear as a memory.
A man, about her father's age, wearing khaki shorts and a blue
Polo. His hair was black and curly. She didn't recognize the

man, but she could see what was happening to him, like a movie going across a mental screen.

Her head throbbed. A scream pierced her mind, so filled with horror that it sent her to her knees in the sand.

"Karmen? What is it?"

Crash knelt beside her, but she pushed him away and focused on the ship, instead.

She wasn't sure what this new ability was, and it was killing her head, but she wanted to understand it. Parrish had said every battle was an opportunity to practice or develop new skills, right? She could handle the pain if it meant understanding what she could really do with it.

Karmen focused on the man in her mind. In a way, she was in two places at once. Her body was there on the beach, but another part of her, some part of her mind was with this dark haired man. All she saw were flashes of action, and each flash sent an awful pain through her.

The man backed into a corner. A figure limped toward him. A scream. Then blood. So much blood!

"What's happening to her?" Parrish asked. "Karmen, are you okay?"

But Karmen waved them away.

She was aware of the action around her, but she couldn't speak or respond. She gripped her head in her hands, trying to lock onto whatever images she'd seen.

She focused on the ship, and she could see the corridors. The dining hall. The casino. Zombies huddled inside in large groups, the walls and floors covered in blood.

The story of the ship's demise came to her as if she'd lived it herself. A woman had been sick when she boarded the boat. Just a cough. It was nothing, really.

Only, she'd spread the virus to everyone else on that ship who'd gotten close to her, and when she died, just like so many others in this world, she'd come back to life as something different.

Something controlled by an ancient evil.

The man Karmen had seen in her vision was just one of many who'd been bitten, died, and turned out there on the cruise ship.

The ship had been the site of unspeakable horrors and bloodshed, and suddenly, she knew with utter clarity that there was no one left alive on board.

As quickly as the visions had come, they were gone. The pain in her head disappeared, and she collapsed onto the sand, exhausted.

"They're all dead," she murmured, trying her best not to let those breakfast cinnamon rolls come back up. "Everyone on that ship is dead."

TWENTY-SIX
NOAH

Noah got cleaned up and changed into some fresh clothes he found in the closet.

Karmen's idea to go to the beach for a little while had been awesome. He'd allowed himself to forget about the world as it was, and that was priceless.

If that cruise ship hadn't come along, they might have stayed out there for hours laughing and having fun, but what she'd seen on board that ship had sobered them all. And it wasn't just the fact that there was a ship full of dead people. Hell, the whole world was full of dead people at this point.

It was also the fact that their powers continued to grow and shift.

How were they really going to fight some ancient, powerful evil if they didn't even know what they were capable of? Or what hidden drawbacks there were that might get them killed?

So far, no one else had really come up against using their

power and nearly dying because of it, but Noah had learned a major lesson back in Philly when he'd helped Stephen.

He'd felt something strange when he worked to heal that illness, but he hadn't listened to his own instincts. He'd been more interested in learning what he was capable of, trying something new and helping out in the process, when he should have been interested in staying alive.

Karmen seemed to be fine after her initial nausea and dizziness out there on the beach, but embracing a new level of magic had definitely taken its toll for a while.

The visions had obviously caused her pain, and she'd been so consumed by it, she hadn't been able to speak or respond to the rest of them while it was happening. That made her vulnerable to attack if and when it happened again.

Noah shook his head and ran a hand through his freshly washed hair.

They needed more time to train and explore any new abilities they could. He was grateful they were going to have a few extra days here, but then what? New York was going to be an extreme test of their abilities.

What if something new came up that got them all into trouble, just because they didn't know how to control it?

"Hey, you okay in here?" Parrish asked, coming up behind him and wrapping her arms around his waist.

Her hair was wet, too, thanks to Crash turning on the power long enough for everyone to get hot showers, and it tickled the side of his arm as she leaned in.

"I'm okay," he said. "Just looking at those ships and thinking about how awful it must have been to be trapped on there when all of this broke out."

There were three ships visible in the distance now, and Noah assumed it had to be part of what Parrish had said earlier. How cruise ships had been quarantined in the early days and forced to stay at sea. These ships must have just been wandering out here for the past month or two with no one still alive on board.

"There are horrors like that happening all over the world," she said. "We have to try not to focus on that. Instead, we focus on what we can do about it. If David is right, we can put an end to this soon. I dreamed of the island again last night. I think it's close."

"I do, too," he said. "I've been thinking that after we get David and Zoe out of the city, we should try to head straight there on the boat. The sooner, the better."

"I agree. And once we're on the water, it will be nearly impossible for the Dark One to reach us."

"Let's hope so," he said, though he didn't think it was good to underestimate or make any assumptions about what the Dark One was capable of.

"Come on, let's get downstairs," she said. "I think Crash wanted to go check the nearby houses for phones and computer gear."

He nodded. "You go on down," he said. "I'm going to hang out up here for a few minutes and just take a breath."

"You sure you're okay?" Parrish asked, tilting her head to study him.

"I just need some time to think," he said.

She squeezed his arm. "Okay, I'll see you downstairs."

Noah stared out at the cruise ships, feeling restless, as if time was slipping away faster than any of them realized.

PARRISH

The day couldn't go by fast enough.

Parrish was anxious to hear from David and Zoe again. They were so close now, she couldn't bear the thought of anything going wrong at this point.

The whole group had gathered together in the living room, waiting for David to reach out to them and let them know what his searching had produced today. Parrish had the fatalis stone clutched in her hand, and she kept turning it around and around, touching each of the symbols and wondering if they'd chosen these for themselves or if someone else had carved them into this stone.

"Stop fidgeting," Karmen said. "They'll be here any minute."

"I can't help it," Parrish said. "I just want to know they're okay."

"I honestly believe if anything happened to David, we'd know," Crash said. "The closer we get to each other, the more I can feel his energy. And my own. If he's fine, I'm sure Zoe is fine, too. We just have to be patient."

Easy for him to say. It wasn't his ten-year-old sister sitting in the most dangerous city in the country.

But he was right about David. Parrish was sure the buzz of extra energy running through her these past few days had a lot to do with how close they were to finally becoming a group of five again.

Also, David had sensed it when she was in trouble and being held by that silver zombie back at the compound. He'd felt her panic and fear. If something had happened to him and Zoe, all of them should have felt it.

She took a deep breath in and let it go slowly, releasing the fear and just being present to the moment.

They were lucky, really.

They'd had the odds stacked against them from the beginning of this mess, and yet they'd managed to find each other. Zoe had managed to stay alive, and better yet, David had found her just before the Dark One got to her.

If their luck continued, maybe this whole thing could be over in a few more days. All they had to do was get through New York and find that island. Then the Dark One would be sealed in tight for another hundred lifetimes.

But what if their luck didn't continue?

What if the Dark One went free before they had a chance to get to the island and reseal the world?

Like she said when she'd held Parrish there by the bus at the compound, they'd never actually defeated her. If they'd been able to do that, she would have been dead, not sealed away.

How powerful did a witch have to be to take on all five of them at full strength and still survive?

Parrish shuddered just thinking about it.

They simply couldn't let her go free. That was all there was to it.

Crash stood and headed toward the kitchen.

"Hey, where are you going? They should be reaching out any second," she said.

"I'll be right back," he said, disappearing into the downstairs bedroom.

Parrish took another deep breath. Okay, so she was maybe losing her patience a little too easily. There were going to be delays and hardships coming up. She needed to chill.

But when David's voice came into her head, she called out for Crash to move his butt.

"Coming," he shouted, running into the room and jumping over the couch to join them around the coffee table.

He placed an iPad he'd gotten from a group trip to raid some of the nearby houses this afternoon on the coffee table and pressed record on the video camera app.

They all took hands and Parrish placed the stone in the center of the group, calling up David's image as if he were there in person.

"You have no idea how good it is to see you again," Parrish said. "How's Zoe?"

"*I'm good,*" Zoe said. "*It's boring here, but we've been doing puzzles to pass the time. It's not so bad, but I miss TV.*"

Parrish had to laugh at that. Zoe had always been in rehearsals. She'd barely ever watched any TV at all, and when she did, their parents limited it to a single thirty-minute show on the weekends.

"How did the recon go?" Crash asked.

They spent the next twenty minutes going over what David had been able to find out in the city that day. From the sound of it the Hudson was completely impassable, just like he'd guessed.

Crash gave him some other places to look at tomorrow.

"Has it been raining there?" Parrish asked.

"*Yes, but I think that's working to my advantage,*" David said. "*I hardly saw any rotters on the rooftops today. It took some time to get the hang of flying in bad weather, but I was actually able to form a sphere of air around my body so I didn't get wet. It was fun.*"

"And it's going to rain again tomorrow?" Crash said.

"*I think so,*" David said. "*I'll check out those places you listed in the morning and we can meet back up this same time tomorrow.*"

"Zoe, you're staying safe in the apartment by yourself?" Parrish asked.

She didn't like the idea of her sister all alone in a strange place after everything she'd been through, but it was better than having her out where the Dark One might see her.

"*I'm fine,*" Zoe said. "*Stop worrying about me so much.*"

But there was a smile in her voice. Parrish couldn't wait to throw her arms around that little girl. She would never let her go again.

They said goodnight and arranged a time to meet up again the next day.

They followed that same pattern for two more nights, with David doing reconnaissance for Crash during the day and reporting back everything he saw, and with the guardians practicing their abilities.

Sometimes, they practiced in a group, sparring and testing each other's abilities, and other times, they each practiced on their own.

They'd fallen into a habit of meeting up by the pool each morning around sunrise to meditate and stretch. It had been Karmen's idea, but it calmed Parrish's nerves. She'd never tried yoga before the pandemic, but she'd always been drawn to the poses.

There was something about the group yoga that made them feel more connected, too. Like breathing together and joining in the same poses synced them up somehow.

She liked it.

Of course, it was funny to watch Crash try to do some of the more challenging poses.

"What?" he said, laughing. "I'm not as flexible as you guys are."

Parrish saw him out there practicing and stretching a few times a day with Karmen, though, and he was getting better quickly.

As for their abilities, everyone was getting stronger by the hour, it seemed, and all of them were anxious to unlock more of their memories and powers before New York.

Parrish, for one, had been working on her fire magic. She'd first connected with the ice side of her abilities, and it was the part of her that seemed to come more easily.

But when she embraced her anger and focused on some ember of passion deep inside, she was able to draw up the flames and sparks of her fire side.

Karmen worked with her on this a little bit, and after a while, Crash joined them. By the second evening, all three of them could conjure flames in their palms. Parrish could create sparks of flame on the blade of her sword, too.

Crash was the only one who could create lightning, though. He was working on trying to light up the bullets in his gun with lightning or electricity of some kind, too, the way she did with her sword, but so far, all he'd been able to produce was a few tiny sparks here and there.

He'd found some extra ammo in the garage of the house next door, but he said he didn't want to waste too much practicing it. Instead, he started spending time working on an ability he called lightning daggers.

"I dreamed about it a couple nights ago, so I'm pretty sure I can get it to work," he said.

When Parrish wanted to work on her ice abilities, she worked with Noah.

Both of them could now draw up frost with a single thought and spread it to anything they touched.

They practiced with the sand on the beach, placing their icy palms deep into the sand and watching as each grain froze over. After a few hours of practice each morning, they'd both been able to stretch that frost about fifteen feet in front of them.

What was cool was that they also realized if they cast the spell while holding hands, they could make it spread wider and farther than before.

Once they realized their abilities could be amplified when they worked together, they started practicing combinations and patterns that might help them get through a large horde more quickly.

They explained this to David on the second night, and he surprised everyone when he gave them some tips on how to work as a group once they got into the city. He might have only been a kid in this lifetime, but there was no doubt he had some experience coming up with strategies for survival and battle.

The next day, the four of them spent most of the morning working on the formation they planned to use once they got to New York City. It was hard to imagine exactly how it would work once there were rotters surrounding them, but at least they had a general idea of what they planned to do.

Only time would tell if it actually worked, though.

In the evenings after the sun went down, they were all way too exhausted to keep training, even though Parrish wished she could. After all, their success or failure in New York held the fate of at least two worlds. They couldn't afford to screw this up.

Noah convinced her that they were more likely to screw up if they were too tired to fight, though, and she had to admit that she'd been pushing a little too hard.

Each night, they'd all stayed up together for a while, playing in the heated pool and letting loose. Crash even pulled up a few movies on the big screen TV, treating them all to a rewatch of the entire Matrix Trilogy.

Karmen had popped some popcorn and passed out big heaping bowls to each of them, along with a few beers.

For a while, they'd all been able to forget the world had ended. They were just a normal group of friends hanging out at the beach.

Later, as Parrish stood on the balcony of her temporary bedroom overlooking the sea, tears involuntarily cascaded down her face. She attempted to wipe them away as Noah joined her.

"I thought you were sleeping, already," she said, sniffing and putting on a smile as best she could.

"What are you doing out here so late?" he asked, draping a blanket over her shoulders. "What's wrong?"

"It's stupid," she said, turning away to watch the lights of the cruise ships in the distance.

"How you're feeling isn't stupid," he said softly, rubbing her back. "Just tell me."

She took a deep breath.

"Is it crazy to say that the last few days have been some of the best of my life?" she asked, the tears falling again just from admitting it out loud. "I mean, I know it's crazy. Everything about the world right now is horrifying, and I'm sad and scared, and I wish everything was different. But at the same time, there's something nice about being here with you guys."

Noah put his arm around her.

"It's not crazy at all," he said. "I know exactly what you're feeling."

"You do?" she asked, wiping the tears from her face again.

God, she hated to cry in front of anyone.

"Of course," he said. "It's like, yeah, I miss my dad like crazy. I miss playing baseball and hanging out with my friends. There are days I still can't believe Aaron's gone or that I'll never see him again. But at the same time, being here with all of you feels like coming home again."

She nodded, glancing up at him and feeling his words to her core.

"That's exactly how I feel," she said. "Except I never had an Aaron. Would you believe me if I said I've never once sat down with a group of friends, or even my own family, and watched a full movie before?"

He studied her and shook his head. "That can't be true," he said. "Your parents never sat down and watched a movie with you on a Saturday night?"

"Not once," she said. "And I know it's so trivial, like poor me in my fancy suburban neighborhood watching movies all alone in my room, but still. Tonight was nice. For the first time maybe ever, I really felt like I belonged somewhere."

"We've always belonged together," he said, placing his hand on her face. "I was just too chicken to ask you out, but I wish I had the very first time I thought about it, years ago. I wish I'd gotten up the nerve to walk next door with a bouquet of roses or something and just asked you to dinner. Or even to just come sit with me on the steps and talk about life, you know? I wish I'd taken you to a dozen movies."

She laughed, moving closer to him.

"Me, too," she said.

He leaned down, then, and kissed her.

TWENTY-EIGHT

NOAH

How long had he wanted to kiss Parrish Sorrows? Years, maybe.

Centuries.

She'd always been the one, even before he remembered anything about their past. His heart had always belonged to her. Why had he been so scared to ask her out for all these years?

He'd wasted so much time worrying what his friends would think, scared she'd reject him anyway if he asked. All of that seemed so ridiculous now.

So pointless.

That was one thing the apocalypse had taught him.

When it came down to it, worrying about what other people thought of you was a waste of your life. Being true to yourself was all that really mattered.

And the one truth of his life was standing right in front of him.

In the moonlight, her beauty took his breath away. He loved her, and in a couple days, he could lose her forever.

Not just for this lifetime. For eternity.

It struck him so hard, he couldn't stand to let another moment go by without making sure she knew just how he felt.

It didn't matter if he'd told her in a thousand lifetimes. He wanted her to know now.

And always.

"Parrish, no matter what happens when we get to New York, I need you to know that I love you," he said. "And not just in an end-of-the-world-panic kind of way. In a true, core of my heart, could-never-love-anyone-else, would-die-to-protect-you way. Even without our memories of who we were back in that other world or how we met or came to fall in love in the first place, I know without a shadow of a doubt that you are the only person I've ever loved. The only person I ever could love. You are my eternity."

Her eyes filled with tears as her arms circled around him, pulling his lips to hers.

"I love you, too," she whispered.

Noah never knew that kissing could feel like this. Like being set on fire, but also like coming home. Electricity and comfort at the same time. He felt her fingers dig into his back, pulling him closer.

He wanted her. Hungered for more. He wanted to lose himself in her softness and her warmth. Maybe they could make each other forget the horrors of losing their families and watching people feast on flesh.

They spent the entire night in each other's arms, holding on as if their lives depended on it, and praying for an eternity of nights left together like this.

In the morning, they didn't join the others by the pool. Instead, they stayed in bed until late afternoon, talking and making up for lost time. Noah felt a little bit guilty about taking time away from their practice to stay in bed all day, but later, when they finally emerged to attend their nightly meeting with David and Zoe, he let go all of his guilt.

"We go tomorrow, then," Crash said. "We'll get the boat ready tomorrow and plan to head to New York day after tomorrow, so long as we get the go-ahead from you."

Noah's stomach knotted, and he gripped Parrish's hand a little tighter.

"*I'll contact you with the final plan before noon,*" David said. "*And hopefully, we'll all be together in just two more days.*"

"Good job, David," Parrish said, but her voice wavered as she clutched Noah's hand just as tightly. "Stay safe, and we'll see you both at noon tomorrow."

When they said goodbye, Noah and Parrish locked eyes for a long moment.

This was it.

Tomorrow they would put their final plan together, and the next day would decide the fate of everything.

But no matter what happened. Noah was glad they would always have this time together at the mansion on the beach.

TWENTY-NINE

THE WITCH

I t had taken the witch days to lock onto the fifth's general location, but she was sure she at least had the right borough now.

At first, she'd only been searching in and around Manhattan, wrongfully assuming that he never would have been able to travel far with a small child like Zoe.

He'd been using his powers more and more over the past few days, though, and the witch had gradually tracked him over the bridge to the Bronx.

Since he was traveling over rooftops, instead of on the roads and sidewalks, it was trickier to follow his movements. He jumped around too much, and his trail was sporadic. He was testing her, she was sure of it.

But she would show him. It would only take another day or two before she found where he was hiding out with the girl.

What surprised her most, though, was that the guardians hadn't come to the city to rescue the little girl. Parrish had seemed so obsessive about the child that the witch had felt certain they'd come to the city as soon as possible.

Was it possible it was really just taking them this long to get here?

Or were they up to something?

The witch couldn't afford to mess up again, which meant that Zoe was not leaving this city. Not alive, anyway. She had to make sure of it.

So, while she had her rotters and trackers keeping an eye out for the fifth, she spent her time setting traps all over the city. She couldn't be completely sure where the guardians would go once they got up here, but there were only so many options. Half this city was destroyed, so if they tried to come over on one of the bridges, they very well could be stuck somewhere, trying to find a way onto the island itself.

Her traps should keep them occupied, though. They'd barely survived the few pets she'd placed in that hospital back in Philly, and compared to some of the special ones she'd learned to create with her new, enhanced powers, those little things were nothing.

The Dark One would be proud of her work here.

A warm feeling spread through the witch's chest. Yes, she would make her mistress proud, and when it was all over and the little girl was delivered to her, the witch would be rewarded with even more power than before.

She would be blessed beyond her own imagination.

She would finally get what she deserved. What she'd dreamed of her whole life.

Laughing, she grabbed another rotter by the throat, forcing her magic into his body through its open mouth.

She'd learned a while back how to turn these despicable

creatures into her pets without ever having to touch them, but she liked the physical act of forcing them all into submission.

And before the day was done, she would do it a hundred times all over the city.

When her work was finished for the day, she stood on the rooftop of one of the tallest buildings in the city and looked out over her domain.

Yes, the Dark One would be so proud.

THIRTY
ZOE

David was late.

He'd told her very clearly not to panic and that under no circumstances should she look out the window or try to come onto the roof to look for him.

For the past hour, it had taken all of Zoe's willpower to follow those instructions. Something was definitely wrong, and she wasn't sure what to do about it.

She nervously tugged on her sleeves and bit at the soft flesh around her thumb nail.

He'd left so early this morning, and he said he'd be back in just an hour or two. He wanted to head toward the river to take a look at the ships and debris to see if there was a clear path for Parrish and her friends to come through on their boat.

That shouldn't have taken all morning. Not with the way he was able to fly around.

Most of his trips the past few days had taken an hour or two at most. He should have been back by now.

Being alone again was messing with her head. Panic kept

swirling around inside her, and she'd bitten the inside of her lip so many times, she tasted blood.

She'd managed to be alone in that hotel room for who knows how long without losing her mind, but having someone else to talk to and hang out with for a few days had changed everything.

Not to mention the fact that now she knew for sure her sister was on her way and about to head to the city. She was so close to feeling safe again. So close to believing she could survive.

Was it really possible she could see her sister by tomorrow? Be hanging out with her and a whole group of people by then?

It didn't seem real, and Zoe wanted it so badly, she was scared she would ruin it somehow.

It was like when she got nervous before a performance.

When she was younger, she used to let those nerves get to her. Sometimes, she could play a piece perfectly a dozen times in practice, but she would still worry herself sick about messing it all up in performance.

Then, it was like she made it happen by worrying, because sure enough, she'd get up there on stage or in the audition and mess up the parts she'd never once messed up in rehearsal.

There was no sense behind it, except that she'd psyched herself out and sabotaged her own performance.

Or at least that's what her teacher told her she was doing.

They'd had to work on that aspect of performance more than her actual technique sometimes.

Her mother would say, *Perfect technique means nothing if you can only do it in practice. Performance is the only time it matters. Fail in performance, and you might as well always be a failure.*

It had been a difficult lesson to learn as a five-year-old back in the day, but Zoe had put her whole heart into mastering her own worry and fear.

By the time she was eight, she had figured out the trick.

All she had to do was learn to trust herself.

When she worried, she wasn't trusting her own talent or her joy. She wasn't trusting her practice and the ability of her hands and body and fingers to remember the music. She was trusting her fear.

And fear always betrayed you.

It was in its very nature to betray.

Instead, she had learned to trust her joy. Her pure passion for playing and creating. Over time, her music had become an extension of herself, so when she stood on stage to play, there was no fear. Only trust.

The funny thing was, this was not a lesson she'd learned from her mom or dad. They were both amazing musicians, but neither one of them had ever reached the level of fame and notoriety they deserved.

Zoe's mom had stopped performing professionally over the past few years, but it hadn't taken much to understand why she'd never been chosen as the lead soprano at the Metropolitan for a show like La Traviata or Madame Butterfly the way she'd always dreamed.

Her mother was exceptionally talented, but she wanted it too badly. In her performances, she let her fear of never being good enough guide her. She tried too hard.

Her father, a cellist, had done the same thing. When he practiced and thought no one was listening, the beauty of his music would bring you to tears.

But when he played for others, he seemed to forget who he

was. He focused on the performance and what others would think, rather than the music.

He focused on what he wanted to get from it, rather than what he wanted to give to others by playing from the heart. That was the best way Zoe could think to describe it, but she'd learned not to give her opinion when it came to their music.

Her mother, in particular, was never one to take criticism well.

The one time Zoe had tried to tell her about letting go of the fear, she'd thought her mom was going to hit her, she got so angry.

"I've been performing my entire life," she'd said. *"I don't need a six-year-old telling me how to improve. Now, leave me alone."*

So Zoe had learned to keep her opinions to herself, and instead, she'd focused on not making the same mistakes. She'd learned to just be herself and to think about what she could give to others, rather than what she might get if she did a good job.

That was a lesson she'd learned from Parrish.

Her older sister was never afraid to just be herself, no matter what anyone else thought of her. She stood up for people even when she knew she wouldn't get any kind of reward. She did the right thing when no one was watching.

She was the same person in the quiet privacy of her bedroom as she was when she stepped out into the world.

Zoe had some idea that Parrish was unapologetically herself because she thought no one was watching her.

But Zoe had been watching.

Learning.

So, over time, that's how she had mastered her fear of

performance and had become one of the best young violinists in the world.

That should have carried over to amazing patience and willpower when it came to dealing with the world as it was now, too, but waiting for David to come back was bringing her to the edge.

Something had happened during those weeks in the hotel room alone. Something inside her had come slightly unhinged. She wasn't sure she could survive that again. He had to come back.

She itched to open those curtains and just take a look.

What if he was out there on the ground, needing her help? She wasn't sure why he had no voice, but so far, they'd only been able to communicate by him writing things down or, more recently, in their minds.

But if he was hurt, maybe he couldn't use his powers to reach out to her.

After another half hour of waiting as patiently as she could, she had practically convinced herself that David was either dead or dying.

There was no reason for it to have taken this long. Parrish and the others were expecting him to reach out around noon, but now it was nearly two in the afternoon. Zoe had no way of reaching them on her own. Not that she knew of, anyway. She needed him, and without David, her sister might never find her.

Zoe curled up on the couch with a blanket tight around her body. She hummed quietly, trying anything to get her mind off those curtains and what might be happening beyond them.

She closed her eyes and tried to rest, but that didn't work either.

Instead, she stood and paced the floor. She even tried sitting down in a meditation pose and reaching out to Parrish on her own.

Nothing worked, and the more time went by, the more she started to worry.

Trust him. Trust Parrish. Don't trust your fear.

She repeated this to herself over and over, but by the time another hour had come and gone, she couldn't wait any longer.

The mantra in her head had turned from trust to panic. Something must have gone terribly wrong, and David wasn't coming back.

Just look outside. He might be out there. What if he needs me? I have to look.

Scared, she took a deep breath and carefully pulled back the curtains.

THIRTY-ONE
THE BOY

David had spent most of the morning searching for some way through the big ships and barriers that blocked the waterways all around the city.

Between private boats, freighters, and Navy ships sent in to try to get control of the area, every river was a mess. It was like a ship graveyard out there.

While the section of the Hudson that came around near his apartment was one of the relatively open waterways, he'd quickly realized that the problem for Crash and the others would be the sections closer to Manhattan. There was no way through, even for a small boat. Not that he could tell from where he was, anyway.

He'd had to travel around pretty far into the city to get a better look at it, but he hadn't seen anything that looked good.

At best, they'd be able to dock somewhere in Manhattan and make their way to Concourse from there, but it was going to take them a lot longer to get there on foot than it would for him if they were flying.

Today, he had been looking at a spot around the Brooklyn Bridge to see if there was any way a small boat could fit through. He was pretty sure there was enough room for a small boat, but they'd only make it so far before they were on foot anyway.

He didn't think Parrish was going to like his suggestion of them just staying put until he could get Zoe safely to their boat, but it was really the best way, even if it took him a week to do it.

The problem, of course, was that the Dark One knew now to be looking for a young boy and girl traveling together. With all her eyes and ears out searching for them, he wasn't sure how best to keep their location hidden.

Even jumping around from building to building throughout the day today had presented some unique challenges.

He couldn't be sure it was the Dark One's doing, but there were definitely more rotters hanging out on rooftops today. Usually, the zombies stayed inside on sunny days. The heat made them decay faster and while these things weren't particularly smart, they did still seem to have at least a little bit of survival instinct left in them somewhere.

He'd been watching these things for more than a month, and he'd never seen so many out in the daylight. Especially not on the rooftops.

Had the Dark One figured out how he traveled?

Were these rotters specifically stationed up here to look for him?

He couldn't be sure, so to be on the safe side, he was extra careful. He kept an eye on any of the rotters nearby and with precise calculations, he only moved from one rooftop to another when none of them were looking.

It took a lot of time, and he had to go from not moving at all to moving very quickly in short bursts, but so far, he was certain he'd managed to avoid any of them seeing him.

Where he ran into some issues, though, was when he'd finally made it home to his own apartment.

There were several rotters hanging out on the roof of the apartment building across from his, and there was one on his own roof.

Because of the way they were staggered, there was never a time when at least one of them wasn't facing his apartment window.

He'd spent at least an hour crouched in his hiding place a few buildings down, timing their movements and waiting for an opening. His legs were cramping up from sitting in one position for so long, but there was never the right opportunity.

He tried to reach out to Zoe through his mind, but every time he tried to connect to her energy, all he felt was fear and panic. She was too freaked out to allow him into her head. To him, it felt like some kind of static he couldn't push through.

He just hoped she could hold on without doing something to compromise her position.

If it had been anywhere else, he might have risked being seen, as long as he could figure out a way to hide again some-where along the way. But this was the worst case scenario.

If they saw him going into the apartment, the Dark One would know exactly where they were. All she would have to do was wake up the rest of the rotters in his building and send them straight to his door.

He knew for a fact there were at least fifty zombies

rambling around in the apartments and stairwells just in his one building. Within a block radius, there might be a thousand.

He wasn't sure he could grab Zoe and enough food to survive for a few days fast enough to get her out of there. Besides, he wasn't sure where he would take her. He wasn't ready yet to make the journey back to Manhattan. Not with so many rotters on the rooftops.

He needed to think of something fast.

Back in his younger days, more than two thousand years ago, he'd been one of the best strategists around. Many people had come to consult with him about their lives, their businesses, and their plans.

Eventually, the Council of Fire had taken notice of his abilities. They'd recruited him to their war council, and he'd worked for centuries as one of the top war strategists in the land. Most of his work there had centered around avoiding wars, not fighting them.

After a thousand years of rewriting or resetting himself here in this world, though, his strategic mind was a bit rusty.

There had to be a way to get back into that apartment without being seen or detected.

He tried the old distraction trick, trying to get the rotters to move away from their posts, but when that didn't work, chills broke out across his arms.

The only reason a rotter wouldn't act according to its own basic instincts was because it had been given a more specific directive.

These rotters were being controlled by someone, and he cursed himself for not realizing this would be the Dark One's next move against him. He should have known better than to leave Zoe behind. He should have gathered up all his supplies and food today and taken her with him when he did his recon. As long as they were together, they could have stayed hidden inside a building for months.

Split up, though, they were in trouble.

He couldn't even contact the others and tell them what was going on. Without Zoe, the connection between them all was too weak. He could still feel their energy and sense their location, but he couldn't speak directly into their minds. Not without a direct connection to Parrish's bloodline and power.

He needed to be physically touching Zoe's body to make that connection, and the dumbest thing he'd ever done was leave her behind.

Parrish and the other guardians would be waiting for him already. He wasn't wearing a watch, but he guessed at this point, they'd been waiting at least an hour. Maybe longer.

He just hoped they were patient and trusting, because the dumbest thing they could do would be to come up here to New York without working through a specific plan with him first.

If they tried to come to New York to find the two of them, it would be like searching for a needle in a haystack. The Dark One would find and kill them all before they ever got to think about going to the island together or reuniting Parrish with her sister.

He hoped they would wait for at least a few days before they made any sudden moves, but he had to admit, he didn't think Parrish seemed like the patient type when it came to her little sister.

Which made some sense after everything she'd been through in her first life. Even if she didn't remember that life anymore, some part of what had happened with her sister must have still been imprinted on her soul. No one ever really forgot a heartbreak like that, even after being rewritten dozens of times.

Zoe would be worried by now, too.

He wanted to wait for dark to see if he could evade them better at night, but he wasn't sure he had that kind of time.

As if to prove his point, a fluttering movement across the way caught his eye, and he stiffened.

Don't do it, Zoe.

But it was too late.

Zoe had done the one thing he'd begged her not to do. She'd moved the curtains to look outside.

The zombies on the rooftops noticed the movement just as quickly as he had. If she'd just looked but not exposed her face, it might have been okay and he could have bought them all some time, but Zoe pulled the curtain all the way back, leaned out the window, and looked down at the sidewalk below.

When she stood upright again, the silver in her necklace caught the light just right, and the zombie nearest to him on the roof touched its hand to its forehead. Its eyes lit up from the inside, a deep blood red that flickered like candlelight.

The Dark One had found them, and he didn't have a second to waste.

He took a deep breath and jumped.

THIRTY-TWO

CRASH

A few years ago, Left 4 Dead was one of Crash's favorite games on XBOX 360.

He played it all day and night, grouping for co-op with random strangers online, until he'd earned every possible badge in the game.

But the truth was, fighting zombies was a hell of a lot more fun when you had the option to restart every time you died.

As he hovered over maps of New York and tried to come up with a strategy that wouldn't get them killed, he yearned for those days when his worst fear was running out of Red Bull after the stores closed.

"Something's got to be wrong," Parrish said, pacing the floor near the windows.

She'd been doing that for the past hour, muttering to herself.

Noah had managed to calm her down several times, but Crash could feel the tension rising with every minute that ticked by. It was about two-thirty now, and they'd heard nothing from David.

They'd managed to use the delay as wisely as they could, riding their bikes out to the marina to choose a good, speedy boat and load it up with supplies. They also raided some of the houses further down the strip and came up with a gold mine of tech at the big white house on the end.

Bluetooth earbuds.

Enough for their whole party, which meant Crash could connect them all together so they could chat without trying to use mind magic or be limited to holding the stone.

He was pretty excited about that, so he'd spent a bit of time setting it up before he'd gone back to the satellites and video feed.

Crash wasn't too worried about David and Zoe. The city was a shit-show, and there were all kinds of things that could have delayed the kid.

In fact, Crash was pretty sure the rotters on the rooftops were the main source of the delay. He'd been keeping his eye on David's building and the surrounding areas, and he currently had an iPad he'd found in one of the houses propped up against a bag on the kitchen counter that was cycling through the four cameras that faced David's street.

From what he could tell, there were now one or two rotters on top of every building in that area. Planted there by the Dark One? Or by Lily?

Maybe, but he couldn't be sure.

They weren't there last night when he'd looked, but they were there today, and after what David had explained to them about the way he liked to travel, that had to be costing him time.

The good news, though, was that none of the rotters seemed to be alerted or concerned about anything in particular. If they'd found David and Zoe, there would be some kind of commotion or crowd gathering.

Instead, things seemed calm.

Besides, worrying about a two-hour delay during an apocalypse where everything was unpredictable wasn't going to help anyone.

What would help, however, was continuing to work on a plan.

He'd meant to do some of this work last night, but he'd spent the greater part of the evening wrapped in Karmen's arms again.

She'd been practicing ways of shielding his dreams from Lily or the Dark One or whoever might be watching in, and for the past several nights, she'd managed to make it so that he didn't have any dreams at all.

Of course, that could have had more to do with being so close to her all night, but he had no regrets there, either way.

In fact, he would have preferred to spend the rest of his life in her arms.

The way things were going, last night could have very well been the rest of his life, but he didn't want to think of it that way. He wanted to think of it as a potential beginning for something even better than late-night gaming by himself.

If he had to face real zombies and the threat of actual death to get to that new beginning, he was going in guns blazing.

"Why don't you all come over here for a second and get your mind off David," he said. "I want to run these maps by you and show you where we're going tomorrow."

Everyone joined him at the kitchen island where he'd

spread out his maps of the city that he'd gotten back at Tank's, as well as his satellite feeds on the laptop.

"Alright, so here's the plan." He pointed to where they were right now on the Jersey shore. "From here, it's a straight shot to New York. We're going to come in through this section under the bridge and into the Upper Bay here. Then, we'll curve around into the East River. I'm thinking we can find a place to dock here near the Queensboro Bridge."

"I thought David said the East River was trashed," Noah said.

"He did, and it is," Crash said, pulling up the most recent images he'd been able to pull from satellite. "But the Hudson is even worse. Look at this."

He shook his head as he scanned the Hudson River side of the island. By the time you got to the Bronx, it wasn't too bad, but they had to get around Manhattan first.

That wasn't happening. There was a massive container ship blocking the entire entrance there. Crash had no idea how that had come to pass, but it seemed to have crashed into the island and dumped half its cargo in the river. Lots of smaller boats and ships seemed to piled around it, as if they'd been trying to go around and had crashed into each other.

It was an epic disaster area.

"Where's Concourse Village on this map?" Parrish asked.

He pointed to an area all the way on the other side of Manhattan. It was just about the worst place for David and Zoe to be. If they'd been in Brooklyn, this would have been a cake walk.

"And where's the Queensboro Bridge you were talking about?" she asked.

He showed her where the bridge was, and she groaned.

"That's so close to the Four Seasons," she said. "We would have been right there."

"Yeah, but Zoe would have been long gone by now if she'd stayed there," Noah said. "We have to keep it in perspective."

"You really think we're going to be able to get around that mess on the Brooklyn Bridge?" Karmen asked, zooming in on some satellite images he'd shown her earlier. "I still think it's iffy at best. It doesn't look passable to me."

"I think I can get us through that with the speedboat," he said. He sounded more confident than he felt. "Anything bigger would be a challenge, but David's supposed to be scouting it out for me this morning before we commit."

Parrish sighed, and her anxiety was making everyone nervous.

Crash chose to stay focused on his explanation, though. David would be in touch soon. He was sure of it.

"From the looks of it, the Brooklyn Bridge must have been blasted by something big. A bomb, maybe? There were rumors on the underground forums that the military was planning to enforce a quarantine on the city by taking out the bridges. At first, I thought that was crazy, paranoid talk, but looking at the bridge now? I can't imagine anything short of a military-grade bomb taking that much of the bridge out."

There had been a full load of cars trying to cross it, too, but he didn't mention that part.

The bridge closest to Manhattan still stood, and even though he couldn't find any camera that could get a good look underneath it, he was pretty sure there was a small space where a boat could pass through.

"If not, we'll have to get out there, but that's going to add a lot of time and trouble to our trip."

"And you don't think we can get any closer to the Bronx than this Queensboro Bridge?" Parrish asked.

"Not a chance," he said, shaking his head. "Look at this."

He switched over to another satellite image and stepped back so they could see.

Parrish did a double-take and then brought a hand to her mouth.

"Is that a plane?" Noah asked.

"That is a plane," Crash confirmed. "A C-130 transport, to be exact. And so is this."

He pointed to a second one just a hundred yards away. The entire river was closed from that point on.

"Wait, what about coming all the way around the other side?" Parrish asked. "Here. Long Island Sound. That looks like a straight shot."

He shook his head. "It won't work," he said. "Believe me, David and I have looked into every possible way to get to them. Long Island Sound is worse than the East River. There was such a huge breakout in New York, and despite the quarantine, so many people were trying to flee the city. To keep them locked down, the National Guard apparently blocked that entire entrance to the sound. The closest place to dock would be New London, and that's over a hundred miles from Concourse Village."

"A hundred miles?"

"What are we looking at in terms of miles from the Queensboro Bridge area?" Noah asked.

"Less than ten," Crash told them. "But we can expect it to be the most difficult ten miles of our lives."

"It's going to be very important for us to stick together," Noah said. "If any one of us gets separated, we're toast."

"And we need to be as quiet as possible." Crash looked specifically at Karmen as he said this. "There were millions of people in New York City pre-virus, so we can assume there are millions of infected there now. Hopefully the sun will keep shining bright all day and most of them will be inside, but the slightest noise could draw them out. Besides, the Dark One knows we're coming. She'll have them out looking for us."

"We can expect some super zombies along the way," Parrish said. "We might even have to face Lily once we get there."

Crash swallowed. Yeah, he was fairly certain they would be facing Lily, if his dreams could still predict the future.

"Maybe the hundred-mile route isn't such a bad idea, after all," Karmen said. "If that way is mostly clear, and the Dark One's expecting us in Manhattan, it might be our only chance for surviving this."

Crash shook his head. "I told you. I spent hours looking over this from every angle. The places north of New York are in terrible condition. The roads and fires and congestion up there makes our trip from Philly look like a walk in the park. It would take us a week to get through there. Manhattan's the only way. When we talk to David, we'll see if he can get closer to the bridge to meet us. Maybe we'll get lucky and get in and out of there before the Dark One even realizes we're there."

Everyone knew that wasn't going to happen, but they could hope, right?

He went over the route with them one more time, just in case. They set a rendezvous point near the Third Avenue Bridge. "If we get separated along the way and the Bluetooth isn't working, make your way to this church here on the corner of Third Avenue and One Hundred Twenty-Seventh Street.

Wait for the rest of the group there. We'll all cross over the bridge together as soon as we can."

"And what if we get pinned down somewhere and can't get out?" Parrish asked.

"Keep in contact through your earbuds at all times," he said. "If we can keep up communication, it will make things easier."

"We'll all stick together," Karmen said. "But while we're waiting to hear from David, I think—"

"Wait. What's that?" Parrish asked, pointing to the iPad. Her voice sounded slightly strangled with panic. "Crash, what's happening there? Is that where Zoe is?"

His mouth went dry as he reached for the iPad and stopped its rotation. He went back to the previous video feed and nearly dropped the device.

Where there had only been one or two rotters in the frame just minutes ago, now there were hundreds, pouring out from every building and side street, appearing in windows, swarming the rooftops.

And every single one was headed toward the building where David lived.

THIRTY-THREE

PARRISH

"We have to move, now," she shouted. "Grab the bags and pack up whatever you can in two minutes. We don't have a second to waste."

No one argued, which scared her more for some reason. They all knew what that horde meant.

Lily.

It had to be her, which meant there were super zombies everywhere, too. Parrish gripped the stone around her neck and tried to connect to her sister or David, but there was only silence.

She ran up the stairs, threw a few things into her backpack, double-checked her weapons and ran right back down and out into the driveway to meet the others.

Crash was the last one to come out, and by the time she saw him emerge from the house with all of his computers and tech strapped to his back, she was already on her way to the marina.

Thank God they'd taken the time to choose and load up

the boat earlier this afternoon. Without that, it would have taken them at least another half hour or more to get going.

Instead, they sped toward the marina, jumped off their bikes, and ran toward the boat. They were on the water in seconds, heading north. The small speedboat bounced against the waves, and Parrish wondered if it might just toss them all off if Crash took it too fast.

Water sprayed into their faces, but she didn't close her eyes. Instead, she kept them straight ahead, waiting. Praying.

Noah held her hand, but no one said a word. All they could do was hold this space, knowing the real fight had just begun.

Finally, after what felt like an eternity, the tall buildings of the Manhattan skyline came into view. Parrish's stomach tightened into knots.

It was surreal to see it this way. One of the most famous cities on earth. A place some people spent a lifetime dreaming to see with their own eyes, but all Parrish felt was dread.

Zoe's alive in there. I know she is.

Parrish went over the plan again in her head. She knew the basic route they planned to take, but everything was up in the air now. If Zoe and David were trapped in that building, it wouldn't take long for that swarm to break through and grab them.

She prayed they were on the move, searching for a place to hide.

But Lily would be on the move, too, tracking them.

She was definitely here. Parrish could feel it.

She tried to calm her mind by touching the stone, but once again, as she thought of Lily, a different image invaded her mind. The handsome man, holding her hand and falling to the ground as his life withered away.

Who was that?

Someone Lily had known?

Parrish couldn't make sense of it. Why did she see that man sometimes when she touched the stone? How was he connected?

She released the stone and the man's face went away. She didn't have time to piece together that puzzle right now. She just needed to focus on her abilities and how they were going to survive that city.

She needed to be at her absolute best. So far, each battle they'd fought had brought out new abilities and powers. She had to believe there were still secrets locked inside them that could help them save David and her sister.

She needed to trust herself.

The only other option was surrender, and that was never going to happen.

She closed her eyes and felt the wind in her hair.

She breathed in the salty scent of the ocean.

She let her worries fall away and focused, instead, on the growing power inside her. She focused on her love for her sister. On her determination to save what was left of this dying world.

She focused on the warmth of Noah's strong leg pressed against hers as they sat side by side.

He'd really been there for her these past few weeks. She grabbed his hand and laced her fingers through his, letting his strength become her strength, too. They could do this.

They could find a way to defeat the Dark One and restore this world.

They had to.

Or they would all die trying.

"This is it," Crash said, slowing the boat as they approached Manhattan.

No one spoke. Instead, everyone's eyes were glued to the scene. The horror of it all. From the looks of the smoke, most of Brooklyn had been on fire at some point. With no organized firefighters in the city, there was nothing to stop even a small kitchen fire from getting ridiculously out of hand. Curls of smoke rose up from a few spots in Manhattan as well, but nothing as serious as the fires across the bridge.

As they passed the Statue of Liberty and got close enough to see the city ahead, the destruction nearly took her breath away.

Massive container ships had crashed into each other, blocking off parts of the river. Some buildings had hundreds of windows blown out. Smoke rose from different areas all around them.

"Dear God," Parrish whispered.

Seeing the smoke from afar or looking at the destruction through satellite images hadn't really prepared her for the horrors of what really had happened here in New York City.

She held her breath as Crash slowly steered them around the wreckage in the water and under what was left of the Brooklyn Bridge.

It looked like a bomb had gone off, and from the presence of military vehicles and boats all around the island, maybe a few had. To control the rotter threat, desperate measures had been taken in the early days to try to quarantine and eliminate.

They'd never had a chance of controlling this, though. There were simply too many infected. Too many dead bodies in the city right from the start. And by the time the dead had started to awaken, it was too late to do anything about it.

All along the river, the city itself told the story.

Groups of survivors had tried to do what Tank had done in Philly. Structures had been erected out of everything imaginable. Fences, barbed wire, even stacks of cars in some places.

Nothing looked to have held for long.

Now, everything they could see from the water was either completely destroyed or packed with throngs of zombies. At the sound of the boat, many of them turned toward the river, their jaws snapping open hungrily as they threw themselves over the sides of the railing and into the water.

"Looks like some of these guys ran out of food a long time ago," Karmen said, shuddering. She was right. Most of the rotters looked emaciated, their flesh hanging loosely from their bones. "I wonder what happens if they don't eat for a long time. Do you think they eventually starve to death?"

"Maybe," Crash said. "I hope so."

The ride up the East River only took a few minutes before they hit a point where the water was too congested to continue. Crash steered them toward the Queensboro Bridge, pulling the boat in between Manhattan and Roosevelt Island. "There," he said, pointing. "Looks like we can dock there just after we cross under the bridge."

It definitely wasn't as close to Zoe as she wished they could have gotten, but for now, it was enough. She was just anxious to get on the ground and start moving toward her.

Parrish had to keep reminding herself to breathe as they pulled up to the docking area. Her heart felt like it was lodged in her throat, she was so nervous.

Crash pulled the boat up to the edge of a platform and

Noah jumped out. Parrish tossed him the rope from the back, and as Noah tied them off, everyone gathered their weapons and supplies.

Luckily, the docking area was clear of any rotters, but from the looks of it, the second they stepped off the docks, they were going to have to start fighting. Their presence was already drawing some attention, and Parrish kept watch for red eyes. She could tell Karmen was doing the same.

"How are we going to get through these mobs of zombies?" Noah asked. "I don't know that our original plan of slash and dash is going to work."

"I wasn't expecting there to be so many out in the open." Crash tried to swallow, but it came out more of a croak. Parrish handed him a bottle of water.

"Thanks," he said.

"We discussed this. Guns are too dangerous at this stage of the game. We're just going to have to rely on our new abilities," she said. "The main thing is we stick together at all times. No stepping away from the group to run after a straggler. We let them come to us, and we keep pushing forward no matter what. Otherwise, we could end up fighting waves of them and still be stuck in the same spot for hours. Karmen, your powers are going to be instrumental here. Do you feel up for this?"

Karmen shrugged, wrapping her arms around herself. She looked scared.

"I don't know," she said. "I guess so. I'm just afraid that if I miss one or two, we're going to get overwhelmed. I don't know for sure how many I can hold at once."

"Just do your best," Crash said, touching her arm. "You can do this. I'll catch any that get through, okay?"

They had a pretty solid plan in theory, but Parrish had no idea how it would really work once it came down to it.

They would stay in a tight group. Karmen would use her mind control to create a circle of zombies around them, like a wall of protection. If possible, she'd make it two or three rotters deep.

"Put in your earbuds," Crash reminded them. "If they get loud, it might be hard to hear each other without them."

Parrish and Noah would slice and bash the ones in the front row, while Crash would keep an eye out for any on the other side who broke through the barrier.

Slowly, they'd inch forward, continuing to stay inside the wall.

If too many broke through at once, Crash would use his chain lightning spell to stop them in their tracks, and Parrish would use the flash of blue light to cut as many down as possible, just like she'd done back at the compound.

Of course, the issue with that was the fact that her light would most likely cut her own group's legs off if she wasn't careful. If it came to that, they'd have to climb onto something like a car or a bus or some steps.

It wasn't going to be fast, but all they needed to do was survive.

Of course, if super zombies attacked in large groups, there was no plan for what they could do. Run and hide. Barricade themselves into a building somewhere and try to take them on one by one? She wasn't sure, but she hoped it wouldn't come to that.

Parrish pulled her sword from its leather strap on her back and poured her power into it. A bright blue flame engulfed the blade, and she'd barely had to even think of it.

Her powers had definitely come a long way in a very short period of time.

"Do you feel that?" she asked as a new sense of power surged through her.

"What?" Karmen asked, turning around, as if to look for something.

"No, in here," Parrish said, placing a hand over Karmen's heart. "Do you feel the power there?"

Crash lifted his hands and smiled as bolts of lightning danced between his fingertips.

"Oh yeah," he said. "There's the juice."

Karmen slowly nodded. "I do feel that. What is it?"

"David," Noah said, lifting his bat into the air. A blue light similar to Parrish's flame pulsed against the wood. "We've never been this close to him before, but I can feel it now. He's alive, and he's only a few miles away."

"Hopefully that means we'll all get stronger as we get closer to him," Parrish said. "We need to get moving, though. We're wasting daylight."

"Oh, wait. Before we go." Karmen grabbed a black duffel bag from the boat and pulled out four long knives. "We have these, too."

"Dang, where did you get those?" Crash asked.

"Tank gave them to me," she said, handing one to each of them.

They were hunting knives, long and sharp. Toward the hilt on one side, the edge was serrated. Parrish was pretty sure they could do some serious damage with those if things got too close for comfort.

Once again, Karmen had surprised her.

Each knife had its own leather sheath that could be

attached to a belt, so the guys strapped theirs on. Neither of the girls were wearing belts, though, so they tucked them into the back of their jeans.

Parrish grabbed her backpack, double-checked she had everything in there she needed, and hoisted it onto her back.

After all this time, hoping she could come to New York and save her sister, the moment had finally come.

And she was scared to death.

They weren't ready for this. Who could ever be ready for something like this?

But ready or not, they were going in. Fate would have to determine the rest.

She took a deep breath, trying her best to calm her heart and her nerves for whatever cruel ideas fate had in store.

"Alright," she said, finally, taking a deep breath and lifting her sword. "Let's go get my sister."

PART THREE
THE CITY

Zoe leaned out the window, looking for any sign of David. He didn't seem to be on the ground, which was a relief. She'd just about convinced herself that he'd fallen and was dead out on the streets.

Instead, she looked up, squinting at the bright sunlight.

There was someone up there, but she couldn't quite tell from this distance who it was. And she didn't have time to think about it.

Within seconds, a terrible roar sounded in the streets, like a chorus of groans.

The sound startled her, and she turned her attention downward again, backing up slightly so she could hide behind the curtain.

At first, she thought maybe a large horde had been pushed their way by chance, but it only took a few seconds to realize this was no coincidence.

These rotters didn't just happen to be passing by. They were coming from every possible direction in swarms, practically falling all over themselves to get into her building. They ran up the steps and tore their way into the building, pouring in like a rushing river.

Something deep inside her reacted to the sight. Like this was the beginning of the end. For all of them.

Zoe stumbled backward, letting the curtain fall back into place.

What have I done?

Her entire body trembled, and she turned in a circle, looking around for anything she could use as a weapon. If they were coming for her, it would only be a minute before that huge swarm got to her door.

And if they'd managed to break down the secure front door of a New York apartment building, how fast would they tear through the door in front of her now?

She fell to her knees, tears stinging her eyes.

There was no weapon that could save her now. There were too many of them.

David had warned her not to show her face, and she'd done it anyway. What was wrong with her? What had she been thinking, risking everything like that?

Parrish would be so angry.

But it was only for a second. She didn't think anyone would see her.

She kept her eyes on the door, just waiting for those things to crash through, the way she'd waited for her father to finally push through the suite door and tear into her. Her breath hitched in her chest.

This was it. She was going to die.

A thud sounded behind her, and she sprang to her feet,

arms up to defend herself. Were they coming from all directions now?

Only, this was a familiar face.

David rolled across the floor, stopped, and grabbed a backpack on the floor next to the couch. He touched her arm.

We have to go. No time.

She nodded once and turned toward the bedroom. Her bag and violin were both in there, along with her shoes.

David gripped her arm tighter and shook his head.

Time stood still then, as she realized what he was saying. There was no time to get her violin. She would have to leave it behind.

"I can't," she said. "You don't understand."

That instrument was a part of her. It was the only thing that had kept her alive throughout this whole thing. Without it, she would have gone insane, and leaving it here felt like leaving herself behind.

Like losing herself.

A memory tugged at her, deep inside. Something about the hotel and her violin, but she pushed it away. She didn't have time to think about that now.

David was right. Her hesitation was costing them too much.

She could hear the rotters climbing the stairs now. It was almost like a low hum at first, then a tapping. But now, it was a pounding. They were just outside the door.

David closed his eyes and took a deep breath. He drew one hand back toward the window, and a strong breeze flew in toward them, ripping the curtain off the wall. He seemed to gather the wind in his hand and push it toward the door.

Rotters slammed against the door, their fingers wrapping

around the edges as they tried to push it open with the force of their combined weight.

I can't hold them long. We have to move.

Zoe ran with him to the window and together, they climbed out. It was so high up, and the ground was invisible through the swarm of rotters still pouring into the building. An endless sea of them spread out in every direction.

We'll never survive, she thought

We have to, David said in her mind. *Hold on.*

She gripped his hand tightly, and together, they jumped just as the door behind them splintered into pieces and rotters filled the room.

Zoe could have sworn she felt the scrape of fingertips on her heel as they flew into the air.

THIRTY-FIVE
PARRISH

I f they'd ever needed a situation that could push them to the limits of their abilities, this was it. Parrish had never seen so many zombies in one location. Even the horde at the compound was small compared to this.

The group came off the docks and stepped into a war zone.

"Bring everything you've got," she said, lighting up the area in front of them with a flash of blue that brought down at least fifty of the rotters running toward them.

They had to step over bodies to keep moving forward.

Karmen worked fast, doing her job by holding a circle of zombies at bay, letting them act as a shield while the others brought as many down as possible. It was elegant the way she seemed to control them with the motion of her hands, as if she were smoothing out the air in front of her, commanding them to stop and form a circle, arm to arm, around the guardians.

Still, it took time to get into the rhythm of working together as a group, despite all their practice.

At first, Karmen was only able to hold about a semicircle

worth of zombies at bay. Whenever she turned around to the other side, the first set seemed to release.

There wasn't a second to relax as the four of them stood back-to-back in the center, each taking out any zombies that approached them. They weren't going to move forward at this rate, though. They would just get stuck in an infinite battle here in one spot as more and more rotters pushed toward them.

"We have to keep inching forward," Parrish said, so thankful they had these earbuds to communicate. Otherwise, they never would have been able to hear each other over the sound of the rotters. "Use whatever you can think of. We have to move or we're going to end up overwhelmed out here."

"Pulling out the big guns," Crash said.

"Do it."

They had originally planned to lay off the guns for fear the noise would draw more attention, but at this point, they already had the attention of every rotter for miles. There was no sneaking around in this scenario.

Crash unleashed a storm of bullets into the crowd around them, and after about a minute or two of inching forward, Parrish noticed the bullets all seemed to have a slight electrical charge to them.

"You figured it out?" she asked.

"You like it?" he asked. "It took me a few to get it working, but I think I've finally got the hang of it."

To prove his point, he sprayed the crowd in front of them. The bodies of the rotters shook like they'd been hit by a taser and then fell to the ground.

"Hell yeah," she said. "Keep it coming."

Karmen was getting better, too, expanding her range and essentially stunning large groups of zombies all at once. Killing them was like shooting fish in a barrel. Hope surged through Parrish as she sliced down rotters and climbed over them to the next group.

They were moving now, and as they approached First Avenue, she called back to Crash.

"Which way do we want to go? Do you think we just keep heading uptown?"

"Yeah, let's head up First and see how it goes," he said. "We might have to adapt our strategy, so pay attention."

First Avenue was teeming with rotters, all pressing in toward them. Parrish knew at any minute they could run into some super zombies, too. It was only a matter of time before Lily or the Dark One sent their pets over this way and the real fight began.

As they moved, though, each person got better at executing their role in the group, and they fell into a rhythm with it, anticipating each other's movements as they kept a tight circle.

Parrish's muscles burned. They'd already been through so much over the past week between the hospital, the compound, and all their training. Her entire body was sore before they even started.

But with every swing of her sword, she reminded herself she was taking one step closer to Zoe every time they moved forward even a little bit.

And then, she heard it.

Zoe's voice. Small but strong.

We're in trouble, Parrish. It's all my fault.

Parrish nearly fell to her knees at the sound in her mind. She faltered in the rhythm, and Noah quickly stepped in with a headshot from one of his two pistols.

"What's wrong?" he asked.

"Zoe," she said. "Where are you? We're coming to you."

The others stepped around Parrish, giving her space in the center of their group so she could talk to her sister. The fighting never skipped a beat.

I don't know. We're on top of buildings. We're moving as fast as we can, but they just keep coming.

"David's with you?" she asked, already sensing the answer but needing to be sure.

I'm here, David's voice now. *We're about to cross over the Third Avenue Bridge. I can sense you.*

"They're on Third Avenue," Parrish said. "Crash, what do we do?"

"Tell them to stay on Third. Keep heading this way. We'll make our way there. Meet in the middle," he said.

Parrish relayed the instructions to David and Zoe, wishing she had some idea of just how far they were from each other. Even though she'd studied the maps, she didn't have a clear enough concept of the city now that she was here to know what kind of distance they were needing to cross here. Served her right for relying on her phone's GPS all her life, instead of pulling out a map every now and then.

Of course, no one had expected life as they knew it to come to a screeching halt, either.

The Third Avenue Bridge was only a few miles at most. They could do this.

"Keep moving toward us," she said. "We'll be together soon. All you have to do is stay alive."

I will keep her alive, David said. *Heading your way.*

The words filled Parrish with a surge of hope, and she looked toward the rotters ahead with renewed determination.

Goosebumps broke out across her arms, and something new awakened inside.

She held onto that feeling, pushing deeper into it, and as she lifted her sword and stepped back into place, sparks of red flame joined the blue light emanating from her sword.

THIRTY-SIX

CRASH

"This way," Crash said, spotting a break in the otherwise endless crowds of rotters.

They'd been fighting their way to Third Avenue for the past half-hour, and he was exhausted. More importantly, Karmen needed a break. She'd indicated she was losing focus and starting to feel light-headed.

He wasn't sure they could push through without her, so he led them into an alleyway between two tall buildings where there were only a handful of rotters lingering. Parrish made quick work of them, and the group crouched down behind a set of trash bins.

Crash leaned against the brick wall and took several deep breaths. They'd been fighting nonstop, and it felt good to finally get a break, even if it wouldn't last too long.

This alley was clear for now, and though they needed to keep moving, he also needed to catch his breath.

"Thank you," Karmen said.

"Are you feeling alright?" Parrish asked.

"I just need a second. Maybe something to eat."

While the others drank some water and searched their bags for snacks, Crash took the opportunity to pull up several cameras and study the area between where they were now and where they needed to go.

David had said they were just crossing the Third Avenue Bridge. That looked to be about three miles or so away. It seemed like such a short distance, but at the rate they were moving, it was still going to take an hour or more unless David and Zoe were moving a lot faster than they were.

The city around them was completely trashed. It was so much worse seeing it with your own eyes than any satellite could ever convey.

Crash could only imagine how terrifying it must have been to be trapped here. Were there still survivors hiding out in their apartments, rationing out whatever food they had left? Or was the city mostly given over to rotters at this point?

He couldn't be sure. All he could do was hope their actions would make a difference to whoever had managed to survive this long in the world.

He pulled up every possible route, trying to navigate them around the larger messes where they might possibly get trapped. New York City was basically a grid, but their trip wasn't as simple as just cutting over to Third Avenue and heading north. There was too much in the way sometimes to make a straight shot, so they were going to need to move in a kind of zig-zag pattern in some places.

Even then, the sheer number of zombies on the streets now was staggering. And it was no surprise to see more and more pouring into the area as they moved. They were acting under orders now, and Crash had a feeling that was all thanks to their old pal, Lily.

But as angry as he was at her, there was something really cool about being close to the fifth after all this time. Like some invisible string of energy was pulling them all toward each other. His instincts kept guiding him in David's direction.

He just hoped he could stay connected to that feeling once they were back out on the streets, fighting for their lives.

Even though Crash was pretty sure they were dangerously close to the day of his vision coming true, there was still a part of him that believed they could make it through this.

That they could still win.

He had to believe.

"We need to keep moving," Parrish said, handing him a bottle of water and half of a Cliff Bar. "As soon as our barrier falls, they're going to swarm this place, and we can't afford to get stuck here."

He devoured the bar, chugged some water, and put the iPad back in his bag. He was pretty sure he'd worked out a good route for them to take for now.

They just had to hope they didn't run into any of the super zombies.

"Let's go," Parrish said as soon as he gave the go ahead that he was ready.

Everyone stood and held their weapons steady, preparing to face a huge cluster of rotters once they stepped back out, but instead, the street beyond the alley was empty.

"I don't like this," Karmen said, rubbing her hands over her arms like she was cold.

"Yeah, why is it so quiet?" Parrish asked.

Crash didn't like the looks of this, either. Just seconds ago, there had been a small crowd out here on the street. There should have been more piling in, not less.

"Every time this has happened, there's been a horde waiting for us," Karmen said.

"This way," he said, pointing in the direction of Third Avenue.

Crash pulled up the surveillance cameras for the surrounding blocks as they jogged forward. There was definitely something strange going on. Every other street in a ten block radius was teeming with Z's. Why was this alley empty?

"'I don't see anything unusual on the cameras," he said. "Except that we seem to be in a small pocket of emptiness. It's weird, right?"

Everyone looked around with nervous anticipation, as if waiting for the red eyes to appear at any moment.

"Does anyone see anything strange or out of place?"

"You mean other than the fact that New York City is a zombie playground and mostly destroyed forever?" Karmen asked. She shifted her weight from one foot to the other, looking impatient and nervous.

"What the hell is that?" Noah asked, pointing straight ahead to the end of the alley.

Crash didn't see anything at first except the throng of rotters on the adjacent street, but when he looked closer, at a certain angle, he could see what Noah was talking about.

About ten yards ahead, a white mist formed on the blacktop. It looked similar to fog, which was impossible on a day like today when it was probably more than ninety degrees out.

"Should we just go around it?" Parrish asked. "We're losing time here."

"I don't think we should just be standing around looking at

it," Karmen said. "While we do this, the Dark One is getting her super zombies in play. We're sitting ducks out here like this."

Karmen was right, but if they made the wrong call here, they could be walking into something much worse. He wanted to be sure they were thinking this through.

"From the looks of it, the mist extends all the way from one side of the street to the other," he said.

He toggled through a few nearby video feeds, and he didn't like what was happening at all.

"It looks like some kind of pattern," he said, holding out the iPad for the others to see.

The mist snaked around them in all directions, cutting off access to any other streets.

Beside him, Parrish gasped. "She's blocking us in. We've got to run."

"Looks like there's one possible path left to us," Noah said, running his finger along a side street. "Here."

"We're like rats in a maze," Karmen whispered.

Crash realized she was right.

New York City was one giant maze right now, and the Dark One was toying with them. One wrong move, and it would all be over.

So, what was the right move here? There was only one route, but maybe that was just the way she wanted to force them to go.

"I don't like the idea of going the way she's sending us. Let's get closer and see if we can run through it," Crash said. "It's just mist, right?"

"Doubtful," Karmen muttered. "This is a bad plan."

She was probably right, but were there any good options at this point rather than to face whatever this was head on?

As they approached the mist at the end of the alley, it rose into the air and solidified, turning into a solid block of ice that extended all the way across the street and went up at least three stories high.

"Dammit," he said, spinning on his heels. "Try this other way."

They ran that way, too, but the same thing happened. She was boxing them in and only giving one possible route forward.

How were they going to get through this? He was sure that if they went the way that was open, something terrible would be waiting for them there, but what choice did they have?

Maybe they could go up? He had no idea how they'd cross from building to building once they were up there, though. If they went up, their only option would be to fight until David found his way to them, and if he and Zoe got stuck somewhere along the way, they were all screwed.

No, they had to keep moving forward.

It was the only way.

As if to prove his point, something very loud and very big seemed to be coming from the direction of the only open pathway. A super zombie? Or a horde? He couldn't be sure, but he didn't want to find out when they were boxed in like this.

"We have to get through this ice," he said, gathering sparks of lightning on his fingertips. "Karmen, if we work together, maybe we can melt this wall."

"I can help, too," Parrish said, fastening her sword behind her back and conjuring flames in both palms.

"Let's go," he said. "Noah, watch our backs. I don't like the sound of whatever she's sending our way."

All three of them concentrated their power on the wall of ice, and slowly, it began to melt.

"Hurry up, guys, we've got something big headed this way fast. Hear that?" Noah asked.

Crash didn't even turn to look. If they didn't get this wall down in the next few seconds, they'd be trapped here indefinitely.

He closed his eyes and focused, not only on the heat he could put into this wall, but also on the surge of power coming from the two girls at his side.

When they were all focused on the same task, it seemed like their power was amplified.

"Can you feel that?" he asked. "Karmen, take my hand."

She did, and the moment they touched, the flames in Karmen's other hand roared to life, bigger and stronger than ever.

Parrish stepped over, touching the side of her arm to Karmen's, and the wall practically disintegrated.

Water ran into the streets, then disappeared into a nearby drain.

There was no time to celebrate, though. Hundreds of Z's rushed at them from behind, and from the sound of it, they had a super zombie with them. They needed to get back out onto the bigger roads so they would be more flexible in their fighting styles, so the group followed him as he sprinted toward Third Avenue.

They would have to face zombies from both sides now, but at least they wouldn't be boxed in with nowhere to go if things got bad.

Crash took inventory of the zombies standing on the street as they finally emerged onto Third. A woman in a black business suit. A cop in full uniform. A priest. A child who couldn't have been more than six years old.

These things used to be people, but now their jaws snapped like hungry animals.

"Run," Noah shouted.

Parrish drew her sword. "Here they come!"

They all moved into action, Crash stunned a few nearby rotters with his lightning power and then stepped forward to put an end to them with his hunting knife. As the first zombie fell, Crash pulled the knife back, then plunged it straight into the eye socket of another.

And just like that, they were back in the thick of it, fighting with everything they had and clinging to what was left of hope.

THIRTY-SEVEN
NOAH

They'd broken through the ice wall just in time.

Noah shouted for everyone to run just as a horde of zombies emerged from the street behind them. He couldn't see the super zombie yet, but he could hear it.

Every footfall shook the ground around them, rattling the debris and glass on the street.

The group moved into action, clearing the rotters on Third Avenue so they could find a better position to face this horde.

Parrish took charge, directing everyone as she struck down several rotters nearby.

"Karmen, focus on the horde. Stun the first wave and hold them back as much as possible while we clear this area," she said. "Crash, seek higher ground and charge up your lightning. Noah, you're with me."

He nodded, reloading his pistols and joining her as she ran up on top of a cargo van to get a better vantage point.

So far as they'd fought, they realized it was almost always better to get to higher ground as quickly as possible. The rotters couldn't bite them if they stayed toward the center of the car, and it was easier for Noah to get a straight shot from higher up.

He didn't hesitate, taking aim and downing ten rotters in seconds. Thanks to Tank back in Philly, he'd gotten some extended magazines for these pistols, so he could hold about sixteen bullets in each one.

He made the most of each shot, aiming for the head and never missing his mark.

They made quick work of the ones on Third while Karmen focused on holding back the horde.

"I can't hold these guys forever," Karmen said, her voice strained.

"Crash," Parrish shouted. "Now."

With a power Noah still could hardly believe, Crash threw lightning bolts toward the crowd on the side street. Several rotters in the front row caught fire and stumbled forward before falling onto the sidewalk.

Others shook and groaned until they fell in a heap on the street.

Everyone outside of Crash's range, though, pushed forward, running over the bodies of the fallen.

Noah took aim toward the horde and brought down as many as he could, while Karmen gathered flames in her hands and lit the sidewalk and street on fire.

These basic rotters weren't that difficult to deal with anymore, even in these larger numbers, as long as they had the space to spread out.

But the hulking man who rushed forward out of the crowd

was no basic rotter. He was a beast just like the one Karmen had tamed back at the compound. Maybe bigger.

Their plan with any of these super zombies was to have Karmen do her best to turn them to their side.

This one, however, went straight for Karmen at the start, moving so fast, Noah barely had time to react.

"Beast heading toward you, Karmen," he shouted. "Watch out."

Unlike with Parrish and the motorcycles the other day, he hadn't sensed this hit coming, but since they'd practiced his shielding several times at the beach house, he'd still been able to throw up a basic shield before the Beast made his hit.

Karmen screamed as the hulking brute swept her to the side with the back of his hand. Her body flew backward and hit the side of an abandoned truck. But it was Noah who took the pain of it.

He cried out and fell to his knees on top of the van. He struggled to keep the shield up as the Beast approached Karmen again, but he would not fail his friend.

With his strength and healing, he could take a beating much better than any of them.

At least for a while.

If pain was his greatest burden, he would bear it with pride.

But luckily, he didn't have to take another hit. The Beast stepped toward Karmen, fist raised, and then stopped as if frozen in place.

"You're mine, now," Karmen said, smiling as she stood.

The Beast turned on the swarm of rotters behind him and roared.

K armen smiled at the giant Beast of a man.

She hated that any human had been turned into such a grotesque thing, but at the same time, she'd really hated to leave the other one behind at the compound the other day.

As someone who had always felt small and weak, having this huge Beast on her side, fighting for her, made her feel strong and invincible.

What she would have given to have been able to sic a dude like this on her father. She could have daydreamed about watching this thing tear him apart for months, but right now, she needed to focus on the fight at hand.

They still had a horde to contend with, but her pet would make quick work of it. She commanded him to attack the crowd still surging in from the direction of the alley, and the Beast turned and did exactly what she asked.

Parrish and Crash joined in, both rushing forward to fight hand-to-hand.

"How are you feeling, Noah?" she called out.

"I'm hanging in there," he said, lifting his shirt to show a large bruise covering his ribcage.

He placed his palm flat against his skin and a blue frost appeared for an instant. He relaxed his shoulders somewhat and lowered his shirt.

"Thanks for the help," she said, cringing at the sight of that bruise. A hit like that might have killed her, but Noah had seemed to take it all in stride. "I'll repay you, I promise."

"I'm counting on it," he said.

A zombie grabbed the sleeve of her shirt with its bony hand, and she conjured a flame in her palm and stuffed it right in the thing's face. To be sure it was dead, she also pulled out her hunting knife and slid the blade into its heart.

"You have to aim for the head," Crash said.

"Do I, though?" she asked as the rotter fell to the ground, its face burned to a crisp.

Crash shrugged. "Well, maybe not when you burn their brains from the inside out."

She tried not to smile, because fighting zombies wasn't supposed to be fun. But at the same time, she was fighting with the people she liked most in the world. And she had to appreciate a guy who could make her smile even when her hand was covered in rotter blood.

Still, they needed to pick up the pace a bit and stop fooling around. They'd probably killed at least five hundred zombies since they'd first come off the boat, but they'd only moved a handful of blocks in an hour or so.

At this rate, they'd be fighting long past nightfall.

The group fell back into their rhythm as they fought the horde to the very last and started their way up Third Avenue.

David and Zoe were headed their way, but she wasn't sure where they'd end up meeting. The key, Parrish said, was just to keep moving. As long as they did that, no matter how slowly, they'd meet up somewhere in the middle and fight their way back to the boat.

If the boat is even still there.

Karmen pushed that thought out of her head, and did her best to focus on holding back another wave of rotters with her growing mind control. It didn't take as much concentration as it once had, which had to mean something, right?

So far, she was holding up okay, but if they hit the point of exhaustion, they were toast.

Karmen could hardly believe they'd made it this far alive, but they were moving too slow. The wreckage here on Third Avenue was harder to maneuver around, too. Cars were packed together like matchsticks, as if everyone had the same bright idea to flee the city at the same time.

What a mess.

And to think they were just a few blocks from some of the best shopping this town had to offer. She used to come here with her mother every Christmas to shop for gifts and check out the decorations, but there would be no Christmas here this year. No fashion week. No marathon.

Nothing would ever be the same again.

She pushed back the emotions she felt as she stared at the ruined city. There was no time for nostalgia now. They had to keep moving forward.

Karmen tried to keep her eyes off the cars as they all fought their way forward, remembering the small child who'd almost bit her arm the first day of their journey outside their neighborhood. Any zombies still stuck in their cars were going to have to just stay there.

But then, thinking about the piles of cars in the middle of the street gave her a brilliant idea.

"Why don't we go on top of the cars?" Karmen asked. "We could run across the tops of them, and as long as we don't get too close to any of the ones trapped inside, none of the others can reach us. The cars are too close together. My pet Beast can take care of any rotters on the sidewalks and stuff."

"Go," Parrish said, slicing through a rush of rotters with more than just her sword. Her blue light made it five zombies deep before it faded, and at least twenty or so fell to the ground.

Karmen pulled herself onto the hood of a blue Toyota. The metal bent slightly under her weight, but it held her just fine. Noah stayed behind to clear the rotters with Parrish while Crash climbed up behind her.

Her Beast kept doing what he did best, crushing rotter skulls between his fists with a single blow.

In a way, she kind of hoped Lily sent a few more so she could have some extra little pets to help them out. But then, she realized just how awful of a thought that was and took it back.

If she could have saved all of these people their fates as zombies, she would have.

Carefully, Karmen balanced herself on the hood, walked a few steps forward, climbed onto the roof, and then back down to the car's trunk. Piece of cake. She just needed to get into the rhythm of it, and then they could make quick work of this entire street.

As long as she stayed in the center of the car and didn't fall, she'd be fine.

She made a point, though, to keep her eyes off anyone trapped inside. It was just too tragic to think about.

"Let's go," she said, getting the hang of it enough to break out in a run.

The others climbed up behind her as the Beast ran alongside, taking out any zombies along the path. It was the fastest they had moved all afternoon, but Karmen had a sneaking suspicion their struggles in the city so far were nothing compared to what they would face ahead.

THIRTY-NINE
THE WITCH

The Witch stood on the rooftop and looked out over the city. She could feel them now. The guardians.

She'd missed them at first, because she'd been so focused on capturing the fifth that all of her mental energy had gone to finding and tracking his magic. The moment one of her lookouts had alerted her to Zoe's presence, she'd sent an entire horde after them.

Not to kill them, of course, but to capture them as her Mistress commanded.

The Witch still hated that there was a child involved in all of this, but it couldn't be helped. There was no reason to hurt the girl, though. It was the fifth the Dark One wanted, after all.

What use was the little girl to her now that Parrish was in the city?

The Witch was good with children. She always had been.

Taking care of the little ones was the one thing she'd enjoyed about her time living with the Council of Fire.

Her favorite little one had been Marilon.

She was the most beautiful child the witch had ever seen. Honey-colored skin and dark, questioning eyes. She'd had a pure heart, always eager for hugs and quick to smile.

Marilon had been taken in as a baby, deserted in the forest like so many girls back in those days. It was the witch who had given her a name, even though it was forbidden to do so. She'd been careful never to speak it out loud, but she'd always used the name in her head.

It meant 'wished for', and to the witch, that's what this child was. Forbidden to interact with men or to have children of her own as a ward of the Council, the witch had taken on the children she watched and cared for as her own.

But she'd never loved anyone as much as she had loved Marilon.

Even now, decades later, she wiped a tear from her eyes as she thought of the little girl. What the Council of Fire had done to her had broken the witch's heart forever.

Watching her death had been like watching the death of love.

The witch had vowed never to love anyone again. All she'd ever wanted from that moment forward was to gain power, so that someday, she could punish people who did things like kill children.

And yet, here she was, searching for a child to turn over to the Dark One.

She wondered if she could get away with hiding Zoe once she found her. If the Dark One wanted the fifth, maybe the witch could convince her Mistress she'd found him but not the child.

He would be like the other guardians, she was sure. Young, too, but nearly an adult by the standards of this world.

Besides, the body he had now would just be a shell of his true self. He was ancient, according to her Mistress. The eldest of the guardians before they came here to be reborn.

She would turn him over, but what about the little girl?

What would the Dark One do to her?

The witch shook her head. It wasn't her job to look after the child, and she needed to keep her mind on what was most important.

How many times would the Dark One have to torture her before she learned to obey?

This was her path to power and fame. To making sure the Council of Fire back home knew who she was and what she was capable of.

She would not let some human child keep her from that.

She'd been through too much to let old wounds like Marilon's death hold her back now.

She straightened her shoulders and closed her heart.

If the girl had to be turned over along with the fifth, then so be it.

She reached out to the rotters on the rooftops, searching through their eyes for the fifth and the child. She wasn't sure why, like Crash and his dreams, she could never quite see the fifth's face when she tracked him.

But she could feel him.

Her zombie minions were doing well, chasing him to the exact location she wanted him to go, near the park.

It wouldn't be long before he flew right into the trap she'd set for him there.

So, while everything was going according to plan on that side of the city, she turned to the south and the guardians.

Their journey had been a bit too easy up to this point, and

though a part of her resisted wanting to hurt them, she had a job to do.

She called three rotters over from the group she'd gathered there on the rooftop.

Yes, these three would do nicely.

FORTY
PARRISH

Zoe was close.

Parrish wasn't sure how to describe the feeling, but it was there, like an undercurrent always rippling beneath the surface of her awareness.

She could feel the draw of the fifth, too, and when she had a second between fights to slow down and focus on that feeling, she could tell he was getting closer.

But she could also feel his anxiety and fear. He was scared, and she couldn't blame him. They were both children, really, fighting all of this mess on their own.

Did either of them even know how to fight? Or were they just running and hoping not to get caught?

Parrish shuddered.

She hated that Zoe had already been through so much alone, and as much as she wanted to protect her from what was to come, that was partly out of her hands now.

She would do everything in her power to make sure Zoe survived this, even if the rest of them would not.

As they fought through the ruined streets of New York, Parrish pushed herself forward by that one thought.

When all of this was over, maybe Zoe and the other survivors could rebuild this world. A world Parrish and her friends had doomed the minute they brought this evil with them.

It was her one true hope and the thing that kept her pressing forward, despite how tired and afraid she was deep down.

For a while, they'd been traveling on top of a row of cars on Third Avenue, but at one point, the pile had stopped due to a concrete police barrier that had been erected to try to control the crowds.

Here, they'd had to get down and navigate rotter-filled streets again.

Just a little farther. We can do this.

So far, their time in the city hadn't been as difficult as Parrish had expected, but she wouldn't have dared to admit that out loud. She didn't want to jinx it.

But maybe it was just that the time they'd spent practicing and honing their powers, coming up with a good group strategy, had really paid off. Maybe they were going to make it to David and Zoe faster than they ever could have dreamed.

If they found the others soon, they might even be able to make it back to the boat before nightfall.

Noah suddenly stopped dead in front of her, holding both hands out to the side.

He lifted his hand to his mouth and doubled-over, like he was going to throw up.

"What's wrong?" she asked, touching his shoulder.

He didn't respond. He just looked up, scanning the area and studying each of them.

They were stopped at the corner of Third and East Seventy-Ninth, and from what Parrish could see, there was nothing particularly special about this location. There were a few rotters roaming up and down the streets, but overall, it was one of the quieter areas they'd been in so far.

But she did not like the look on Noah's face. Was he having another one of his premonitions?

"I don't know how to save you all," he said, his eyes growing wider as they locked on something behind her.

He breathed in, his body taking on a bright blue glow as he threw both arms out to the side. Threads of blue energy extended from him like ropes to the three others in their group.

She spun just as something swooped down from the top of a nearby building. Razor-sharp claws scraped across the skin on her arms and face, but all she felt was pressure as the giant bird-like zombie dodged the first swing of her sword.

She fell to the ground from the knock-back but quickly scrambled to her feet, her eyes following the creature as it flew up and joined two others, nearly identical to itself.

"Parrish."

Noah's voice was barely more than a whisper in her ear, and she turned just as he fell to his knees on the asphalt.

Her mouth opened in a scream as she ran to his side. His entire body was covered in thick gashes. The right side of his face had taken the injury intended for her, and blood poured from his wounds, covering his shirt.

Crash and Karmen had also been knocked to the ground, but neither of them showed any sign of injury. Noah had taken it all on his own.

With trembling hands, she dropped her katana and threw her backpack to the ground.

"I have to get you fixed up," she said, sounding so panicked she hardly recognized her own voice.

"No," he said, gripping her forearms tightly. "They're circling back around. I can't take another hit. You have to get up. We have to fight."

The urgency in his voice startled her back to the present moment. And he was right. Of course those things were coming back.

They'd never fought something that flew through the air like this, though. Her katana wasn't going to do much damage to them if they were fast.

"Here they come," Crash said, standing and gathering his lightning powers in his hands.

Karmen stayed on the ground, closing her eyes. Parrish prayed her friend could manage to turn at least one to their side quickly, but they were moving so fast she barely had any time to gather her own energy.

She stood and slid her katana back into its sheath at her back. Instead, she gathered a ball of flames in between her palms. Instead of heading for each of them, this time, they seemed to all be taking aim at Noah. They must have realized he'd taken their hits, and they wanted to take him out before he could do it again.

"Over my dead body," she muttered.

She swirled one palm over the other, flattening her flames into a disc before rearing back and hurling the spell toward the first creature.

It shrieked as the flame spell made a direct hit, but that didn't seem to slow it down at all.

The thing's claws descended toward Noah.

"Karmen," she shouted.

"I can't get into its head," Karmen answered. "I'm trying."

"I got it," Crash said, sending a stream of lightning toward the bird-like creatures.

A steady stream of electric energy poured from his hands, hitting the first bird-woman and then erupting in a web of lightning bolts that flashed between all three.

The birds trembled, but they didn't stop.

The first one kept on its path, swooping toward Noah and slashing at his back and neck.

To Parrish's relief, the thing's claws couldn't damage him. His stoneskin was in full effect, despite his injuries. He could only be hurt if he was shielding someone else, so the birds had done them all a favor by going after Noah.

Parrish acted fast, running forward as she pulled her sword from its sheath, flames igniting across the blade. With a single slice, she took the first bird's head clean off before it could fly away.

She set her sights on the other two, but they swiftly changed direction and swooped high over Noah's head, realizing they wouldn't be able to hurt him.

These were smarter than some of the other super zombies they'd faced, and she was reminded of the silver zombie she'd faced back at the compound.

Had these also been sent directly by the Dark One? Was she watching them, even now?

Or had Lily's powers advanced just as much as theirs had?

She glanced around, looking for any sign of a rotter like the one who had spoken to her at the compound that day, but she didn't see many rotters around at all. Karmen's Beast pet had taken care of almost all of them.

All they needed to do was get rid of these last two bird-like creatures before they managed to do any more damage. Noah's wounds looked deep, and blood had already pooled around him.

Somehow, he still found the strength to stand, but it took everything Parrish had not to run to him and try to help.

But right now, the best thing she could do for him and everyone around was kill these things. She glanced up, raising her hand against a stream of sunlight coming down from above.

There was no sign of the two that remained at first.

"Do you see them?" she shouted, turning around in a circle.

"I think they landed on top of that building," Crash said.

"Be ready," she said. "They'll come back. I'm sure of it."

But their group wouldn't be able to sit and wait for that to happen, because just as she said it, a loud chorus of groans approached from the north.

What had so far been a relatively easy trip into New York City had just gotten a hell of a lot more complicated.

FORTY-ONE

He'd never pushed himself this hard before, but if he stopped, he was certain they'd be dead or captured.

And he didn't want to find out what plans the Dark One had for him.

Or for the girl.

What significance was a girl with such a small piece of a guardian's magic in her? Why did the Dark One want to get to her so badly?

Could she somehow use Zoe to free herself from the prison they'd created centuries ago?

Or was it really like Parrish had said—that the Dark One just wanted to make her suffer?

They had to get to the island, because while he was sure he remembered more than the others, there were still gaps in his memory. He remembered, for example, that it was his job to reset their memories and their lifetimes in each cycle.

What he didn't remember was exactly how he did it or what role the fatalis stone and Tobias played in that cycle.

He yearned for those memories, because without them, he wasn't sure what the Dark One needed to do to go free. He was certain he'd been the one to come up with the original reincarnation spell. He'd thought it was impossible for the Dark One to ever cast magic again. He'd put in so many fail-safes to make sure they'd never be fighting this war again.

But he needed his full memory back to figure out what fail-safes were still in place and how they could defeat her now that she was gaining power.

Memories or not, she was definitely gaining strength. If she could truly take control of any human she'd awakened from the dead and speak through them with her own voice, she had to also be dangerously close to freedom.

This was never supposed to happen.

He shook the thought from his head and focused on his flight over the rooftops. He'd been right about being able to fly farther distances than before, but he couldn't fly indefinitely. He still needed to land every quarter mile or so to regain speed and momentum.

He'd been lucky to get over the Third Avenue Bridge into Manhattan, but ever since they'd crossed over to this part of the city, the number of rotters had grown even more dense than before.

These zombies had definitely not been up there several days ago when he'd first gone after Zoe at the Four Seasons. He had only encountered a handful at best that night, despite the fact that they were traveling during the worst time after dark.

Now, though, there were hundreds in the hottest part of the afternoon.

Each time he had to land, they had to fight against more and more rotters.

Zoe had no way to fight them, so he made sure she stayed behind him at all times.

He was actually a little smaller than Zoe, but he had played around with a few tricks here and there that came in handy against rotters on rooftops.

First, he could draw a strong wind together with his mind, even if there was hardly a breeze out. He could manipulate and control the air around him to create wind. He could also direct that strong wind wherever he chose, forcing it into one space like a gust of wind in a storm, or sending a steady, even stream.

With the zombies on these rooftops, he'd gotten pretty good at sending them over the edge of the buildings with a strong gust of wind. When there were too many all at once, though, he wasn't strong enough to move them all.

For this reason, he chose rooftops carefully.

He did his best to stay near Third Avenue, since he knew the other guardians were fighting their way north to meet up with him there, but lately, the rooftops on Third Avenue were the most crowded. If he landed there, they might end up trapped.

He had to be careful which direction he went, though, because if he got too close to Central Park, he'd run out of rooftops entirely. There were trees over that way, but since he'd never practiced flying between trees, he wasn't sure he could keep his balance with Zoe holding his hand.

"Watch out," she shouted.

He'd been looking for the next rooftop to land on, and he'd nearly missed a large antennae. He had to swerve around it, knocking them both off-balance. He needed to land and get his bearings back, or he was afraid he might fall.

He'd only managed to glide or fly through the air, because he was keeping the wind moving beneath them. If he lost focus, he might also lose the air stream. And losing it for even just a few seconds could mean death for both of them.

His heart raced as he aimed for a nearby rooftop with ten or so rotters in sight.

That was a lot, but he didn't have much choice at this point.

He needed a break to get his focus back. He'd allowed his mind to wander too much.

Besides, if they could reach out to Parrish and the others, they might be able to get an idea of how close they were to each other.

When he landed, he didn't have a second to waste. Several rotters lunged at them, and Zoe screamed, grabbing his shoulders and crouching behind him.

David sucked in a deep breath, imagining the air flowing into him. He pulled it back, almost like a slingshot, and then sent it out in a whoosh of air toward the zombies, putting everything he had into the motion.

They were so close to him, he hadn't had room to build up enough momentum to push them off the building.

This particular building was large and had a big area. There were lots of places up here for rotters to hide, too, and as the first group groaned and pushed against the gust of wind blowing them backward, five more appeared around the corner.

Crap. He didn't have enough power behind this to keep them back. Not when there were this many.

He had to try something different.

Frantically, he looked around, searching for anything he could use as a weapon.

The building they were on must have been an apartment building, because there on the far corner, he noticed a small greenhouse garden filled with potted plants both inside and out.

That would have to do. He took Zoe's hand so he could be sure she'd hear him.

Take cover.

He pointed toward a wooden bench nearby.

Climb under there and cover your face.

"What are you going to do?" she shouted back.

He pointed again, and she ran. He didn't have time to check that she'd followed his directions. There were too many zombies up here, and they were getting too close.

He moved his hands in a circular motion, compressing the air into a tight ball. With great concentration, he sent the ball of air flying toward the greenhouse, shattering the glass as he brought it through one window and then back again.

Then, he redirected the airflow, creating a kind of funnel that swirled up from the ground, picking up the shards of glass from the windows and some of the flowerpots.

He moved his hands faster, gathering momentum and power as he pulled the funnel of air through the line of rotters. The glass sliced through them, severing limbs and tossing them aside like ragdolls.

He repeated the motion, careful not to lose any power or

concentration as he sent his miniature tornado across the entire rooftop.

When every rotter in sight was decapitated or neutralized in some way, he released the funnel and fell to his knees, exhausted.

Zoe ran to his side, and he took her hand.

Are you okay?

She nodded, self-consciously tugging at the collar of her shirt. He saw a small cut there, but it didn't seem to be bleeding.

He sighed with relief.

They couldn't stay here long, because he had no doubt whoever had sent these zombies after them today would send more up the stairs here if they sat for more than a few minutes. But for now, they were okay.

He held Zoe's hand tighter and reached out to her sister with his mind.

His breath hitched in his chest as an intense wave of fear washed over him.

The others are in trouble.

"And here I thought this was a boring trip so far," Crash said, broadcasting his voice to the others through their earbuds.

"New York City never disappoints," Karmen said, winking at him.

"How are you holding up over there, Noah?" he asked.

He could hardly believe the guy was standing with the amount of blood he'd lost already.

"I'm good," Noah said, placing a frost-covered palm over the claw marks on his shoulder.

"Yeah, you look good," Crash said, wincing.

Would Noah be able to heal those scars? Or would he be forever marked by those talons?

There was no time to stand there and consider it. A new horde of rotters was headed their way, and Crash had no doubt the bird-like creatures would be back soon. Probably when they least expected it.

He made a mental note to keep his eye on the sky as he gathered lightning in his hands.

He was going to try something different this time, building on a technique he'd practiced at the beach house a few times. With David getting closer by the minute, Crash's power surged to new levels.

If he was possibly going to die today, he might as well have some fun before that happened.

As a test, he moved his hands back and forth in front of his body, nodding as he perfected the timing. With this type of motion, he could create a surge of electricity that worked like daggers, slicing through the air.

Now, to try shooting them.

He widened his stance and repeated the motion, this time sending the slicing motion forward, like he was throwing a dagger or a ninja star through the air.

The first few he sent sliced the shoulder off a rotter on the front lines. Not bad, but he needed to work on his aim.

"Whoa, what was that?" Parrish asked. She'd already reached the front row of rotters and sliced through them with a flash of blue light that separated a dozen heads from bodies.

He couldn't let her show him up like that.

Crash licked his lips and took a deep breath. "Just something new I'm trying," he said.

He set his sights on a group off to the far left, away from the rest of his group.

He breathed power into his hands, amplifying the energy sparking at his fingertips.

With rapid motions, he threw lightning daggers at the group, aiming for the head and not letting up until he'd unleashed a barrage of at least fifty. The magical daggers made a cracking sound like miniature lightning as they left his hands, and Crash whooped as they hit their marks, knocking one rotter after the other down to the ground.

Hell, this was more fun than a machine gun any day of the week.

He'd played video games his whole life and never dreamed he'd be some kind of superhero in reality, so despite the extreme danger and the threat of death at every turn, there was a part deep inside that was enjoying this.

"Don't get too cocky there, lightning-boy," Karmen said, knocking him down a peg. "We've got incoming."

He'd forgotten to look up until she said that, but now there wasn't a second to waste.

The bird-like women were back, claws stretched toward him. They were too close for him to send daggers at them, but just as the long, razor-like claws reached him, he had a sudden flash of memory.

It was like some ancient, buried part of him awakened at a moment of heightened focus and fear, and instinct took over.

He pushed both palms forward, creating a shield of pure light that crackled with a familiar web of electric energy.

The bird-woman shrieked and pulled back, her wings flapping frantically as her claws sparked. Still acting on instinct, Crash reared back and sent his lightning-disc toward the creature's underbelly. The disc sliced through the woman's wings, severing them from her body.

Crash pulled the hunting knife from his belt, gripping the hilt with both hands as he brought the thick, jagged blade down through the top of the woman's head.

Her eyes widened and then went dark.

He was about to let out another whoop of celebration until he looked up to see that the second bird-woman was headed straight for Karmen.

FORTY-THREE
KARMEN

Karmen locked eyes with the bird-like creature swooping toward her. She wanted inside that thing's mind, but it was locked down tight.

"Karmen, move. I've got this," Crash shouted, lifting some kind of lightning disc into the air.

"Leave it," she said. "I can do it. Help the others."

He hesitated, but she knew what she was doing.

"Go," she said.

Crash ran off to join Parrish and Noah on the front lines of the horde, and Karmen's confidence wavered just a touch.

I'm insane.

But getting inside this thing's mind was a challenge for her now, and she wanted to figure it out.

Her Beast roared and ran toward her, which was a surprise. She hadn't given it any instructions to keep her safe, but it seemed to have a natural instinct to want to protect her. Good to know.

She told him to stand down and focused all of her energy on the winged-woman above.

Searching the woman's mind was like searching for a keyhole. If she could just find it, she could unlock the woman's brain and command her the same way she'd taken hold of the Beast at her side.

But where was it?

Dammit, this thing was getting too close. She needed to crack this, but she was rapidly running out of time.

"Karmen, watch out."

"Leave me alone," she shouted, anger bubbling up inside of her. Not that she was really angry at Crash for wanting to help, but she was angry and frustrated at her lack of skill with this woman.

She knew she could do it, and the whole group needed for her to be able to turn these super zombies over to their side, but she was failing.

As she embraced her anger, though, orange flames broke out across her arm and hands. She forced her emotions into that flame, and it flared.

Okay, new plan. If she couldn't turn this thing's mind, she'd light it up and see if she could get it to turn around. She needed to buy herself more time.

Raising her hand in front of her, she blew out, sending a stream of flames out in front of her like a flame-thrower. The flame widened as she poured her anger and determination into it, and the bird-woman flapped her wings harder, flying backward away from the flames.

"Yes," Karmen shouted, laughing as the woman flew higher and then circled back around.

This time, Karmen kept contact with her flames as she focused on the woman's mind, searching again for the keyhole.

"Cutting it close there, Barbie," Crash said.

"I told you never to call me that again," she said, letting her annoyance at the nickname fuel her rage.

She locked eyes with the flying woman, forcing herself into the thing's mind. She didn't need a keyhole. She needed a crowbar.

But the moment she connected with the woman's thoughts, it wasn't the Dark One she heard in her head.

It was Lily.

The fifth was on the move again. The witch tracked his energy signature to about six blocks away when he'd suddenly stopped. She'd sensed a larger output from him for a few minutes, but then he'd started moving faster than ever.

He can sense the others fighting.

This wouldn't do.

She'd put all of this time and work into getting him to Central Park and into her trap, where he wouldn't be able to leap across rooftops anymore.

She couldn't have him heading back toward the others. That was the opposite direction of where she needed him to go right now, and if she wanted to keep her plan on track, she was going to have to think fast.

Luckily, she'd put a few barriers up between the fifth and his friends, just in case.

One of those barriers was hiding on a rooftop near where the fifth was jumping right about now.

The witch wasn't sure if she should make her way over there or stay put, but before she could make up her mind, something very strange happened.

A voice entered her head.

A familiar voice.

I know you're here. I've taken some of your toys away from you, and they're going to lead me right to you.

The witch stopped in her tracks, shaken by the invasion into her own thoughts.

She'd done the same thing to other people plenty of times, even watching their dreams or listening to their thoughts, but she'd never had anyone besides the Dark One do it to her.

It was an unsettling feeling, hearing the voice of someone you couldn't see in your head like that. Knowing from their tone just how badly they wanted revenge.

What surprised her most, though, was how much it stung to hear Karmen's voice dripping with such disdain. It wasn't like she'd been the easiest person to get to know in the first place, and she had a tendency to sound snarky or rude, but the witch had liked Karmen.

Maybe her most of all.

They were very similar in their powers, which was something that usually bonded witches in her world. Witches of the same elemental side who shared core abilities were often like sisters back home, and the witch had longed to have someone close to her to discuss spells with and share secrets.

Of course, back there, the witch had barely even known what she was capable of herself. She knew she possessed some fire abilities, but she'd had no idea she could track. She'd used it instinctually when she tracked Tobias through the forest that fateful night, but that was the first time she could ever remember following someone and just knowing where they were headed. Sensing their power.

The coercion abilities were fun, though. The ability to see into people's minds and twist them to her will.

Karmen enjoyed it, too, and the witch had no doubt that they could have been good friends under different circumstances.

But now, they were on different sides, and she would destroy Karmen if she had to.

I know you can hear me, whether you want to respond or not. I will find you, Karmen said.

The witch smiled and shook her head. Maybe a slight change of plans was in order.

Not if I find you first.

P arrish's mouth dropped open in shock as the bird-like creature who'd attacked her earlier swooped across the crowd of rotters, slashing them with her sharp talons.

For a split second, she'd thought that thing was coming for her when it flew over her shoulder, but now it was clear what had happened.

"Good job, Karmen," she said. "I take back every mean thing I ever said about you."

"Wow, that's years' worth of stuff, I bet," Karmen said.

"Eh, only if you count everything I wrote in my diary about you," Parrish said with a laugh as she continued working her way through what was left of the horde.

"Oh, I bet I know who you wrote about the most. Dear diary, I have the biggest crush on the hot guy who lives across the street," Karmen said.

Parrish's face warmed, and she glanced over at Noah.

He was holding back a smile, and when he winked at her, she could hardly believe this was real life.

After all these years of dreaming, she was finally hanging out with him on a daily basis, and instead of lying in the grass holding his hand and talking about the future, they were fighting their way through a horde of zombies in downtown Manhattan, both covered in blood and guts.

She winced as she studied his face. That did not look good at all.

"Hey, Noah, how are you feeling?" she asked, sliding her blade through the neck of a woman in jogging gear. She'd still been wearing a pair of fancy headphones with an iPhone strapped to her arm.

"I'm feeling a little woozy, to be honest," he said, bringing his bat down on another rotter's skull.

Something deep down turned in her stomach.

Was it possible he could get infected from taking on one of their injuries? He'd discovered a while back that his skin was hardened against zombie attacks or any kind of cuts and stuff, but when he shielded them, he got at least some of their injuries.

So the question was whether or not those bird-women had any of the virus in their talons.

Parrish's mouth went dry just thinking about it, and as she stared at the sea of rotters still heading toward them, she wasn't sure she had the patience to deal with all of them.

She needed to check on Noah a little more closely. See if he was showing any signs of infection.

And if he is, what do I think I'm going to do about it?

She didn't have an answer to that, but she needed to know.

They needed to make faster work of these zombies, and she was about to tell her friends that when Karmen's voice interrupted her thoughts.

"Um, guys? I might have done something really stupid," she said.

"Oh, well, I guess there's a millionth time for everything," Parrish said.

"Haha, very funny."

"What did you do?" Noah asked.

"I reached out to Lily and kind of threatened her, so I think she's coming for us," Karmen said. "So, we might want to make quick work of this horde and figure out a plan for facing her."

"You did what?" Parrish asked. "How?"

Karmen explained it as though she'd simply tuned into the frequency of Lily's mind and reached out to her.

Parrish rolled her eyes. Great. That was just what they needed right now.

But hey, if that meant Lily was looking for them instead of Zoe, she was okay with that. They were bound to have to face her at some point, anyway.

Parrish still wasn't sure why Lily had decided to help them back at the hospital, or what she would do when they met up again, but she guessed they were about to find out.

"Okay, let's do this," she said. "Give it all you've got, and then we'll slide into one of these buildings and take a break to make a plan."

The four of them lined up side-by-side in front of the oncoming horde while Beast and BirdWoman watched their back, cleaning up any rotters who dared attack from behind.

Parrish smiled. Time to show off what they could really do.

So far today, she'd been mostly going back and forth between her fire and ice abilities, practicing the switch between. For the most part, changing from one to the other was a pretty clumsy process for her. It was like trying to do math with someone shouting random numbers in her ear.

Focus was the main issue, but once she got into the rhythm of the new ability, she was getting better at controlling it.

Like now, for example. She sheathed her katana and allowed a cold chill to crawl through her. It took a moment for her to embrace the ice side of her energy, but when she connected to it, her hands glowed with a bright blue light.

She blew air across her lips and smiled as the air came out like a cold fog that crackled in the heat.

Reaching forward, she pressed her icy hand on the forehead of a rotter who lunged toward her, its mouth open. Frost travelled quickly down its decaying body, freezing its jaw in place.

She pushed her power just a little and the rotter's entire body froze to the spot.

But she wanted to see just how far she could take this, and how easily she could switch from ice to flame when she needed to.

She inhaled, drawing as much breath as she could hold. When she exhaled, she turned her head from side to side, sending a cloud of white snow and ice in an arch in front of her body.

Whoa.

She'd frozen at least fifteen zombies in place.

Noah caught on to what she was doing with the ice and contributed his own power to hers. At first, they combined efforts to freeze another row about twenty deep on Noah's side.

Unlike before, when she and Karmen and Crash had all touched skin to amplify their power, Parrish and Noah were able to boost each other's spells just by focusing together as one.

She wasn't sure if it was due to the fact that they'd become so close in so many ways over the past couple of months, or if it had something to do with the fact that they were using the ice element side of their power, but either way, she could feel his energy infusing with hers.

With every second, her power grew stronger alongside him. She reached deeper, pushed harder, and together, they sent a wave out over the horde, encasing them all in a harsh blue coating of pure ice.

"Whoa," Crash whispered, stepping back as every rotter in the area ceased to move.

But their awe and excitement was short-lived as a blast of heat rolled back toward them in a widening rush of pure flame.

The frozen horde disintegrated into ash, and in her fear, Parrish reached for the second half of her power. For the first time since she'd gotten to New York, she managed to access both sides of her abilities, tapping into the combined power she'd only just discovered back at the beach house by accident.

Back then, she'd wondered if it was some kind of fluke. Something she'd done but could never replicate or understand.

Now, though, she was sure it was a skill she had the innate ability to use, which meant that some part of her, deep down and still buried within a series of trapped memories, still knew how to use it.

She gave herself over to that subconscious part of her own

mind, and everything slowed to a crawl. Time was suddenly hers to control, and in that moment, a memory took hold.

Parrish, standing in a field of flames, her face bloodied and burned on one side. A woman with dark hair stood on the other side of a raging fire, a purple glow surrounding her form.

In her mind, she saw herself clap her hands together, a purple orb forming between her hands as she brought them apart. With a thrust of forward motion, she sent the purple orb toward the woman in the flames just as another blast of fire came toward her.

The fire moved in slow motion, and this ancient version of Parrish threw up a wall of ice to shield herself.

She snapped back to the present and repeated the motion, creating a wall of ice that protected her and her friends from the flames.

She continued to pour her energy into the ice wall until the fire on the other side subsided. The ice quickly melted onto the asphalt, combining with the ashes of the dead.

Parrish's heart raced as her combined power slipped away from her and time sped back up to normal.

She'd managed to use it this time, but she wasn't strong enough yet to hold onto it for very long.

And from the looks of the fresh horde approaching them from all sides, she was going to need it.

Up ahead, flames dancing on her fingertips, a woman stepped forward.

Black hair. Pale skin. Parrish recognized her instantly, despite the distance between them.

Lily.

Parrish was glad to see her, because if Lily was there with

them, it meant Zoe and David were still okay. She hadn't gotten to them yet.

Parrish raised her sword, eager for the chance to put an end to this, once and for all.

Fate was pulling them forward, unrelenting, and all they could do was surrender to it now.

T he intensity of emotion was almost more than the boy could handle.

He was so close to them now, the fear and hope his friends felt was almost a part of him. It echoed in his own heart, and he longed to be with them. Coming back to them was like coming home after a lifetime away.

He had to get to them before it was too late.

He couldn't remember what would happen if one of the other guardians died, but he had a feeling it would mean the end of hope.

I can't let them die. We have to see this through.

They needed to get to the island and put a stop to all of this.

And they were so close now. Just a little farther, and they would be reunited. With their full powers restored, the Dark One would be unable to defeat them as long as she was still trapped beneath the earth.

These basic rotters would become trivial. Almost nothing would be a threat anymore, short of facing the Dark One herself.

Hold on tight, he said to Zoe.

She gripped his arm tighter and nodded.

He jumped off the edge of the building and caught a stream of air, moving it beneath them so that it lifted them both higher. To propel them faster, he also wove a stream of air behind them, using the same technique he'd used with the miniature tornado earlier.

It was more effective than he'd expected, and they shot forward. Zoe clung to him, burying her head against his shoulder.

He'd been heading in the direction of Central Park, hoping to avoid too many rotters on the rooftops, but now they'd switched directions and were on their way back toward Third Avenue.

Maybe ten more blocks, and he should see them. Seven. Six.

He pushed himself faster, gathering more air beneath them.

The second he crossed over the trap, though, he understood just how stupid he'd been. He was a strategist, after all. He should have known he was being drawn toward something this whole time.

He and Zoe both fell from the sky as the wind was sucked out from under him.

He barely had time to summon a fresh stream of air to cushion their fall, but he managed it just at the last second.

Startled, Zoe blinked and looked around at the empty rooftop where they'd fallen.

"What happened?" she asked. "Where's Parrish?"

He shook his head, still trying to make sense of it in his mind.

He touched her arm.

Something pulled us down. A trap, I think. Be careful.

Zoe's eyes widened and she looked around, scrambling back against a wall near the door to the stairwell.

David stood, surveying the area and trying to figure out what exactly had been triggered that could make him simply fall from the sky.

"Do you see anything?" Zoe asked, and he shook his head.

Not yet. But he could feel it.

Some new energy drowned out the guardians. Something dangerous.

Something close.

To be careful, he conjured a sphere made of air, gradually enlarging it until it was big enough to cover him and Zoe from the front. It wasn't quite as effective as a full shield, but it would keep them safe from a surprise attack.

His ability to control and manipulate air the way he did was a bit unusual in his homeland. Technically, he was born with power from the ice elemental side, like Noah. But he'd always been able to manipulate air better than ice or water the way most of the iceborn did.

In all of his years, he'd only known a handful of people in his world who'd had a similar type of power to his.

When he wanted to, he could conjure a layer of ice on the outside of a sphere of air like the one he had now, but those types of shields were more difficult to see through, and he had a feeling he was going to need his eyes.

"Do you hear that?" Zoe whispered.

It was a high-pitched kind of sound. Something faint, at first, that would never have been noticed on a normal New York City day with cars passing on the streets below.

But in the dead quiet of the afternoon, he heard it approaching like a hum.

And then a roar.

He realized too late that the sound was coming from inside the building.

His shield of air had been designed to protect them against an attack from the front. When the group of zombies pushed against the door behind them, it flung both him and Zoe across the roof.

Thinking fast, he was able to send a quick cushion of air toward Zoe so that she landed softly, but there was nothing he could do for himself. He grunted as the wind got knocked from his lungs and his head banged against the side of a metal pipe.

Zoe scrambled toward him, grabbing his hand and attempting to pull him backward as five zombies stepped out of the building, their mouths snapping hungrily as some kind of green acid dripped from their teeth.

"What's wrong with them?" Zoe asked.

A strange question, considering there was something very wrong with the entire world right now. But she was right that there was something particularly wrong with these.

It was the first time he'd actually encountered zombies with special abilities, like Parrish and Crash had talked to him about. Super zombies, they called them. He'd been hoping they wouldn't face any up here on the rooftops, but he was the one who'd been dumb enough to trigger the trap.

The five super zombies in front of them now seemed to

move as one, and David realized the high-pitched humming sound was actually coming from their throats.

He gathered a ball of compressed air between his palms and hurled it forward, hitting the zombie in the middle with a direct blow. A hit that hard should have knocked it backward or blown a hole straight through its chest, but it barely fazed this one.

The group continued to move forward, their red, glowing eyes locked on his face.

He was going to have to try something new with these. If they moved as one, maybe he'd have to hit them all at the same time to do any damage to them.

He stood and pushed Zoe out of the way to give himself some room. He only had seconds to perform the move before the rotters would be too close to build momentum, but he had to try.

He'd done this move before, he was sure of it. Maybe not in this lifetime, but it was familiar enough to his soul.

He jumped into the air and spun around, sweeping his leg through the air as he kicked a steady, compressed formation of air toward the group. They flew backward, their backs hitting the brick wall behind in unison.

David repeated the move, this time focusing the kick toward the heads of the rotters. He was hoping maybe the force of his kick would be strong enough to incapacitate them completely, but even with him putting everything he had behind it, the kick only seemed to disorient them.

They recovered quickly and started heading toward him again.

He wasn't sure he had enough experience with this kind of

offensive magic to survive against these kinds of zombies for long. He'd always been more of a behind-the-scenes guy in battle, rarely ever taking to a fight alone.

He could hold his own for a while, but he really needed to focus on getting back to the rest of the group. Once the guardians were all together, it would make all the difference.

The two of them couldn't afford to get stuck up here fighting for a long time. It was too dangerous, because there could be more of these things on their way. It would also be difficult for Parrish and the others to reach them up here. They'd have to make their way through the whole building, which would be extremely dangerous.

He had to keep moving.

He gathered all of his strength and tried the move one final time, spinning twice in the air and on the final turn, kicking his leg forward. A wall of compressed air spun toward the five rotters, this time knocking them completely to the ground.

He took Zoe's hand.

We need to get out of here.

She nodded, holding tightly to his arm.

He swirled his hands in front of them, creating a sphere of air around them like a shield, this time careful to cover all sides like a bubble. He ran forward, catching a gust of wind as he jumped to the nearest rooftop.

He wasn't sure how far the trap that had pulled them down originally extended, but he wanted to be careful not to fall again.

The problem, though, was that the rooftops were now teeming with undead. Just minutes ago, they'd been relatively clear, but whoever was tracking them knew he was close to rejoining with his friends.

As they flew through the air, he could see that the path between him and the guardians was now completely blocked.

Red eyes glowed from crowds of zombies that pressed together, arm to arm on top of the buildings. There wasn't a single place to land, even if he'd wanted to.

He shook his head, seeing now what he'd failed to see before.

He'd been guided this entire time. Ever since he'd first fled his old apartment with Zoe by his side, the witch tracking them had been leading him toward the same location.

Central Park.

He didn't think this was the work of the Dark One, though. This was that witch the others had told him about. Lily.

They'd told him not to underestimate her, but he had. Despite his knowledge and experience, he'd failed to see the patterns. She'd been placing rotters on rooftops, knowing he'd avoid them at all costs, even if it meant going out of his way.

She'd wanted him to fly toward the park and away from the rest of the group. And when he'd changed direction, she'd grounded him and forced his hand.

So, where was she now?

Waiting for him at the end of the path?

He couldn't be sure, but as he looked across the crowded rooftops, he realized he had only two choices. He could follow her trail and face her head on, hoping the other guardians would be able to reach him before she captured him.

Or he could turn around and head back toward the Bronx, undoing all of his work and taking them right back to where they started and away from the guardians.

At this rate, if he turned around, he might not be able to get this close to them again for days. The witch could track him, so she'd know where he went and try to box him in anyway.

Besides, there could already be traps back the way he came. She would have anticipated that he might turn back if things got too hard.

No, the only way out of this was to face her head on and warn the guardians about what was happening.

We need help, he told them, broadcasting his anticipated location to the other guardians and praying they could win whatever battle they were facing before it was too late. *Can you hear me, Parrish?*

It took a long time for her to respond, but when she finally did, David nearly cried in relief.

Where are you? Parrish asked. *We're in a bit of a tricky spot ourselves. Can you get somewhere safe and wait for us?*

Exhausted, he landed on a rooftop near the park where there were very few rotters to be seen. For a moment, he had a glimmer of hope that they'd be able to hide out here and rest for a few minutes.

I think so, he told her.

Carefully, he walked to the edge of the rooftop in a crouch and looked down on Fifth Avenue.

There, standing on the steps of the Metropolitan Museum of Art, was a woman with pale skin and a long, black dress that trailed after her in the wind.

Her eyes snapped up toward his, and she smiled.

David gasped, his stomach twisting at the sight of her.

He was finally face-to-face with the witch they'd warned him about, but when he tried to reach out to Parrish again to tell her, his brain erupted in static.

Was Lily doing this to him?

He wasn't sure, but no matter how hard he tried, he couldn't reach Parrish now.

They were on their own against the most dangerous witch in the city.

G oing after Karmen and the others had been so tempting, but the witch had not come here for them.

Instead, she'd sent one of her many pets out to greet them, knowing this one would keep them occupied for a little while. At least, the witch hoped her decoy looked enough like her at a distance to make them all believe they were facing their old friend.

It had taken her all night to find a human who could pass for a twin, but it had been worth it.

The question was whether they'd be reluctant to kill someone they'd once cared about, or if they'd be eager to get revenge.

Either way, the fake witch would be a nice distraction while she captured the fifth and the little girl.

These next few minutes were critical to her plans for the future. One wrong move and the Dark One would be done with her forever.

The witch couldn't bear the thought of disappointing the Dark One again. Love and adoration welled up inside her, and she was flooded with the confidence that someday, she would return to their home world as a champion, revered by many and feared by all.

She'd longed for that kind of recognition and respect her entire life, and she was so close to it now, she could feel it the way she could feel the warmth of the sun on her face.

With that kind of power, she could change the world. She could make sure that no child ever grew up the way she had, unloved and tossed aside. Treated like a nobody, undeserving even of a name.

With that kind of power, she could have anything she wanted.

She just had to do this one last thing. Infect the fifth and capture the girl.

He'd triggered her trap on top of the building a few blocks away, and soon, her pets would steer him this way. She was sure of it.

She needed to get him away from the buildings, and then he would belong to her. She imagined the look of pride and excitement on the Dark One's face when she handed him over.

Maybe she'd let her keep the child as a reward.

Parrish wouldn't like that at all, but once the Dark One had control and was free again, it wouldn't matter what Parrish wanted. Besides, the witch would keep the little girl safe. She'd make her just as happy as any sister could.

She would protect her in a way Parrish never could.

Something snapped the witch out of her daydream, and she looked up, catching the eyes of a human looking out over the top of the building. She couldn't see him from here. He was up incredibly high.

But she could feel his eyes on hers.

She smiled. She'd been waiting for this moment her whole life. A chance to finally prove herself and claim her prize.

In her mind, she reached out to the rotters she'd stationed there on the roof. They'd been hiding there for hours, just waiting for the fifth to fall into her trap.

A young girl screamed, and even at this distance, the sound rang out in the relative silence of the dead city.

Don't hurt them. Just bring them to me.

Excitement hummed through her entire body. She could hardly stand to wait down here, and she wished she'd joined her pets on the rooftop, instead.

But she knew her plan was a good one. Get him to the ground, lure him into the park where more of her special pets were waiting for him. A single bite was all it would take.

She absently ran a hand across her arm, as if checking to make sure her skin was still smooth and beautiful. She'd gotten used to the textured feel of her scarred skin, but today, there wasn't a mark on her.

She planned to keep it that way.

The witch looked up, impatience stirring in her heart. What was taking them so long? Her pets should have grabbed them both by now and dragged them down here. She'd given them wings for a reason.

But instead of her beloved pets, she saw a cone of air rise high into the sky above the tall building.

She tightened her jaw. The fifth had reacted faster than expected, but it was okay. She had a backup plan to force him down here.

The witch closed her eyes and summoned a pack of dogs she'd stationed inside the building. It was amazing how many humans had died inside some of these buildings. They'd all just been trapped inside their apartments and offices for weeks, rambling around mindlessly until she'd come along to turn them into something new.

These days, she didn't even need to be near them to turn them into her special pets, the way she'd needed to that first night in D.C. when she'd met the guardians. Over time, she'd taught herself to cast the spell and turn them with nothing but her mind's powers.

A gift from the Dark One to be able to reach inside these undead humans and create whatever she wanted out of them.

That was real power.

Who cared that she'd had to pay such a high price for it?

She shuddered at the memories and pushed them deeper. She wouldn't think of that now. She had a job to do, and it was almost done.

She gave the dogs the attack order, but only moments later, she gasped as their bodies flew off the rooftop and crashed onto the pavement below. She closed her eyes, not wanting to see what the fifth had done to the poor creatures. They'd barely even had a chance to serve her.

She was going to have to take matters into her own hands. There was no more time to waste. She couldn't allow Parrish and the others time to make their way here, so it was now or never.

As long as she could feel her decoy fighting, she knew she was safe from any attack from Parrish or the others, but how long would that horde keep them away? She needed to move quickly.

The fifth would be hers, and nothing could keep her from her goal.

The witch summoned a ring of fire in the air in front of her. It started small, only about as big as her own torso and thin like a hoop.

She poured her power into it until it burned so hot the red flames turned almost white with heat. When she was sure it was as hot as she could make it, she pulled back and rolled it toward the building, turning it faster and faster. As it rolled, it grew taller, too, until it was maybe seven or eight stories high and so hot, it melted a hole in the asphalt.

With a push, she shoved the ring into the building, expanding the flame until it consumed the first fifteen to twenty floors in a brilliant white light that made the air surrounding it wave.

The witch breathed in, and then, with a final upward thrust, sent the flames toward the rooftop and waited.

The fifth would have two choices.

Burn or flee.

And by now, the buildings surrounding him had no place left for him to land. She'd sent rotters up there in large swarms to fill every available inch of space.

She had him now, she was sure of it.

When he jumped from the rooftop, he was nothing more than a speck, really. A small sphere of air, covered in frost to protect them from the flames.

As he grew closer, though, the witch's heart raced and she could hardly keep herself from laughing with excitement.

He'd fallen right into her hands, and there was no one here to save him now.

She stepped forward, conjuring more white-hot flames as

she moved, sending them out in every direction in order to box him in as he landed on a cushioned bed of compressed air.

Her mouth went dry in anticipation as she sent a final wave of fire rushing toward the sphere.

But as the ice encasing the sphere melted and the two figures inside appeared, the witch dropped her hands to her side in surprise, taken aback by the innocence of it all.

She'd never expected this, and for just a moment, the shock brought her to her senses.

The fifth was just a child, his dark eyes tugging at a piece of her soul she'd locked away a long time ago.

I can't hurt a child, she thought.

The voice that responded was not her own, but it was in her mind.

The voice of the Dark One.

You can, and you will. He is only a child in this lifetime. He is more ancient and cunning than you could imagine.

As the Dark One spoke, the witch could feel her trying to regain control.

How could she have been so easily manipulated? She hadn't even been in control of her own mind these past few days.

The Dark One had somehow taken her over, forcing her thoughts toward loyalty and revenge. Toward hatred and power, at whatever cost necessary.

But this.

This was too much to ask.

She could not hurt this child.

Infect him now, the Dark One said with a hiss. *End him now, or I swear you will suffer worse than before. I'll make you suffer for lifetimes, if I have to. You belong to me, witch. You have since the moment you stepped through that portal to this world.*

A tear fell down her cheek as she struggled to hold back the Dark One's control.

My name is Lily, she said, placing both palms against her temples, forcing the Dark One out of her head.

With a deep breath, she reached out to the one person she knew she could count on to hear.

FORTY-EIGHT
KARMEN

The fight against Lily and her minions was unrelenting, and Karmen wasn't sure how much longer she could hold out. She was convinced the only reason she'd made it this far was because of how close they were to David's energy.

She kept hoping they'd see him descend from the sky any minute now, but Parrish had said she'd had contact with him and told him to stay put until they got through this horde.

Karmen had managed to tap into the minds of four additional super zombies so far, bringing her total to six. She didn't think she could handle more than that right now. Not at this level of exhaustion. She was afraid taking even one more into her control would make her lose all of them.

Besides, she was also still having to cast her fire magic and hold as many of the regular zombies back as best she could, so their whole group wasn't overrun.

She had actually tried tapping into Lily's mind again, just to mess with her and try to distract her from the fight, but each time she focused on the woman inside the flames just ahead, she got no response. Only a strange type of static, as if she was tuned to the wrong station or something.

But then suddenly, out of nowhere, Lily's voice sounded in Karmen's brain, as if she'd tapped into the earbuds Crash had given them.

It was so clear and distinct, Karmen actually wondered if everyone could hear her, too.

"*Karmen, I don't have much time. I need you to listen to me,*" Lily said.

She shook her head, unable to pair the desperate tone of Lily's voice with the confident witch at the end of the street sending a nonstop barrage of rotters their way.

How about you let up on the attack and we can have a nice, little chat, then?

"*I know the woman you're fighting looks like me, but she's just a decoy,*" Lily said. "*I sent her to distract you so that I could capture the fifth and Parrish's sister. They're here with me now, and the Dark One wants me to kill the boy.*"

Karmen wasn't sure how to react. She couldn't get her mind around what she was hearing. Was this some kind of trap?

"*You have to listen to me,*" Lily said, her voice filled with pain and sorrow so deep it resonated inside Karmen's heart in ways she wasn't expecting. "*I don't have much time before she takes my mind again, and I'm afraid this time, I won't ever recover. You have to send Parrish. Tell her if she ever wants to see her sister alive again, she has to come now.*"

Karmen stood still in the middle of the battle there on 79th Street, knowing she had one of the most important decisions of her life to make right now.

Did she send Parrish away and risk sending her into a trap? Or did she ignore Lily and keep fighting, possibly only to risk Zoe and David's lives if she was telling the truth?

In the end, it wasn't a decision she could make on her own.

"Guys, we have a problem," she said. "Pull tight to me for a second."

"We're kind of in the middle of something here," Parrish said, sending another blast of flames toward the horde.

"Zoe's possibly going to die if you don't listen to me right now," Karmen said, knowing that if that didn't stop Parrish in her tracks, nothing would. "Now, come to me."

The others let off whatever magic they'd had building up, and then ran toward her. Karmen connected all six of her new pets in a web of thought and sent a single directive out to all of them.

Circle around us and protect us, no matter what.

Her pets did as they were told, closing the gaps so that their small group of four could huddle inside.

"What's going on?" Crash asked.

Karmen explained Lily's message as quickly as she could.

"I can't make this call on my own, but from the tone of her voice, I don't think we have much time," Karmen said. "She made it sound like the Dark One has had control of her mind this whole time."

"And you believe her?" Noah asked.

Karmen bit her lip. "I do. I know it's crazy, and it's a huge risk. But yeah. I think she sounded sincere."

"We can't trust her," Parrish said, but there was panic in her expression.

One wrong choice, and her sister could be lost to her forever. Karmen didn't want to be the one responsible for that.

Crash grabbed Parrish's arm, his eyes wide.

"Go," he said, the absolute certainty in his voice drawing out goosebumps on Karmen's flesh. "I dreamed all of this, the night after the hospital. Us fighting Lily, and then Lily capturing your sister and David. I didn't tell you, because I thought it meant we were going to lose. I thought it meant we died at Lily's hand and then she captured the others. I never even dreamed of the possibility that she could be in two places at once."

"Go," Noah said. "We'll be right behind you."

Parrish didn't hesitate.

She reached inside the collar of her shirt and grabbed hold of the fatalis stone. She placed her thumb on the spiral symbol as a glowing purple light formed around her entire body.

"Come find me," she said.

Then, with a flash, she disappeared.

FORTY-NINE
PARRISH

Parrish disappeared into a darkness so complete, she saw and felt nothing.

When she emerged from that darkness, her feet landed on a sidewalk several blocks away. The jarring change nearly took her breath away. She blinked through watery eyes and sucked in a breath as the face of the friend who'd betrayed them all just a few short days ago came into view.

She had no idea how she'd known to touch the symbol, or how she'd teleported herself to his location, but she could feel the surge of power at her back.

One glance behind her brought fresh tears to her eyes. Zoe and David huddled together near the ground, a tower of flames burning across the street behind them. Zoe's eyes widened, and Parrish wanted nothing more than to grab her sister in her arms and kiss her face, but there was still one final battle to fight.

She straightened and pulled her sword from its sheath, the twin flames of fire and ice dancing across the blade.

"I won't let you hurt her," she said, expecting a fight or a trick of some kind.

Instead, Lily fell to her knees, tears streaming down her face.

"I was so afraid you wouldn't come," she said. "You have to hurry before she takes control. I can't hold her back much longer."

Confused, Parrish stared ahead, unsure what Lily wanted her to do.

"I hope you can understand," Lily said, pressing her fingertips hard against her temples. "This is not what I wanted. This isn't who I am, but the second I stepped into this world, she was here in my head. Telling me what to do. I couldn't stop myself."

Lily cried out in pain, and Parrish took a step back, unsure what to do next.

"All I ever wanted was to be loved, the way you love Zoe," Lily continued. "I wanted my life to matter to someone."

Lily doubled over, as if in agony.

"I'm so sorry, Parrish," she said through gritted teeth. "I can't hold her back. You have to do it quickly."

Parrish shook her head, not wanting it to end like this. If Lily was telling the truth, none of this was her fault. She'd been manipulated by the Dark One's power this whole time.

It all made sense, though. The way she'd told her about the Dark One's plans, let her know Zoe was still alive, given her the stone. The way she's saved Zoe's life today, when she could have killed both her and David with a flick of her wrist just now.

Everything Lily had done was because of the Dark One.

"There has to be a way to save you," Parrish said. "If we

can get Karmen over here, maybe she could shield your mind the way she shielded Crash's dreams. We can still fix this."

Lily's mouth opened in surprise, and she lifted her eyes to meet Parrish's.

"Thank you," she said. "Thank you for giving me a name and for being my friend. It has meant more to me than you will ever know. But I'm out of time, Parrish. Please, let me do this one thing to make my life meaningful. Let me die while I'm still here to remember."

Parrish shook her head. She didn't want to kill her. Not like this.

But Lily cried out again, and this time, as she looked up, her eyes took on the hint of a glow. A dark, purple glow Parrish recognized from the rotter she'd faced back at the compound.

The Dark One was taking over, and there was no time to stop her.

"I'm sorry," she whispered.

She plunged her sword deep into Lily's chest, putting an end to her life.

FIFTY

PARRISH

"Parrish, is that really you?"

Parrish turned and ran toward her sister, her legs nearly giving out from exhaustion but her heart pushing her forward.

"Zoe," she screamed, stretching out her arms.

Zoe's face was dirty and stained with tears. Her clothes streaked with blood.

But it was her. It was really her.

Parrish fell to her knees and gathered her baby sister in her arms, sobs shaking her body. After all this time, she had finally found her.

"I thought I'd never see you again," she said, running her hand down the back of Zoe's hair and kissing her forehead. "I missed you so much. I love you."

"I love you, too," Zoe said, smiling through her tears.

"I was so scared you didn't know just how much you meant to me," Parrish said. "I never got the chance to let you know how much I loved you when you left."

Zoe shook her head. "I've always known," she said. "I was so scared, though, Parrish. I can hardly remember how scared. I thought I was going to die up there in that room."

She scratched at her arm, and Parrish stood, looking her sister over to make sure she was really okay. It had seemed so impossible that this moment would ever come, and now that it was here, it didn't feel real.

"Are you okay?" Parrish asked. "You're not hurt?"

She just wanted to hold her sister close and never let go. She was never going to let this little girl out of her sight again. To see that she was here and she really was okay made all of the struggle worth it.

"David took care of me," Zoe said, reaching for Parrish's hand. "Come on, I'll introduce you to him."

Parrish smiled and wiped the tears from her eyes.

David was even younger than Parrish had realized. Smaller than Zoe, he couldn't have been older than eight or nine years old, but his eyes held the wisdom of his years.

"Hi, David," she said.

The boy looked up at her and smiled. *"Hi,"* he said. His voice was as clear in her head as if he'd spoken out loud. *"I've missed you."*

He glanced around, frowning at Lily's lifeless body and shaking his head.

"Where are the others?"

Parrish gasped. She'd forgotten they were still back there fighting that horde and the decoy zombie.

"We need to get back to them," she said. "Here, take my hand."

They both grabbed onto her, and she used the fatalis stone again to teleport the group back to the fight.

"Hell, yes," Crash shouted when they appeared.

Hell, yes, was right.

The moment Parrish touched down, her entire body lit up with power, as if someone had finally turned on the lights in a dark room. If they thought they'd known power before this, it was nothing compared to what it was now that the five of them were together.

"Welcome back, old friend," Noah said, nodding at David.

"We've missed you," Karmen said.

Parrish lifted her sword into the air and smiled at the zombie horde that remained.

This wouldn't take long.

"Shall we?" she asked. "Zoe, stay by me. Everyone else? Let's end this."

"Where do we go from here?"

Parrish grabbed Zoe's hand and pulled her close, making Zoe want to cry in relief. She still could hardly believe her sister had come all this way to save her.

All those nights alone in the hotel room, she'd dreamed of this day, but she'd never really thought it was possible.

"We should find a safe place inside to talk through our next moves," Crash said, looking up toward the darkening sky as the sun began its descent. "We don't have much daylight left, and we're all too exhausted to keep fighting tonight."

"Noah's bleeding," Zoe said.

"She's right. Those bird women really did a number on you, huh?" Parrish ran a finger across Noah's cheek, and from the look of tenderness he gave her, Zoe was pretty sure her sister's secret crush wasn't such a big secret anymore.

She hid a smile against her shoulder, not wanting Parrish to see her blush.

"Besides, I'm anxious to get inside somewhere and make sure Zoe's okay."

Zoe frowned. "I'm fine now," she said.

"Well, I want to be sure for myself," Parrish said, squeezing her hand.

"What's a good spot?" Noah asked, looking to David for his opinion.

The boy pointed to the building across the street.

Apartments. Rest. Then, when we're feeling ready, we'll go to the island together.

"Do you know where it is?" Parrish asked.

"What island?" Zoe asked, though she had some faint memory of an island.

Didn't she?

David smiled.

Not much time now, he said. *I will lead you all there soon.*

The warmth of excitement spread up Zoe's cheeks. Yes, there was something exciting about this island, even if she couldn't quite remember what it was. Some part of her had been looking forward to that for a long time.

Together, their group settled in an apartment close to the first floor, and Karmen whistled as they entered the foyer.

"Well, we're sure getting our fair share of luxury this week," she said. "What do you think a place like this goes for?"

"Nothing, anymore," Crash said, and Karmen slapped his arm playfully.

"You know what I mean."

"Ten million?" Parrish said with a shrug. "I honestly have no idea, but if it's safe, it's priceless. Let's check the place for stragglers and block the doors."

Zoe sat on the couch as the others checked the apartment

and set up their computers and other tech. Karmen had this huge zombie man with her that she kept calling Beast, and when he stomped through the house, the floor shook.

He scared Zoe a little bit, but Karmen kept telling her she was in control of him.

"Where will he sleep?" Zoe asked.

"He'll keep watch outside the door," Karmen said with a wink. "Zombies don't need to sleep."

"And you're sure you've got a lock on him?" Noah asked. "It won't drop if you fall asleep or something?"

"No, I've got him," Karmen said. "I'll have the others set up all around the building and I'll keep the bird in the sky, watching out for any hordes and making sure we don't have any surprises while we rest."

"How are you holding up?" Parrish touched Noah's hand, and Zoe blushed again.

Yeah, they were definitely an item now, which made her happy. Her sister had practically swooned over the dude since the day he moved in across the street.

He was cute, too, but he was a mess. From the looks of it, he'd gotten hurt worse than any of them today.

"I'm going to go clean up a little bit, and then I think we all need to eat something. It's been a long day," he said.

But before he took off to one of the bedrooms, he crouched down in front of her.

"Hey," he said. "Remember me?"

Zoe laughed and rolled her eyes. "It's been a while and your face is messed up, but it hasn't been that long," she said. "We did live across the street from each other all my life."

Noah smiled. "I can't tell you how glad I am that you're safe," he said.

Zoe threw her arms around him.

"Thank you for coming with Parrish," she said. "If there was anyone she'd have wanted at her side, I know it was you."

"Well, thanks," Karmen said. "What about me?"

Zoe made a face. "I didn't think you guys liked each other much."

Karmen laughed. "No, I guess we didn't back then, but we're all in this together now."

Parrish introduced her to Crash, and for a while, they all sat around talking and going over everything that happened.

Even though she had been reunited with her neighbors and her sister, Zoe couldn't help but feel a little bit like the odd one out in this group, though. Sure, she'd known Parrish, Noah, and Karmen her entire life, but the five of them had apparently known each other for over a thousand years.

She curled up against the corner of the couch with a blanket, listening to them talk about the island and their plans for tomorrow. Every once in a while, Parrish touched her leg or asked her if she was feeling okay, and Zoe always smiled and nodded.

But there was something bothering her.

Something more than just being the only outsider in their guardian group.

Her arm was itching more and more the past few days, and for some reason, she'd been terrified to look at it. As if some part of her didn't really want to remember that night back at the hotel.

She'd been playing her violin, even though she knew it agitated the zombie locked away in the bedroom. She'd done her best to follow her dad's orders before he'd died, but she wasn't strong enough to move the heaviest furniture in front of his door.

After he turned, the lock on his door had seemed to hold him in there good enough.

Or at least she thought it was enough.

But then, in a moment of weakness and loneliness so deep, she thought she'd lose her mind, she played her violin.

A stupid mistake, just like with the curtain earlier. She wasn't cut out for this survival life the way Parrish was.

She remembered it now.

The terror she'd felt when her dad pushed through the door, his eyes glowing red as he sought her out. She'd been afraid he would tear her apart until there was nothing left but a pile of bones.

Instead, he'd left her with this.

She peeked around the blanket to make sure no one was watching before she carefully pulled back the sleeve of her shirt, her hand trembling.

It was just a small bite, really.

And so far, it didn't seem to be turning her into one of them. If it was going to turn her into a zombie, it should have happened already, right?

She was fine. Parrish was here now, and she was going to make sure Zoe was safe from now on. It was all going to be okay.

"You sure you're feeling alright?" Parrish asked.

Zoe quickly slid the sleeve of her shirt over the bite and smiled nervously. What would Parrish or the others do to her if they realized she'd been bitten? Should she tell them?

Let's keep this our little secret, a voice inside said to her. It was a voice she was sure she'd heard before, and it soothed her as much as it scared her.

"I'm fine," Zoe said. "Just tired."

"Me, too," Parrish said. "Let's get some rest. Come on."

But Zoe stayed awake long after the others had all gone to sleep, clinging tightly to her sister's hand and trusting that somehow, Parrish would make everything alright.

T he Dark One opened her eyes and sat up, taking a moment to get used to her new body.

The streets around her were littered with the dead. All her beloved servants, slaughtered mercilessly.

She smiled.

And each death had brought her just a little bit closer to freedom.

The guardians believed they were in control now, their powers too great to be challenged, but they had no idea who they were dealing with.

Every time they unlocked a new level of power, they gave more to her, as well. A little trick she'd set up from the start, thanks to Lily, the fatalis stone, and a handsome young farm boy.

David thought he was so clever when he'd turned her own creation against her by using the stone to seal her powers, but he'd failed to see the one major flaw in his strategy.

Admittedly, it had taken her time to see it, too.

But time was something, it turned out, she had plenty of.

While they'd been rewriting their memories and living mostly oblivious, human lives all this time, she'd been trapped inside her prison of ice for a thousand years, making her plans and biding her time.

So far, they'd played into all of it beautifully.

She stood, testing out her new legs and feeling more alive than she had in a very long time.

This wasn't like taking over the body of some rotting human without an ounce of power running through their veins.

No, this body felt like her old self again. The power coursing through her now was close to her own in so many ways. Not perfect, but it would do.

She walked over to the building where the guardians had retired for the night and caught her reflection in the window.

Beautiful, but she was going to have to do something about this wound in her chest.

The Dark One placed a hand on the gaping, bloodied hole where Parrish's sword had run her through, and in an instant, she was healed.

It was too bad the witch they'd called Lily had to die. She'd had so much potential, really, but in the end, she was unable to do what needed to be done.

Not that the Dark One had ever really planned to bring her home again, anyway.

She could never have shared her power and glory.

So, it was only a matter of time before she'd have killed the girl, anyway. So what if it had happened a little sooner than she'd planned? At least this way, Parrish had done the dirty work for her.

Besides, now she had this beautiful new body to play with.

A Beast of a man growled at her from the steps of the building, and she hissed back at him. He whimpered, backing away into the shadows.

She thought about killing him, along with the rest of the blonde girl's pets, but in the end, she decided to let her presence remain a surprise for another day.

For now, she had work to do.

After all her careful planning, there was still one chance for the guardians to defeat her. One chance for them to save this pitiful world and those beyond, if they were smart enough and willing to make a few sacrifices of their own.

She knew better than to underestimate their power, but at the same time, they were just children in this lifetime.

And without the island, they would never be anything more.

Besides, Parrish would do anything to keep her little sister alive.

The Dark One laughed as she made her way down Fifth Avenue, a sea of fresh rotters kneeling as she passed.

Tonight, she wouldn't worry about the guardians.

Tonight, she would celebrate this victory, because deep beneath the earth, in a prison made of ice, after a thousand years of praying for revenge, a single crack had finally formed.

Soon, when she was free, entire worlds would bow to her once again.

And that was something that no one, not even her daughter Parrish, could take away from her now.

ABOUT THE AUTHOR

Sarra Cannon is the author of several series featuring young adult and college-aged characters, including the bestselling Shadow Demons Saga. Her novels often stem from her own experiences growing up in the small town of Hawkinsville, Georgia, where she learned that being popular always comes at a price and relationships are rarely as simple as they seem.

Sarra owns her own publishing company and has sold three-quarters of a million copies of her books. She currently lives in Charleston, South Carolina with her programmer husband, her adorable redheaded son, and her beautiful daughter.

Love Sarra's books? Join Sarra's Mailing List to be notified of new releases and giveaways!

Also, please come hang out with me in my Facebook Fan Group: Sarra Cannon's Coven. We have a lot of fun in there, and I often share exclusive short stories and teasers in the group. Join now.

Want more? Come join us LIVE several times a week on my YouTube channel.

Connect With Sarra Online:
www.sarracannon.com

www.ingramcontent.com/pod-product-compliance
Lightning Source LLC
Chambersburg PA
CBHW051944240626
47153CB00005B/1615